UNDER THE SAME SKY

DIANA KNIGHTLEY

For mom, I think you would have loved this story, I wish I had told it to you before you had to go...

ONE - MAGNUS

My wrists were bound in front of me as I was shoved stumblin' forward. Twas dark, wherever I was, humid and verra hot. The heat made it hard tae breathe. I dinna remember where I was at first, or how I arrived, but then it came tae me: I had been captured.

General Reyes had me. A firm hand shoved my back propellin' me staggerin' forward. The mosquitoes buzzed thick around my face. My head hung heavy but I managed tae look behind, through the darkness, tae see I was surrounded by soldiers. They looked overly heated, exhausted, and enraged.

I kent Kaitlyn escaped, though Reyes had shot toward her as she jumped, so I dinna ken if she survived, if any of them survived.

I tripped over a root in ankle-deep water and thick mud that made walkin' difficult.

I forced the words out, "Where are we goin'?"

Nae one answered my question.

Ahead of us stood a fortress with high, sharp-angled walls, topped with cannons, standing in dark relief against the moonlit sky.

The sound of waves crashed nearby. I smelled the familiar scent of the sea. I guessed that I was in Florida from the air's humidity, but this wasna Fort Clinch. The walls of Fort Clinch had been straight and tall, nae angled like this.

Archie, when grown, had warned me that General Reyes spent a great deal of time in St Augustine and Kaitlyn had said twas south of Amelia Island. This was a guess, but it felt true.

I was led through the front gate and across an open courtyard down a hallway tae a hole with a pile of bricks beside it.

"I want tae speak tae general Reyes."

The soldier beside me grunted and shoved me tae my knees. "Crawl."

I dinna want tae go intae the hole. I dropped and kicked the closest soldier as hard as I could. Three men descended on me kicking and pummeling as I struggled until I couldna fight anymore. My ribs ached as I lay on the ground afraid of the injuries that might have been inflicted.

One man crawled through the opening, grabbed the rope bindin' my hands and dragged me through.

He crawled out and left me inside a tight cave. The ceiling lay verra close. Then the soldiers piled bricks at the opening makin' my prison dark and quiet as a tomb. My breaths echoed within.

A shufflin' sounded a bit away.

"Who are ye?" I asked.

Twas nae answer, just another shuffle.

I was fearfully hungry. I lay on the stone floor, in total darkness, listenin' tae the crash and rumble of the waves outside, trying tae figure out what tae do.

TWO - MAGNUS

Many hours later I heard clatterin' as the bricks buryin' me inside were removed.

A voice called through, "Campbell. Out."

I crawled tae the opening where a soldier brusquely grabbed the rope around my wrists and dragged me from the hole.

"Where are ye takin' me?"

The soldier dinna answer.

The day was hot and wet, rain ran down the stone walls. I was dragged along the ground, down a hallway, tae the outer courtyard. The sky was overcast and stormy.

I struggled tae see every direction of the building's construction: a castle, high fortified walls. The men wore uniforms of blue coats with wide red cuffs. They spoke tae each other in Spanish and ignored me as I was dragged, my skin raking across the stone and sand of the courtyard.

I was tossed in through a door tae the feet of General Reyes.

He spoke in Spanish tae the men and they left us alone.

I was prostrate. He walked around me slowly, drew his sword, and swung it in an arc from both directions above me, menacin' me with it. Then he kicked me, hard. I groaned and curled around my knees tae protect my sides.

He said, "Do not worry yourself, Mags the First, I would not dream of hurting your precious ribs. I need you in fighting shape." He slumped into a chair, his legs splayed out as if he was relaxed. He was wearing the same uniform as the other soldiers, a blue coat with red cuffs. Beads of sweat rolled down his face. I found a comfort in the fact that he was suffering in this sweltering heat.

I raised my head tae find the doors: there was one behind me, the only exit.

Reyes asked, "Are you looking for the closest escape route, Mags the First? I will tell you where it is: through me."

"Twas what I was hopin' ye would say. I do plan tae go through ye."

Reyes chuckled. "Maybe you have not realized the dire situation you find yourself in, but let me—"

"Where am I?"

"Your beloved Florida, Lady Mairead tells me it is your favorite place. I rather like it as well."

I scowled. "How dost ye ken Lady Mairead?"

"We have been in business together for a while now."

When I tried tae rise he shoved my shoulder with his boot.

I asked, "I am tae remain on the dirt floor for our conversation?"

"Yes." His eyes traveled over me. "You have grown to be a strapping young man, Mags the First."

"My name is Magnus."

"I know who you are."

"There, I am at a disadvantage, I have only just met ye and I haena any idea why ye have me bound on a dirt floor."

"Your mother hired me."

My stomach sank. "Why would she...?"

"She hired me to kill Donnan so you could ascend to the throne. Your wife accomplished the killing before I could complete the—"

"So ye failed. You should be the one bound on the floor. What did Lady Mairead give ye tae murder the king?" As soon as I asked it I kent the answer. "She gave ye a vessel."

"Yes, she willingly gave me a vessel. Then I tricked her into giving me a vessel tracker. The vessel tracker is, perhaps, the only one of its kind. She quickly realized how dangerous I had become: unstoppable. She has given me some powerful machines, wondrous really... she was very forthcoming."

"Why would she do that?"

"Because she wanted to protect you. She wanted you to sit on the throne. Her judgement was horribly clouded."

I scowled. "Tis nae her usual style tae be taken advantage of."

He shrugged. "She had not met me."

"So why am I nae dead?"

"I have a task for you. I have been thinking on it, Mags the First. We are all fighting over this throne, in the year 23-something, but why did we pick that time to conquer the world out of every other time?" He waited.

I answered, "I daena ken."

"We didn't choose it. It was chosen for us by a barbarian highlander in the 1500s, a Johnne Cambell. He got the vessels, he killed and stole and conquered and built an empire where he decided to. The rest of us, you, his great-great, on-and-on, grandchild, and your dear mother, are just the descendants, taking your throne wherever it is. His nephews and sons and cousins are all fighting over the throne, and it exists where he put it."

"His name was Normond. He was from the year 1686."

"I thought you were smarter than this, Mags the First. No, his name was Johnne Cambell. I met him in the year 1557 a couple of days before he found the vessels. I was there. I fought alongside him."

I closed my eyes, this was too much tae think on, and it meant that Reyes kent the original date of the vessels. He was even more dangerous than I had believed. "You haena explained why I am a captive."

"It came to me as I have been hopping from place to place with the vessel gift from your mother, that I would make an excellent king. It also came to me, why should I fight the sons of Donnan for the throne? I would be a better king than any of them, my apologies, Mags the First, I am quite sure you tried, but you do have limitations. But me, I am not a barbarian anymore; I am well-read, highly educated, and I have seen the world. I have studied history; I know where things went wrong. I could prune back this branch of the tree and start it all anew. All I would need to do is go back there, to that battlefield, and kill Johnne Cambell before he gets the vessels. It is simple really. All of history relived a second time, just with a better outcome."

"A better outcome for whom?"

"Why me, of course, have you been listening?" His smile slithered across his face, reminding me of the sickening charm of Lord Delapointe and causin' me tae wonder why the hell my mother wasna a better judge of character.

"If you were there and ye have a vessel, why daena ye go back there? Why am I involved at all?"

"Well, see, there is a problem. You have probably discovered, I would assume, on the banks of the spring in Florida, that traveling back to relive your own life causes time-irregularities?"

"I daena ken, but Kaitlyn has told me it did."

"Ah yes, you are the less wizened version of yourself. You have not lived through all that you could have done. You have to rely on your lovely wife to tell you what to do, how to think, how the world works. How is she, by the way? I imagine she is as feisty under your hands as she is in the video with that other man. Who was he, the man who had her before you? He seemed apt at giving her pleasure. I have watched it, she is quite something to behold—"

My bound hands were in the dirt within my line of vision. I concentrated on the point between my fingernail and the dirt and scratched a line tae the stone. "Ye should begin tae beg your maker for forgiveness because ye will be speakin' tae him in person verra soon."

"Says the man in the dirt in front of me."

"My situation looks dire but ye are givin' me strength, daena fool yourself."

"Fine, I will not discuss how well your wife would move under me. You do not need to know about it. You will be nothing but a distant memory by then."

"And where will I be?"

"I am not sure, but I assume that when your great-great grandfather is dead you will be nothing. Not Mags the First, not Mags, just a pile of dusty molecules within a pile of dust within a pile of dust going back... what is it, five generations or so of piles of dust? That's why from now on I am calling you Mags the Dust."

"If I am nothin' but dust, ye daena need the ropes on me. You just had tae kill my forefather and I would nae exist..."

"That is the complicated part, Mags the Dust. I was there, on the battlefield of Inchaiden, at the origin of the Tempus Omegas. I had been to meet with the king and I was traveling through Campbell lands when I met up with your great-great-whatever-grandfather, Johnne."

His slithery smile widened. "If you want to talk about barbarians, your great-grandfather Johnne could do more barbaric things before breakfast than most men would do in a lifetime." He waved his hand as if this accusation was a mere nothin'. "He was gracious, though. He allowed me to rest at Balloch. I found him to be good company. Then in the dawn hours, after Samhain, there was a storm and a commotion. My men and I rode with the Campbells to see what was happening in the woods. That was when we found the men, lying on the ground. Johnne was afraid. He ordered his men to massacre the time-jumpers, down to one man. That man Johnne imprisoned in the castle."

I quieted, listening. His tale fit the one Kaitlyn discovered in the book.

"I lived at the castle while Johnne learned how to use the Tempus Omegas, but I soon figured he would not want any witnesses, so I left. I returned to Spain and lived peacefully until Donnan arrived. He questioned me about that day with the Tempus Omegas and was terribly persuasive, he is where you get your propensity for violence, I think. I told him what he wanted to know. Then Lady Mairead found out about me and she was very persuasive as well, just in different ways. That was when I was given my first Tempus Omega, yet I believe the case could be made that it should have been mine all along."

He continued, "I have since used it to collect wealth, houses, antiques, art. I have had many adventures, but through the years the realization came to me," he punctuated the thought with his palm on the arm of his chair, "I should go back in time to that moment on the fields of Inchaiden and I should take all the vessels now that I know how to use them."

I took a deep breath.

He finished quickly, "I cannot travel back into my own life and make changes. I've tried four times and each time the battle scene was worse, the deaths more horrible. Numerous times I barely escaped. I thought I needed more of the Tempus Omegas so I forced Lady Mairead to bring me them, but they didn't help. I cannot be the one to do it. That is where you come in."

"What am I to do?"

"You will travel to the year 1557, the night of Samhain, and you will find the younger version of myself and ask him to help you. You will tell the young Nick Reyes all about the Tempus Omegas and how to use them. You and I will wait in the woods for the Campbell men to arrive. After the Campbell men massacre the time-jumpers, you and I will kill the last remaining Campbell men. That way I will have all the vessels and the knowledge to use them."

"And I will be dust."

"Yes, I figure about halfway through the battle you will just fly away on a night breeze, Mags the Dust. Do not let it bother you though, you will die a hero: save the world and all of that. It is one of those things that the people of your chosen time love, a good superhero. Selfless acts in the name of rescue."

"How have ye learned of this?"

"I studied. I watched and listened and asked questions. I lost my accent and my barbarity and my ignorance and now I am a gentleman officer and soon I will be a benevolent king. I have lived for a time in every century. I know what needs to be done and I am prepared to do it."

"You could ask anyone tae do this for ye, for me it is tae die. Why dost ye want me tae do it? How will ye make me?"

"There is no one else that I can trust to be so compliant and I think you know how I will make you."

"By threatenin' the lives of my family, my wife."

"No, see, that would be barbaric. I am not threatening, I am promising. I will let them live. They will not remember you, there is a sadness in that, but they were not meant to know you anyway. They will have their own lives but I will make sure that within their century they will be provided for, comfortable and protected. It will be like having a wealthy benefactor. The wealth you have collected, I will see to it that they receive it. They will not understand where it came from but it is fair that it belongs to them. I will make sure of it."

"You are askin' me tae die."

"You are already dead, Mags the Dust. It is 1740 right now. You were born when, 1681?"

I nodded.

"You would be an old man of sixty years now, and with your propensity for battling I doubt you would live that long. And who would want to? In a few years you would meet your end in the Battle of Culloden anyway, along with your grandchildren." He shrugged as if twas an easy thing tae consider.

"Think of it like this, I am telling you to do one last important thing before you go: to save the world, to provide for Kaitlyn, and to end this future kingdom of barbarians, you included, pardon my bluntness."

I watched that scratch in the dirt I had made, one mark, one moment. On a timeline of history this mark would be a century, a line that meant all that had happened between then and now. Magnus, he existed, he lived for 24 years. He was a child in Scotland in the 17th century and a man in Scotland in the 18th century and a husband in the 21st century and a father in the 24th. Twas a great many things tae have done, and through a great deal of time.

"I am verra hungry."

"I imagine you are." He poured a cup of water and put it within reach. I was desperate for it. I got the handle into my shaking hands and my head up enough to pull it to my mouth. I gulped it down, splashing most of it down my chin. It was gone too soon.

"I need more."

He sighed and didn't move to bring me another.

"Since you have had the Tempus Omegas have you traveled to any beautiful spots, dust boy?"

I remained quiet.

"I have traveled extensively—"

"Where is Lady Mairead?"

He ignored me. "I live here, in Florida, but some of any year I live in Scotland, very near Inchaiden and Balloch Castle."

"Ye daena strike me as someone who would live in Scotland. Tis too rough for ye, why daena ye move somewhere else and leave us be?"

"But see, there is much happening around the banks of the River Tay. There is the stone circle of Croft Moraig, the castle Balloch, Inchaiden which is the cradle of time-travel, and someday, far in the future, as you know, the kingdom of the ancestors of Magnus the First."

He shifted in his seat. "With that much magic and mystery I feel I must stay close to the River Tay to keep my eyes on the comings and goings of Magnus and his mother Lady Mairead. Which brings me to your question: I have not seen her in a long time. I would guess that means she knows she has lost."

He brushed dust from his pants. "I returned today to help my men. James Oglethorpe is laying siege to this fort. I wanted to assist their defense of it and see how it goes. Of course if a time-jumper assists in a battle they don't want to change it too much. I would not want to change the course of history."

He chuckled. "We will win of course. It is exciting to drop in and out of history, no?"

I simply said, "Nae."

"Nae? Nae to what, the excitement, the fun?"

"Nae tae it all. We should nae involve ourselves in the history of the world, we arna gods, tae create and destroy."

"Says the king sitting on an inherited throne in a borrowed time."

He picked up the cup and tossed it to the desk beside him. "I see we are in agreement, I will have you returned to your room until I need you."

Soldiers entered. They yanked me to standing then shoved me out into the rain-soaked courtyard. I noted the position of the sun through the thick storm clouds. A guard shoved me toward the North. The front gate was behind me tae the south. A scan of the walls showed trees on three sides, and tae my right in the far wall, a man entered through a small door with a string of fish hangin' beside his leg.

Soldiers gathered and joked with him about his catch and I kent that door was the postern door and through it was the shore.

The guards shoved me down the hall and returned me, wet and hungry, into the same dark hole.

THREE - MAGNUS

I tried tae sleep. My thirst was very painful and was makin' me afraid for my life. I dinna think Reyes wanted a dead man but he wasna workin' tae keep me alive.

There was a groan from the other end of the room.

"Who are ye?" I asked. "Dost ye need help?"

Twas pitch black in front of my eyes and I was so thirsty there wasna anythin' I could do tae help someone without the strength tae answer. Twas verra frightenin' tae be in the same room with someone who was takin' their last breaths and I couldna see or help them.

"Dost ye need me tae pray?"

There was no sound but I began tae pray without an answer. I needed the sound of my voice tae take my mind from my thirst. Twas a comfort tae speak tae the heavens while in a pitch dungeon afraid for my life.

Many hours later, I heard it for the first time, the loud blast of a cannon. The ground shook from the impact. I sat up and listened. There was yellin' and hurried activity, the sounds of soldiers moving cannons and barrels and carts, and another cannon blast.

This was the battle Reyes had spoken of—

I scrambled to the bricks that had been piled in front of the hole and pressed as close as I could tae listen. Men were shouting and calling in Spanish. I had heard it spoken in the English court when I had lived there in London. I dinna understand what they were sayin' but it sounded as if they were preparing tae fight. It sounded verra much like a war at the walls.

The hallway though, seemed eerily quiet.

Another blast reverberated.

I aimed my feet at the bricks and shoved and kicked them from the entrance. Then I pulled back, waitin', listenin'. If there was a guard outside I would expect him tae come in and beat me for doin' it, but there wasna a guard—

I said tae the room, whoever was in there with me, "If ye can get up, I have opened the door. Dost ye want tae come?"

There was nae response.

"Hello?"

Again, nothin'.

I dragged m'self on m'elbows through the dust and dirt. I paused at the opening of the hole and listened tae the movements of the soldiers outside.

The loudest cannon shot of them all, close, just outside the wall. I tried tae cover my ears, but my bound hands were useless. Rubble fell and a dust cloud filled the hallway causin' me tae cough compulsively.

As soon as the dust settled enough tae see, I scrambled out of the dungeon.

There was nae one here, but down at the end of the hall soldiers ran by toward the north wall.

I pressed my shoulder tae the wall as I climbed tae my feet thinkin' on the impossibilities of blending in while wearin' a kilt with my hands bound in front of me. I raced down the hall, clung tae the opening, and watched left and right.

Soldiers were shooting from the walls. Cannons were firin'. A great many men were running and yellin', there was dust and rubble and chaos. Cannons blasted in the distance.

From where I stood I saw the sun risin', the front gate guarded, the dark corners of the fort.

I skirted the courtyard, headin' toward the east, hidin' within the shadows, hopin' tae reach the postern door and gain my freedom.

Somehow I had a clear path tae get there through the dust and chaos and managed tae remain hidden. I rushed through the door and emerged intae a spray of water and falling stone rubble. A large ship was anchored just off shore with its cannons firin'. Cannons on the fort returned fire, guns were shootin' all around. I was exposed, bound, defenseless — a cannon fired and heavy shot crashed beside me, breakin' the ground.

I stumbled toward the bank and dove intae the water just as shot broke the surface and the concussion of the blast knocked me deep down tae the silty bottom.

FOUR - KAITLYN

I woke up in a bed in the guest-room, barely remembering that I had woken up in a chair in the living room with a terrible crick in my neck and had carried Archie in here. He was still fast asleep, with his little soft breaths. I held his warm hand for a moment then realized I had to pee, so after placing pillows around him securely, I went to the bathroom. Then I took the shower I desperately needed.

There was a pile of clothes from the last time I was here, and I lost myself for a moment staring down into a drawer at Magnus's clothes. There weren't many, a shirt and a pair of pants, dark and in a style I really liked on him.

I took a deep breath and dressed to meet the day.

I carried Archie with me down the hall to the living room, where Zach's family was already busy. Ben was toddling around touching everything and Emma was racing behind him trying to move antiques to higher shelves. "I'm so sorry Kaitlyn, he's broken a tea cup and—"

"Well, no wonder, this place is not at all toddler-proofed."

He gleefully rushed to a shelf where some ancient books were well within reach. Emma was frazzled. Zach was exasperated, running his hands through his hair. "It's not fucking baby proofed, what are we going to—?"

I said, "This whole house belongs to Magnus, what do you think he would say if he was here?"

Zach answered, "He'd probably laugh as Ben broke stuff, but I don't think that's a great parenting—"

"True, he's a highlander, he doesn't necessarily get the inherent worth of these ancient artifacts." I pulled a stack of books off the shelf ahead of Ben and placed them higher.

Ben rushed to the china cabinet. "The point though is he wouldn't care. So we shouldn't worry as we move everything up or shove it into closets." I scooped up some tea pots just before Ben's fingers got to them.

Emma said, "You don't mind?"

"Nope, all this can go in a back room." I put Archie in his carrier. " Give Ben the box of silver spoons, let him bang those. We'll find more stuff." I picked up the box of silver coins and moved it higher.

Zach moved a china vase to the closet. Mrs Johnstone entered and gasped. "What are you doing?"

I said, "We have to move everything up for Ben, he wants to play."

She said, "You could just tell him no."

Emma picked Ben up, looking mortified.

Zach looked embarrassed and not a little pissed.

"You know, no. I won't tell him no. He is King Magnus's guest here in Magnus's home and Magnus told me to make his guests comfortable. As a matter of fact Magnus told me to tell you that he wants this whole downstairs child-proofed for Ben."

She scowled.

I said, "I'm just telling you what Magnus said. He wants Ben and Archie and all the guests to be comfortable. If it means moving everything of value out and putting mattresses all over the floor then that's what I'm going to do."

"I've finished making breakfast, Queen Kaitlyn, if you're ready to eat."

"Perfect, thank you."

She stalked down the hall.

Emma said, "Thank you Katie."

"You don't have to thank me, not at all. Ben is a little boy who just freaking time-traveled to the future. As far as I'm concerned he gets to play wherever he wants." I watched Ben bang a spoon against a marble top table. My chin trembled. "Magnus loves him so much."

Emma put an arm around me. "I know he does."

"So let's just remember that. Magnus is a king apparently and he loves Ben, so seriously, don't worry about it. Treat Ben like you want to treat him and don't worry about anyone being a judge. Especially Mrs Johnstone, her opinion doesn't matter at all. She thinks Donnan was a king of men."

"And he was...?"

"Magnus's father. That one that... you know."

"Yeah, right, so she doesn't matter."

"Exactly. Anytime she complains just tell her that Donnan's son, Magnus, told you what to do. That's how we go forward."

"You'll be channeling Magnus?"

"We all have to channel Magnus. Hammond told me not to tell anyone he's missing. We have to pretend like we expect him any moment."

Zach said, "I do expect him any moment, seriously Katie, I saw his eyes when we were leaving. He'll kill that guy. He'll come home."

"Yes, of course he will."

Quentin came down the stairs leading Beaty. "Did I hear food?"

"Yes, breakfast is ready."

FIVE - KAITLYN

We were all eating when Hammond entered. "Can we speak, Your Highness?"

"Have you eaten?"

"No."

"Then join us." I had Mrs Johnstone bring another place setting.

"Can I speak freely?"

"Definitely, these are all friends of Magnus and they were there when he was captured. This is Colonel Quentin Peters: he's head of Magnus's personal security. This is Zach and Emma: Zach is Magnus's private chef, Emma is in charge of his household, but really you can think of them as our family."

Hammond nodded and opened his mouth to speak when the loud sharp voice of Lady Mairead sounded from the foyer. "I need to speak tae her right now!"

When she stalked into the dining room her face was flushed, her expression furious. She banged a fist on the table and bowed over me. "Where is Magnus?"

"Why, I—"

"You tell me right now, right now do ye hear me!"

"He's with General Reyes, I—"

"How could you let this—? How long has he had him?"

Hammond said, "Mairead, maybe you should sit down so we can speak—"

She banged her fist on the table. "Nae, I winna sit down." She turned on me pointing at Hammond. "Kaitlyn, what is he doin' here? You canna trust him." She said to Hammond, "Not one more word from ye or I will have ye strung up for treason."

Hammond sighed wearily.

Everyone else at the table had expressions of shock, which was normal, Lady Mairead enjoyed taking over a room.

Lady Mairead said, "Where is Archie?"

"He's here, he—"

"Good, we canna tell anyone that Magnus isna here."

I said, "I agree."

She sat stiffly in a chair. "Hello Chef Zach, Emma. Did ye have safe travels?"

Zach said, "Yes ma'am."

"Quentin, explain yourself, you are supposed to be his guard."

He said, "General Reyes snuck into our dinner party. We didn't know who he was. He showed up with Hayley and we were overpowered."

She cut her eyes at Hayley. "And how are ye, Madame Hayley? You have a wound on your head."

Hayley's hand went to her bandage.

"And this is?" Her eyes cut to Beaty as if she just noticed her.

I said,"Beaty Campbell, she is newly married to Quentin Peters."

"Oh my, I supposed she had the look about her. Are you Jimmy's child?"

"Yes, Lady Mairead."

I see. "Well, you carry the looks of your family, I am sure not much else. That was probably a verra entertaining marriage contract."

"Your son struck the deal and seemed fine with it."

She looked down at her hands.

I asked, "How do you know General Reyes?"

"I have been in business with him. He is conniving, and deadly." She leaned back in her chair. "I canna believe he has gone against me and taken Magnus." She looked left and right. "Madame Johnstone!"

Mrs Johnstone stuck her head in the door. "Yes?"

"I will need tae be served some food."

"Of course Lady Mairead."

Lady Mairead leveled her eyes on me. "Tell me everything that happened."

I wanted to ask her what her business was, and to make her explain what was going on so I could figure this out. But also, I kind of figured I wouldn't know how to figure this out even if she told me, and maybe Lady Mairead would be more capable. So although I knew she wasn't trustworthy and I knew I couldn't rely on her, I really needed her help solving this.

I told her everything.

Except that I had the book.

At the end, she narrowed her eyes, letting them settle on me. They were full of suspicion. "Is that everything?" she asked.

"Yes."

Hammond asked, "Lady Mairead, I am head of Magnus's armed forces and one of his most trusted advisors and I—"

"Does he ken ye dinna help me when I asked ye tae?"

"Yes, he knows I chose duty to the king over treason. He is okay with my decision."

She scoffed and took a bite of her eggs and beans. "He is not really here tae speak for his thoughts on it is he? Kaitlyn, heed my warning on this. Hammond Donahoe has proven himself tae be unreliable; ye would do well not tae trust him."

"Magnus trusts him. So will I."

She scoffed again.

Hammond said, "Where do you think Magnus is, or when, and what should our next step be?"

She took a long deep breath. "I daena ken where he is. I met with General Reyes in Scotland once. Also in St Augustine. I am nae sure where he would take Magnus, but he wants his throne."

Hammond said, "If he wanted Magnus's throne, why isn't he here fighting for it?"

Quentin said, "Or why didn't he kill Magnus right then? He could have killed all of us and then just jumped here and taken it. He didn't, he kept Magnus alive."

Hayley said, "Maybe he's not sure if Roderick is going to win the kingdom. If he holds onto Magnus, lets Roderick take the kingdom, makes them fight each other, then kills the victor — I'm sure it would work like that in the movies."

"That's a good point," said Quentin, "but he could still kill Magnus and then come kill Roderick. The simplest plan is probably the truest one. It must be bigger than simply killing Magnus and taking his throne."

Hayley said, "He is pretty evil, maybe he wants to torture him first—"

I said, "Hayley, can you not?"

Quentin said, "No, I think it's even bigger. Like what if he figured out a way to control Magnus, to brainwash him? Maybe he wants Magnus to be king, like a figurehead, while Reyes controls him."

I cut my eyes to Lady Mairead. "He could use one of those metal neckpieces like you used on me."

She looked away. "I would never relinquish one tae him. It must be something else."

I said, "So we think he wants Magnus's throne. He might be willing to wait to see if it's Roderick's throne. Or he might want to control Magnus. These are all possibilities. These are all big, evil possibilities and sadly almost-impossible-to-stop plans."

Zach shook his head, "I don't know, I feel like it might be bigger than those..."

Emma said, "What's bigger than wanting Magnus's throne?"

Zach said, "Just spitballing here, no wrong answers and all, but if you could time travel you'd want Magnus's great-great-great grandfather's throne. Forget dealing with all this shit, you'd want to start all new shit."

I opened and closed my mouth. He was right. I knew it. Zach had figured it out. And shit — I needed to burn that book.

Lady Mairead looked speechless. Then she looked right at me and said, "Where is the book?" Her face was terrifying.

"Book? What book? I don't know what you're talking about."

She grabbed the table knife beside her plate and held it clutched in her fingers. "You tell me where it is."

I shrugged.

She lunged at me.

Hammond jumped up and held her off. "If you threaten the queen again, I'll have you arrested."

She laughed a high cackling laugh. "The queen, *really*! Fine." She dropped the knife and sat. She gestured for Hammond to sit back down. "Relax, you are correct Hammond, I winna threaten the queen."

She addressed me. "There is a book. It was here. Donnan told me about it. He kept it within his writing desk. He told me it was verra valuable because it carried the date of the beginning of the vessels. You understand the danger associated with that date, I am sure?"

I said, "I understand the danger."

"Well, that book isna here anymore. I have looked for it all through this house and I have searched the other places Donnan might have hidden it. You were here in this house when it went missing so I am sure ye must have it."

"I don't. But that's a good thing, maybe Donnan destroyed it, then Reyes won't know when it—"

"Reyes already kens the date, as he was there."

"Reyes is from the time of Magnus's great-great-great grandfather?"

Hayley said, "Wait, how old was he? I swear I'm getting more furious with every second. That's got to be illegal to be — what, 800 years old and dating a 24 year old? Gross."

I ignored Hayley and asked, "So what does he want with Magnus?" But my stomach sank when it slammed into me—

He wanted Magnus to go with him to the past. He was going to make Magnus go get the vessels from the very beginning. Because Reyes was there and he couldn't loop back on himself.

He was going to make Magnus do it.

And if Magnus went back to that battlefield in 1557 all of this would disappear...

Lady Mairead said, her voice level and scary, "I need tae ken the date, I need ye tae tell me where the book is so that I can go back there and help Magnus."

My mouth opened and closed. "I..." I had no idea what to do. I knew not to trust Lady Mairead. She was helpful sometimes but she could also be very dangerous. In this one instance I held more information than she did. I felt like I should keep my hard-won advantage.

I needed to think on it, to buy some time, and right then Archie started crying from the other room.

Emma read my face. "Kaitlyn, we should probably check on him, you know how he only wants to see you."

"Yes, that's true." I pushed my chair from the table. "Zach can you entertain Lady Mairead for a few minutes? Maybe tell her how much you're enjoying her wedding gift? Hayley, maybe tell her how the house is? Quentin can you come with me for a moment?" I stood, my hands shaking. "Okay, I'll be back in a mo—"

"Where is Bella tae tend tae her baby?"

"She's in the guest quarters."

"Here on the grounds? Tis verra protective of ye." Her eyes squinted. "What of her beau, John Mitchell"

"Do you know him?"

"Of course I ken him, John Mitchell works for me. He informs me of everything Bella does. If it involves Archie, the next-in-line for the throne, then it involves me as his grandmother."

Archie's cries grew stronger, sounding desperate.

"I need to check on him." I performed my best sweep from the room followed by Quentin and Emma.

SIX - KAITLYN

I gathered Archie into my arms. "I'm sorry sweetie, Kaitlyn is going through some stuff and your wicked grandmother is here and I..." I looked at Quentin, "What am I going to do?"

"You're not going to tell that bitch anything. She thinks she knows what Reyes's plan is but I'm not convinced."

"Well, I'm totally convinced; this is the reason Reyes has Magnus."

"It could be any of those other reasons: he's trying to control him, he's biding his time; the whole going back to the beginning is pretty complicated. Zach is kind of a stoner, this might not be the most plausible—"

"He's not really a stoner anymore and this situation kind of requires that kind of thinking. I'm sure of it. This is exactly right."

Quentin sighed. "Okay fine, if Magnus is being taken to the way long ago past, I should go get him. I know how to ride, to fight, and I'm his guard. Plus I'm a colonel in his future-kingdom-army whatever the hell that means."

Emma handed me a bottle for Archie and I got him to calm enough to start suckling. I kissed him on his sweet little forehead.

I waved my hand around like a crazy person, "See all this? There's so much crazy happening, where is Magnus? I haven't even been able to think or rest or — It's *breakfast* and I have to deal with Lady Mairead and crazy time-jumping stuff, and all it will take is one person going back in time and getting those vessels and—" I snapped my fingers. "This all disappears. I don't want it to disappear. Maybe Lady Mairead, but not you or you, Emma, or Magnus or this little guy. Crap, I need to get back in there and protect Zach and Hayley from her."

Quentin asked, "Do you have the book?"

I shook my head.

Then I chewed my lip.

I said, "Don't make me answer."

"Okay, you don't have the book. I questioned you and you don't. It's clear." He ran a hand over his hair. "Firmly tell her you don't have it. Tell her we'll all look for it and we'll let her know as soon as we find it."

"Yeah, yeah." I pulled up some tissues from the night stand and wiped my face. "Yeah. I can fix this. I know what to do."

Emma said, "You do? Because I have no idea."

"It's easy. I just have to be stronger than Lady Mairead."

They followed me back down the hall to the dining room.

~

The conversation looked strained. All eyes turned to me.

I rocked Archie back and forth and stood behind my chair. "First, Lady Mairead, I don't have the book. I don't know the date and so all I can tell you is we will look for it and when we find it you'll be the first to hear. Secondly, thank you for dropping by, my apologies you can't stay longer but as you know we are here because of a war and really don't need new drama brought into our safe house."

Lady Mairead said, "Your safe house will hold for about three more days before it falls tae Roderick. He has already guessed your location and is now plannin' tae corner ye."

Hammond leaned closer listening.

She continued, "He would like to draw Magnus out tae fight. He will be surprised tae learn Magnus isna here."

Hammond said, "How do you know this?"

"I have people who tell me things. Unlike here, amongst my own family and my household, where things are kept from me, hidden, as if I am tae be tricked."

I tried to keep my voice steady. "I am not trying to trick you. I am trying to understand where Magnus is and come up with a rescue plan."

"Well, you better go fast, ye have three days. I canna help because ye have hidden the book from me."

"I have not." I took a deep breath. "What are we going to do about Roderick, Colonel Donahoe, any ideas?"

"I will need to discuss this with the board and my commanders. I will have a working plan in a few hours."

Lady Mairead cut her eyes at him. "I will need a room."

"You don't have anywhere else—?" I remembered the old adage keep your friends close your enemies closer. "Forget that, you'll stay in the—" I looked around confused at this big ass house that was mine apparently, a part of the kingdom I now ran without Magnus.

Lady Mairead said, "Is Bella in the East Wing? I'll take the West." Her brow lifted. "The rest of you are all sleeping here together in the main house, how very friendly of you."

We, all of us, gave each other a look. Mine was overwhelmed. Zach's look was astonished. Emma showed pity. Beaty — confusion. Hayley looked murderous.

Lady Mairead sighed. "The awful part is I have a remembrance of the book, in the top drawer of Donnan's desk, and I canna return for it as I canna loop back on my life, twould make..."

She kept speaking but I stopped listening.

Archie done feeding, looked up at me sweetly. *Yeah, little guy, terrible stuff is happening, but don't you worry — I'm that dragon I was telling you about when we met. I'm going to go back there to the middle ages and breathe fire on a really, really bad guy.*

I said to Lady Mairead when she finished, "Yeah, well too bad you can't find the book. Um, anyway, I need to go sit down in the other room in a comfortable chair. If you'd like to go to your rooms, we'll let you know if we discover anything."

SEVEN - KAITLYN

Ben was toddling around banging shit and I didn't care because he was all sweetness and normalness and I needed some of that right now. Emma followed him around attending to him, worrying and watching, and I thought about how this motherly business was so *her*.

I looked down at Archie and sighed.

Mrs Johnstone bustled in. "Bella has sent word she wants Magnus's son brought to her right now."

All eyes turned to me, holding my husband's mistress's baby in my arms.

"Oh, yes, of course." I placed him gently in the baby carrier. "Will you make sure there are full bottles for him?" I tried to be a grownup while she carried Archie from the room but my heart hurt. With my hands on my hips I said, "Great."

Hayley, watching Mrs Johnstone carry Archie from the room, said, "Yeah, that is not the right word, sweetie. That shit right there isn't great, it's a complicated, big, heaping pile of bullshit and I'm sorry you have to deal with it. I have half a mind to go over to that bitch's guest wing and give her a piece of my mind. But I might kill her and–"

"I know you mean well, Hayley. I know you do, but I have a lot of stuff to worry about and I don't need to worry about whether you can handle yourself like a grownup. I need you to handle your shit and be strong and help me. I'm dealing with a lot of people. I'm supposed to be strong and dignified and respectable. So when I'm alone with you and my family, I would really like to be the one who gets to throw temper tantrums and threaten to kill people and for you to be the one who talks me down."

"Oh, yeah, right. I'm not going to kill her. Only a terrible friend would say something like that and I'm your best friend in the world. It was just my head wound talking — momentary insanity. What do you want to do?"

"Kill her. In some horrible way, like with a pit involving alligators."

She grinned at me. "You shouldn't kill her, sweetie, she seems like a lovely person."

"Now that might be going too far." I sighed. "I don't really want to kill her, she's Archie's mom, you know? And she's had a really difficult life. Donnan raped her, I'm sure of it. He collected her like she was some kind of an artifact and kept her in his castle and she really thought Magnus was going to save her from that. I feel sorry for her. I love Archie and the truth is, when it all comes down to it, she's his mom. I have to accept it and live with it."

"When did you grow up?"

"I don't know," I joked, "but I'm furious it happened." I slumped down in the chair. "What are we going to do?"

Quentin said, "Hammond is working on a strategy to keep the kingdom from falling to Roderick. I'll meet with him in a few hours."

"Perfect."

Zach said, "I intend to relieve Mrs Johnstone of her duties as cook, do you think she'll mind?"

We all groaned. "I hope not."

"Cause those beans were for sure straight from the can. I mean, add some spices, get creative."

I nodded.

Emma said, "I'm not being much help, sadly. Maybe I'll figure out if there are any extra clothes, make a list of things we need from the store... are there stores?"

"Your guess is as good as mine."

"Who do we ask?"

I shrugged. "Mrs Johnstone?"

"So don't piss off Mrs Johnstone, Zachary."

"I won't, but I also can't fucking sit by and watch my loved ones eat beans from a can."

Hayley said, "We all thank you."

Quentin said, "So now I have to rescue Magnus. Where is he? Reyes could have him anywhere."

I said, "Lady Mairead's thoughts are the best I've heard on the matter. General Reyes is going to send Magnus back in time to fight the original men for the vessels. Winner takes the spoils. I think he will be there."

Hayley said, "What would happen then?"

"All of this, everything that happened since Magnus appeared in my life, would be over. Like it never happened."

"No more Magnus?"

I nodded unable to say it out loud.

Quentin squinted his eyes, "So that's all we've got to go on. I'd like to say that it could be any number of things, but if everyone else agrees, I'll go along with this."

Hayley said, "It won't hurt to go check, I suppose. If he's not there then you can go look somewhere else."

Zach said, "I know I brought this up, but now that it's a working plan it sounds kind of crazy."

I said, "But if I say it's not crazy, if I say I know this is it?"

Zach nodded. "Then I say okay, Katie. That's what Quentin should do."

"Thank you. Is everyone in agreement?"

They all nodded.

Quentin said, "I'll go back in time, stop Reyes, rescue Magnus, and keep them from making a big mistake, but you don't know where because you don't have the book—"

"I do know where and when. I'm trying not to tell anyone else though, so I will go with you. You and I will go rescue Magnus."

"Just tell me, is it in the long ago past, in Scotland? I need to pack the appropriate weapons and for my kilt to be color coordinated with the landscape."

"Yes it is."

Beaty who had been listening but so quiet I forgot she was in the room spoke up then. "I needs be goin' with ye, Quenny."

We all turned.

"If ye are a goin' tae Scotland ye need me. I can speak tae the men, and I ken the lay of the land."

"I'm not sure that makes sense..."

"You are goin' tae long ago Scotland, where I hail from, accompanied by a queen from some future place and ye are a black man from the New World. I daena think ye will last for a day. Ye needs a Scottish lass tae lead ye through the lands."

Quentin chuckled and shook his head. "I mean, you're not wrong, Beaty."

She laughed. "I ken it, Quenny, I am nae wrong. I can ride and I can speak Gaelic. I am the daughter of a farmer and I have fought with a pig and I have plucked a chicken and I can keep ye from the trouble that is always followin' ye. Ye need me."

Quentin took her hand. "I suppose we do. Do you agree Katie?"

"Yes, I can't believe I'm saying this, but yes, I suppose we do need Beaty, and I'm very glad you feel better."

"I do I feel much better. The food this morn was delicious. Dost ye think ye could find me some of the clothes ye be wearin'? I wants tae be wearin' the man-breeches, like Emma has on."

Emma laughed. "I'll look through closets. Here I was worried about how you would acclimate, but you seem to be doing it faster than Magnus."

"I like this verra much. Tis a grand house and I like tae be reclinin' in this great chair." She wiggled her bottom in her seat.

I said, "I'm not good at riding horses. What if I got two of those all terrain vehicles from Hammond? Then, as soon as we see the storm, we can cover ground faster, because we need to get there before the Scots get there."

Quentin said, "ATVs will be noisy, but they'll give us speed and more firepower, so yeah, let's do it."

Hayley said, "I'd like to go too."

We all turned to her.

"Nick is my fault, we all know it. And I have ATV skills. I can shoot. Michael and I used to go to the range all the time. I know how to ride a motorcycle. I've taken self-defense classes and I've been CrossFit training. And Katie, you owe me because last time you took me to Scotland you deserted me. You can show me the country proper this time. I'll help you rescue Magnus and then you'll forgive me for almost getting him killed."

"What do you think Quentin?"

"I think it's too many women with questionable skills."

I scoffed. "Seriously? Too many women, right."

"It's not the women part but the questionable skills part that you should focus on."

"Yeah, but you said *women*. If there are only three of us we run the risk of getting separated and someone would end up alone..."

He said, "I want Hammond."

Zach said, "I could go."

Emma looked at him sharply. "Think about it, my love, what if something happens to you?"

I said, "Zach, you're out of the question. I'd love to take you but on a happier journey, this is too dangerous. I need you here, with your family, in charge of my shit."

Quentin said, "I want Hammond to go with us."

"No, I need Hammond here. He's the only one keeping the kingdom from Roderick."

I stared off into space. "What I kept telling Magnus is we are better when we stick together. Well, let's stick together. Hammond will protect this house. Emma, you'll help take care of Archie. Zach, you'll watch to make sure the house is safe, and I'll give you a vessel to use in case you have to leave in a hurry."

I looked over at Hayley. "Hayley will come with us. That will make four. Beaty is our guide. Hayley will need to be a super badass woman but also wear a bodice and seem old-school and demure. I could use a bestie. Sound good, Quentin?"

"You're the boss."

I gulped. "Yes, I guess I am. We'll leave once we've gathered all our supplies. We'll definitely need the two ATVs." I hoped I sounded confident.

EIGHT - MAGNUS

I kicked tae the surface, broke from the murky water, and my aching lungs gasped for air. It was painfully loud above, the surroundings filled with smoke and roar and splash, and the yellin' of men. Shot broke the water just beside me, splashing water intae my mouth, chokin' me and forcin' me back under.

Another cannonball struck the water a few feet away, its force throwin' me limply through the underwater mud and muck. I kicked for the surface once more, gasped some air, and dove under again.

I shoved up for air. I was havin' tae rise for breaths more often, diving down tae escape the fightin' then shovin' tae the surface tae breathe again, growin' weak from the effort and takin' in mouthfuls of water.

I dinna like tae swim submerged, but twas quieter under there. When my lungs were pained from the want of breaths and

I burst through the surface twas all smoke and blasts and terror and death above.

I gasped for more air and went down again, kickin' for the life of me.

I dinna think I could do it anymore.

I was too tired and afraid. My wrists were bound, twas too difficult tae continue... When I went under there was solace. It made me think twould be good tae just let go, tae stop swimmin', tae cease fightin', tae end in peace, in the quiet muck of this unknown river.

I canna do it Kaitlyn. I tried, but I canna—

From the clouds of murky water the curve of a large sea monster drew close and bumped against my side, liftin' me tae the surface for another breath.

The air filled my lungs with a harsh gasp. I choked and coughed and floated there for a moment, my arm across the beast's back. Twas quieter, the water calmer. Then the beast submerged and swam away.

I was north of the battle and close tae the shore. I found the strength tae kick and pulled myself tae the oyster-shell covered bank. I dragged myself up, elbow over elbow, raking across the shells and fell face first intae thick dark mud. *Och.*

I lay there thinkin' *what tae do now?* but kent I dinna have time tae consider. The battle was close. I heard the blasts, the ground shook from the explosions. I was in no condition tae fight so I needed tae get clear of it. I rose tae my knees and searched the landscape for cover. The trees were a great distance away.

I climbed, achin' and exhausted, tae my feet, and found enough strength tae run.

NINE - KAITLYN

I was strapping knives on myself and really, really missed Magnus doing that for me. *Really*.

Quentin said, "How did I let you talk me into this?"

"You didn't let me, you didn't have any say in the matter, as I'm your boss or your queen or whatever."

"You could just tell me what year to go to and I could go."

"I tell you, sure. Then I know. Magnus knows. Reyes knows. There are time-travel vessels laying on a battlefield on this date — anyone could just go pick them up. What if someone tortures you for the information? What if you tell Beaty in a fit of passion?" I teased him, "I've heard about your fits."

He teased me back, strapping his gun belt on under his coat. "I've actually heard your fits, your highness, queen of the bossy ladies. Fine, when Magnus asks why I brought you and my teenaged wife and our friend Hayley, I'll tell him you bossed me into it."

"He'll believe you because he knows me. And he'll be alive so he'll forgive us on it."

Zach walked in to check on our packing.

I said, "Since you are both here I need to ask you something."

Quentin stopped his packing. "Sure."

Zach said, "I'll help if I can, since I can't come and actually help-help. Wife won't let me be a hero."

"Your wife, your better-half, the love of your life, mother of your kid, yeah, she doesn't want you to time-travel — she's also the brains in your family."

I sighed and straightened my skirts. "I'm thinking this whole thing through — Magnus is going to be forced to go back in time to... sometime, by General Reyes. The present General Reyes. And the past General Reyes is back there in the... some time that I'm not telling you. He's there, Lady Mairead said so...."

Quentin nodded. "I know what you're saying, we need to kill him."

"But can we? I mean, he had a whole life of living since that moment, and ever since Lady Mairead gave him the vessel, he's had a whole life of being a time-jumping asshole. Who knows what he's done, whose life he's screwed with? Can we kill him without repercussions?"

Quentin said, "I don't have to think about it. It's done. Then he just disappears and that whole moment by the pool doesn't even happen. Magnus isn't held hostage. It all turns out okay."

I considered that for a moment. Then asked Zach, "What do you think?"

He said, "It's kind of like that, 'would you go back in time to kill an evil guy in history' question—"

Quentin said, "Exactly! We have to do it."

Zach said, "But it's not always that cut and dried. Out of strife comes good, sometimes. From a broken heart a beautiful song is written, maybe the best song anyone has heard. Would you want to stop that broken heart?"

Quentin said, "I can't believe you're saying you don't think we should kill Reyes."

"Nah, you should totally fucking kill him. You can't really consider all the other stuff: what ifs and who is its. He's a creepy sewer-slime monster and he shouldn't get away with it. You guys have been given the chance to get to his time, to a moment where you know he'll be, and you can surprise attack him. How long did Magnus fight him in that alternate reality?"

"Like 25 years. It completely broke him."

"Yeah, you can't let that shit stand. You should kill him if you've got a clean shot, Katie."

I nodded. "Okay, thanks guys. I'll consider the philosophical portion of this decided."

Hayley entered a moment later with Beaty. "What the hell is this anyway — tight as hell." She struggled against her bodice.

Beaty said, "Tis a terrible thing. Tis verra tight and constrictin' I did so love those pants. Are ye sure I canna wear pants, Queen Kaitlyn?"

"No, we have to look the part as best we can." I surveyed the four of us. We did not look the part. I didn't have a bodice. We were wearing parkas over our dresses. "And we should carry a lot more weapons." We strapped on more guns and knives and then gathered up our backpacks, full of food and supplies, and went out to get the ATVs Hammond had found for me.

Hayley asked, "So you don't get to say goodbye to the baby?"

I pulled a strap tightening a belt on the ATV. "Nope. Bella said 'over my dead body,' and I'm trying to remember that I'm not the kind of person who takes that literally." I leaned against the vehicle. "I can't believe I'm leaving him without saying goodbye."

"He's a baby! What does he know?"

"I know."

She patted my back comfortingly. "We'll be back tomorrow, you'll kiss his sweet forehead and tell him good morning and he won't know you were gone on this fool's errand. I'm not going to die, right?"

"I haven't lost anyone yet."

"Awesome. And I'm never the first in anything."

"We'll be fine, just don't ever, ever, *ever* find yourself alone with a Campbell man."

"Why? What – Magnus is a Campbell man: do they look like him, because that might actually be worth it."

I sighed over-dramatically and we finished our packing.

Emma's job was to watch over Archie. Zach's job was to make sure Hammond knew we were returning tomorrow and to make sure Lady Mairead didn't know that we were ever gone at all.

TEN - MAGNUS

The mud was deep. It tugged against my boots so that walkin' was a struggle. I yanked a foot free, leapt ahead, then yanked m'other foot free. I was at the verra end of my strength when I finally made it tae the stand of oaks and collapsed. I needed water. I couldna imagine takin' another step without it but hadna the strength tae find it.

"Och." I said intae the dirt.

A voice nearby said verra quietly, "Wheesht."

Someone was here but I hadna the strength tae put up a fight. I slowly turned my head. A man crouched not two feet away. I groaned.

He put his fingers tae his lips tae tell me tae be quieter still but made nae move toward me.

He was dressed in the coat of a soldier but underneath he was clothed in a tartan and clutchin' a Scottish dirk. Verra stealthily he inched closer, reached for my wrists, and with a clean slice, released my bindings.

He sheathed his dirk, uncorked a bottle, and passed it tae me.

I raised myself and drank, drainin' it of the water inside. I passed it back tae him empty.

The heat was oppressive, steam rose from the mud. Mosquitoes bit around my neck. I swatted at them, but they were impossible tae beat back.

A moment later he rose, gestured for me tae follow, and began tae run through the trees, headed north.

I followed him as I had nae other plan.

~

Occasionally he froze, went dead silent, and waited and watched. Once, he made me drop tae the mud. We went as still as we could go for a verra long time, covered, waiting and listening. Verra faint footsteps travelled by in the other direction.

When I was stopped like this my middle pained me for want of food. It was only when we were in motion that I wasna constantly hounded by hunger.

~

We stayed motionless, hidden behind a log, while an army traveled by headed south. Twas many men, weapons, and horses. They were nae Spanish and looked fresh and well-provisioned.

I would have asked them for guidance or sustenance but followed my travel companion's conduct and remained hidden.

I heard him whisper a prayer until they passed.

~

We came tae a spring late in the day. The man filled his bottle while I fell at the edge, half in and out of the water, fillin' my hands with it and drinkin' thirstily.

Once satiated, I turned tae my back and stared up at the sky. "I am fearfully hungry, friend. You have saved my life with the water and guidance, but I need some food or I canna travel any farther."

"How did ye come tae be at the fort? I haena seen ye afore." The man was as big as me, about the same age, but twas hard tae tell as he had a full beard. He also looked weary and though he wore a uniform was unkempt, as if he had been tae battle. He dug through his sporran for a stick of dried meat.

My mouth watered at the sight but he dinna offer it, instead he carved a slice for himself with his dirk.

I licked my lips. The pain was great and I would have fought him for it if I could survive it.

I rolled tae my stomach and drank some more water then rolled tae my back again. "I canna tell if ye are friend or foe."

The man chuckled, "I have the same questions of ye, the man who is lost and near dead, but as I could have killed ye when yer hands were bound — instead I freed ye, seems as if I have naethin' else tae prove tae ye. You should tell me what ye have been doin' at the fort, or I will stop askin' ye."

"I was prisoner. A man by the name of Reyes was holdin' me in a dungeon there."

"And ye escaped? What did he have ye for?"

"He was—" I couldna say twas involvin' future-kingdoms, thrones, and time-jumps. "Twas an old family grudge. He was trying tae end it by endin' me."

The man nodded. "Och, and ye escaped."

"Aye. And what of you, why are ye hidin' from soldiers wearin' yer same uniform?"

He scoffed under his breath. "I have decided tae go the other way."

I sat up. "You art a deserter? How can ye leave your men, your fight? Tis terrible."

The man shrugged. "Tis nae my fight. I traveled all this way tae the New World tae have some land and tae find a wife, nae tae lose my life outside the stone walls of a castle I daena want tae live in — have ye ever seen such a swamp?" He batted a mosquito away then smacked his neck. "The bugs will eat us alive. The heat, tis nae for man tae want tae live in it. I am ready tae go home."

"Where is yer home?"

"The highlands, Glen Coe, on Loch Leven."

I stared at him for a long moment then shook my head sadly. "Och, you and I — we arna friends. You art a Donald?"

"Aye, I am Fraoch MacDon—" He stopped tae stare at me then let out a long breath. "Ye art Campbell?"

"Aye, I am Young Magnus, nephew of the Earl of Breadalbane."

We stared longer still. I was too tired tae judge the situation fairly and if he wanted tae fight I would lose.

Finally, he said, "Och. You are weakened and near death. I could stab ye through the heart right now with barely any trouble at all—"

"I would try tae cause ye some trouble."

"But would ye?" He smiled. "And I have a'ready shared m'water with ye and have kept ye alive for most of the day, twould be a waste tae kill ye now."

"I might die from want of food anyway."

He chuckled, "That ye may." He cut a hunk of meat from the stick and passed it tae me on the end of the blade. I grabbed it, shoved it tae m'mouth, chewed it barely, and swallowed with a moan.

He laughed again. "By m'accounts tis the eighteenth time I have save yer life taeday. Daena kill me in my sleep, Og Maggy, I haena wanted tae die taeday or I would have continued stormin' the St Auggie fort."

"I daena understand how ye could desert them."

He shrugged. "The fight is lost. I could see twas not ours tae win. I daena want tae die on the shores of the river, there are monsters in the water wantin' tae devour us. Twould nae be a Christian death. There is one just there."

I followed his gaze to a low log downstream, half in and out of the water. "Tis a fallen tree."

"Nae, tis a vile, water-soaked, deamhan uilebheist with teeth that would rip ye tae pieces if ye are nae careful."

"Och, I daena like the sound of that." I pulled myself up and crawled away from the water's edge. I leaned beside Fraoch against a tree.

"Now that ye art on the run, where will ye go?" I asked.

"I needs tae get north, upriver, where I will catch a boat tae take me tae the Port of Savannah. Then I will return across the ocean, headed home tae the highlands. What will ye do?"

I said, "I need tae return tae the fortress, Reyes has somethin' of mine—"

"Och, ye have a desire tae die. There is nae good that will come of goin' back."

I thought about it as the light dimmed with night coming on. The familiar sounds of Florida hummed around us, but this was a hostile Florida, without my comfortable home, without Kaitlyn in a bed a'waitin', without the cool wind of the air conditioner blowin'. I had tae retrieve a vessel. I was empty-handed and therefore trapped. I couldna return tae her and she would never find me. The only vessel was inside the fort held by General Reyes.

I lumbered tae my feet with a groan. "Thank ye friend, for savin' my life. I—"

"Many times taeday."

I brushed off my kilt. "Aye, I am grateful for it. Someday I hope tae repay ye—"

Fraoch said, "Where are ye goin'?"

"Tae the fortress."

Fraoch stood. "I winna let ye. I just met ye, we arna friends, but we both hail from Scotland and I winna let ye die out here."

"I daena think ye have a say in the matter." I tried tae look firm and strong but my knee buckled and I held ontae a tree branch for support.

Fraoch waved his hands in irritation. "Och, ye are gòrach, Og Maggy, ye will die in the mud here."

"Tis nae matter tae ye and I will be gone either way." I turned and left the clearing, but hadna gone for more than a few moments when Fraoch scrambled behind me and slammed intae me, knockin' me face first in the dirt. He drove the breath from my chest and close tae m'ear said, "Wheesht."

He pinned my shoulders, wrenchin' my arm behind my back, and held me down with all his weight. I was nae match for his strength and would die then if he wanted tae kill me, but he stilled and quieted and after some long moments I heard it, faint, a movement through the brush, the footsteps of a man, two men, then a fourth. They were verra close. I went as quiet as I could be and listened tae their sounds as they passed, the bugs stilled, the birds, twas all quiet until the human sounds were nae more and then longer still. I listened tae the woods as the bugs began tae vibrate through the leaves and then longer again I waited, the heaviness of Fraoch across my back.

I bucked him off then and shoved him away and lumbered again tae my feet. I was full of fury.

He stood in front of me, his hands clenched in fists. "Ye canna survive it, Og Maggy."

I was weavin', unable tae stand straight from weakness.

He pulled his fist back and swung, directly for my stomach, connectin', knocking me stumblin' back a couple of steps. He followed.

I swung at him but he ducked, stepped away, swung and hit me against the side of my head and dropped me tae my knees.

He stood over me. "Ye will die. I daena want tae keep hittin' ye, seems a waste tae fight ye as ye are weak as a bairn. I have told ye ye arna in any condition tae fight or even walk. Tis nothin' but death ahead of ye."

"I daena want tae die, but I canna live without returnin' tae the fort."

"Dost ye have a brother?"

"Aye." I tried tae stand but couldna get my feet under me and fell back tae my knees.

"He will thank me for savin' ye from this mischief. It makes nae sense. You should return home. Where is your home?"

Home is where you are, Kaitlyn. She was in Scotland in the year 2382. "Balloch castle." I wiped my mouth on my sleeve. "On the River Tay."

He shoved me down tae my side in the leaves and mud of the clearing. I had nae idea how tae get up again, much less from here in these woods tae there in the future. My only choice was tae get a vessel.

Fraoch sat down and leaned against another tree.

"Ye almost got us killed. Twould be a pity for two Scots tae die here because they couldna agree on whether tae live or nae."

I tried tae calm myself. I focused on the dim light as it filtered down through the trees above us.

Finally he said, "You should say somethin' Og Maggy, ye almost killed us, I saved yer life again, and ye have gotten the beatin' ye deserved for it."

I tried tae rise over my fury. "I will kill ye when I have a chance."

Fraoch said, "Nae, ye winna. Ye ken if your brother was here he would have fought the sense intae ye. He will thank me for doin' it."

I groaned. "He would, tis true."

Fraoch said, "What is his name?"

"Sean."

"And ye wouldna fight him back because ye are a good obedient brother and ye ken that he would be in the right on this."

"Dost ye have a brother? My brother wouldna be in the right, but he would demand I follow him anyway."

"I have a brother, he is young and he daena listen tae me though I am right in most things, as I am now, in this. You need tae sleep, Og Maggy. In the morn ye will see my side on it."

I sighed and turned tae my back. "Will we stay here taenight?"

"Aye, we shouldna move, but we needs tae keep watch for men. They are in search of fresh water." He adjusted his back lower against the tree, settlin' tae keep watch.

"I ken ye daena want me tae, but in the morn I have tae return tae the fortress. I must find a way tae break in, tae retrieve what I left."

He shook his head sadly. "Og Maggy, ye are mistaken on it, ye should let it go, tis nae worth yer life. What is worth a man's life? I have been thinkin' on this question: family, a bonny lass, some land of yer own. Tis what I was promised here in the New World but all I have been given is a rash-covered arse from the heat, and a New World where the logs have teeth. Now I am supposed tae die for it? Nae. Nae I have come tae it, Og Maggy, tis nae worth yer life tae fight for anythin' but your home."

"I canna agree. In this I have tae fight here, for what I lost."

"Do ye have a bonny lass back home?"

"I do. She is..."

"Och, ye should get tae her and daena leave searching for yer fortune nae more. I tell ye, there is naethin' good comes from it. Start yer farm, love yer woman, live tae be an auld man with your bawbels hangin' below yer kilt for all the world tae see and daena care. Tell them tae nae look if yer gingamabobs hang low." He laughed and got me chucklin' too.

He added, "We have been walkin' much of the day, tae return tae the fortress will be tae do that distance once more, ye are too weak for it. Do ye ken tae talk tae the Timucua?"

"Nae."

"The Timacua daena want ye here. Ye have tae ken how tae talk tae them tae pass through their lands. And ye daena have provisions. I can share but I canna give it tae ye. And Og Maggy, ye haena been payin' attention tae the soldiers, they are in movement, and they have been speakin' on the siege. It has turned. The Spanish took Fort Mose. We are bein' pushed north. You canna walk intae a territory that is held by the Spaniards, nae alone. And I have proven myself untrustworthy as a fellow soldier."

"So what do ye propose we do?"

"We are verra close tae the river, at dark we will steal a boat."

"Och, ye are a deserter and a thief."

"I am also verra good at navigatin' and I am the only friend ye have in the New World."

"We are friends?"

"Unlikely, but aye, we are friends."

I let out a low breath. "Can ye spare some more meat?" He broke off a large hunk and passed it tae me on his blade. I ripped it apart with my teeth and chewed hungrily.

ELEVEN - KAITLYN

I woke in a clearing, face down in a Scottish forest. I looked over at Hayley, she was staring up at the sky and for a red hot panicked moment I thought: *dead.* Then she groaned. She turned her head to me. "How come you do this?"

"I haven't ever really had a choice."

Beaty groaned nearby, "Beaty, how are you?" I couldn't sit up to see, but had to hope she would answer.

She said, "Tis fearful and verra painful. Why is it so dark? It looks as if tis mid-day but I can barely see."

I was able to lift my head. Quentin was sitting up, unlocking the chains that locked him to the ATVs.

Hayley and I slowly got up bit by bit, groaning and not over-dramatizing at all.

She asked, "How do I look?"

"Like you've been through an ordeal, brush your bangs down to cover your bandage." She did. "Now you can barely see your head wound. And 'just been through an ordeal' is basically how everyone looks in the 18th — I mean in this century."

I felt around me in the dirt and leaves for the vessel. Nothing.

Wait...

I searched some more.

I got into a crouching position and flailed around wildly, "Where is it?"

Quentin said, "What, the vessel?"

"Did you take it?"

"No, I didn't."

Hayley said, "But my eyesight is making everything super dark, is yours doing that? How can you even see it?"

I said, "I can't, that's the point, I can't see it."

Quentin drew his handgun and went into guard-mode in case someone was with us. Hayley, Beaty, and I crawled around searching and digging in a wider and wider diameter.

Finally I said, "This is fine, I have another one. It's on the, you know, thingy..." I waved my hands in the direction of the ATVs unable to form the right words.

I rifled through one of our bags for the second vessel, the one I brought just in case, the one no one else knew about. Shit. It was gone.

I looked through all our bags, and my searching grew more and more frantic. By the last one I was throwing our stuff all over *everywhere*.

My breath was coming fast.

We were in the fucking — where were we? God, we were in the freaking forests of Scotland in the mid-16th century and we lost — I lost the vessels. Holy shit. I dropped down to my butt and looked around at my friends. "What are we going to do? The vessels are gone."

Quentin said, "We must have been robbed."

"But no one is here. Why would they just take the vessels and would they know what it was? How would they also know where the second one was?"

Hayley asked, "Has this ever happened before?"

"No, whenever we travel it's always lying right beside us. It falls out of our grip but it's there, always right there."

We all looked around at the space. It was like they just disappeared.

Unless.

"Could it — I mean, that would be weird — could it be that we traveled to the day before the vessels all got here? Could it be that our vessel isn't here because the aliens have them all? Did we just discover the back edge of where they could travel to in the past...?"

"Shit," said Quentin, "I seriously hope you got the date right."

I gulped. "Yeah. Um. Yeah. I hope so."

He said, "And we, of course, didn't tell anyone the date, so no one knows where we are..."

I drew in a breath but then couldn't let it out and gasped for another. Then that wouldn't go in or out. I doubled over, clutching my skirts, trying to get any air at all.

Hayley said, "Wait, Sweetie, you breathing?"

I managed to shake my head.

Then I fell forward onto my hands.

Hayley got down beside me. "See me? Look at me? You aren't looking at me. You've got crazy eyes, stop the crazy eyes and look in mine. Now purse your lips like this — see me? Now breathe in. Try it."

I pursed my lips and drew in a short jagged breath. I shook my head.

"No, do it again, purse your lips, breathe in. Breathe in. Now do it again, breathe in. That's a girl, do it again. Good. See, you can breathe like a normal human again."

"You're being so nice to me but I just killed you. I just stranded you in a medieval forest. We're as good as dead."

Beaty looked down at her clothes. "I am nae dead, Queen

Kaitlyn, I am standin' afore ye with a breath in my lungs, tis nae as dark as ye are makin' out."

I moaned. "To me it's dark as hell."

Hayley looked around at the trees, "Yes, it's very dark, but it looks exactly like a 21st century Scottish forest and Quentin and I got out of one of those, so I'm not convinced this is that drastic."

I moaned. "Oh this is very, very drastic. We can't leave. We're stuck here. We might have to live our whole lives—"

"Does anyone know this date?"

"Magnus does. Me."

"Well, you don't matter, you're stuck."

Quentin said, "But Magnus will come get us."

"We're getting him."

Quentin said, "I don't know. I just know Magnus will be here in the morning. He might be a prisoner but he's also sure to have a plan. A bunch of aliens with vessels will be here in a few hours and we have to get a vessel from them before the Scots get here. We have tasks. But we can do them. We just don't have any room for mistakes."

Hayley held out a hand and helped me up. "Right, no mistakes. When the aliens land we'll rush over, grab a vessel, and run away before the Scots get there. Easy. We'll find Magnus, he'll be there somewhere — maybe we should divide up the jobs."

Quentin said, "I'll go in, search the aliens, steal a vessel, and then I will kill Reyes."

"From a safe distance, in a way that doesn't affect any of the rest of the moment, while you're getting the vessel you won't kill anyone, or fight anyone, or even get seen, right? Your job is total stealth."

"One hundred percent."

I said, "The rest of us will keep watch for a sign of Magnus."

We didn't want the noise of our ATV engines to attract the attention of the Campbells, especially when we didn't have a vessel for an escape, so we decided to push them out of the clearing to a hidden spot in the forest. I said, "No worries, we got this. Our plan is perfect, we'll get this all done. For now we just watch for the storms."

~

We all pushed the ATVs to a place that seemed good to wait and watch. It was hidden in trees but on a bit of a rise for a view. It was exhausting to push them here, but we were warm at least. Quentin and Beaty sat together and talked and whispered.

Hayley asked me, "You know what's cool about this?"

"What?"

"You know something now. You know that the vessels can only loop back to this date for some reason. Even if you wanted to you couldn't go see the dinosaurs."

"Or Cleopatra's time."

"Yep. You can only go back to this time, when is this by the way?"

"Not telling you, but it's way before the signing of the Declaration of Independence."

"We aren't even Americans yet?"

"Nope, weird, huh?"

Beaty loudly said, "Queen Kaitlyn, dost ye have your camera? I was thinkin' ye could take a photo for my Insta."

"Beaty what are you—"

She started giggling. "Quenny told me tae say it tae ye. I daena ken what it means..."

"Well, it's very funny, and funnier if you do get your own Instagram account long before Magnus figures out how to use a phone."

I tried to push down my growing fear. We were stranded in

the 16th century. Again, totally responsible for these people. Trying to rescue Magnus. What if we couldn't?

Night was coming on.

It was crazy cold.

We had parkas and mittens to put on over our clothes. We were too close to the castle to start a fire so we just had to shiver together. Beaty was wrapped up in Quentin's arms. Hayley and I were huddled listening to Quentin as he showed Beaty how to work her flashlight.

I thought about how weird it was that the Scots from the castle didn't come to check out our storm. They would come to see the next storm though, that was a part of the story. What made them do that? Was it because there had been so many storms, ours and then theirs? Had this all happened before? Was our loop a part of all the loops? It was mind-boggling and I didn't want to think about it anymore.

Hayley said to me, "This is just like that night, remember, when we told your mama that we were staying at my house and told my mama we were staying at yours and we knew they wouldn't call to check on us because they hated each other? We wanted to spend the night with those boys, remember?"

"That's right, the ones from the country club, down visiting Amelia Island for the summer, from Atlanta."

"Yeah, they were really hot and they said a bunch of sweet things about wanting to stay out all night and the one, he played guitar, right? I'm a sucker for that."

I snuggled in closer for warmth and comfort. "Who isn't?"

"True. So we arranged to stay out with them and then they got busted and had to go in for the night, but we were stuck, out, nowhere to sleep."

"We slept in the sand dunes."

"Exactly, like hobos, it was just like this."

"I love you Hayley. I'm sorry I put you in this much danger."

"I love you too, sweetie. And what I'm trying to say is this doesn't feel like that much danger. I can't wrap my head around it, so whatevs. Love ya Quentin. Love ya Beaty."

Quentin said, "Ya'll need tae quiet down, the aliens are comin'."

Beaty said, "What is an alien, Quenny? Tis like a beast?"

He said, all heroic and romantic, "Don't worry about any beasts, Beaty, I'm going to keep you safe."

She murmured, "Good, because taenight feels the kind where uile-bhéists be lurkin'."

"What do you mean by that?"

"It feels like Oidhche Shamhna, the night of spirits."

"Oh." I said.

"But it wouldna be, I daena think anyone would be heedless enough tae sleep outside on that night."

I said, *och*, to myself and tried to remember through the sounds of bugs and the wind rustling through the trees and the high dark sky and the freezing cold, that I didn't believe in monsters.

Though, of course, we were waiting for aliens.

So I tried to relax while we waited for the night to turn to day.

TWELVE - MAGNUS

A few hours later, Fraoch woke me with a nudge. "Tis time tae find the boat."

"Och." It hadna been enough rest, but twould have tae do.

"You arna plannin' tae leave this morn?"

I held my head in my hands trying to find the strength tae rise from the dirt. Fraoch had been right, I wasna strong enough tae do what needed tae be done. "Nae." I lurched tae my feet.

We dinna have tae walk far before we found the banks of the river, sparklin' in the moonlight. Fraoch warned me that there would be encampments along the banks so we crept along silently and used signals tae communicate as we searched for an unguarded boat.

We first found three skiffs tied tae a low hangin' branch of an oak but there were men stationed nearby. We waited for some long moments but the guards were awake and watchful.

We crept around their camp and walked farther north.

Then we found it, a lone skiff, pulled up ontae the rocks and brush of an unguarded shore. We watched and listened and then I fell in behind him and we crept closer.

On investigation it looked recently used, watertight, but as we drew near it, a verra long beast, its tail directly under Fraoch's foot, shifted, causin' Fraoch tae yelp and jump intae the air. With a heave the beast tossed itself intae the water and slid away.

Fraoch lunged for the rope that bound the boat, untied it, and together we shoved it clear of the shore. I dove intae the skiff tryin' nae tae drag my feet in the water where the vile beast was still swimmin'.

Fraoch and I both lay as quiet as possible on the bottom of the boat and allowed it tae drift from the shore.

Twas a big boat, with seats across. It did a lazy spin, then the current grabbed ahold and pushed us north. We rose, took our seats and oars, and in the dark moonlight we paddled. Soon enough we found a rhythm tae our rowin', propelling our boat along with the current, fast, headed up stream.

~

As it neared dawn we sighted someone on the shore. Fraoch slumped tae the bottom of the boat and I joined him there, keeping a hand on an oar, but hidden within. We let the boat float along followin' the current until we passed the encampment, then we climbed up tae our seats and continued along.

I daena ken how long we traveled or how far. I thought about how Fraoch would likely never ken the true distance, but I might someday ride along this river in my Mustang and track the length of distance on Kaitlyn's phone. Then I would ken how much of it I conquered, but until then I only paddled without knowledge of where or how much longer tae go.

This place was foreign: the river overgrown, the trees, live oaks, thick and wet with moss growin' down. Kaitlyn called it Spanish moss, much like these were Spanish lands with English fightin' over it, and like Fraoch said, twas nae my fight...

When we had a time tae speak I said, "Remind me what the year is?"

"Tis 1740."

"Och." Thirty-seven years in my future, still hundreds of years in her past. I thought about Kaitlyn, in the future in my kingdom, and with the steady row of my oars in the predawn, passin' the drippin' trees in the heat of a summer night, I began tae pray that God would watch over her, and if twas in his divine wisdom, tae please help us get back tae each other.

I couldna imagine how though, without a vessel, in a year she wouldna expect me, in a place she wouldna ken.

THIRTEEN - KAITLYN

The storm built fast and loud, the trees creaking as it pummeled them and whipped around us.

We scrambled to standing and climbed on our ATVs. Beaty wrapped her arms around Quentin and pressed her face into the back of his coat. I held on around Hayley's waist. We started them and the sound was so freaking loud, louder than anything in this entire century, and bringing them here now seemed the craziest thing in the world.

I wondered if our sound and not the storm was maybe why the men came from the castle to check at all — did we bring this whole time-travel-thing into play?

We were on a bit of an incline, in thick woods, but the ATVs were nimble and could easily weave through the trees as long as we concentrated and tried not to let it slow us down. We went down, headed toward the clearing where we landed. The coordinates I used to jump must have been very similar to the ones the aliens used, and wasn't it weird that aliens would use latitude and longitude at all — wasn't that an earthbound construct?

We wove through the trees, and stopped in a small glen just

within the tree line: the sky, the woods, the whole place completely dark, the storm whipping the trees.

Through our headlights we could see there were bodies there — lots of bodies, dark and quiet, unconscious from the jump but oh freaking crap, there in the middle, four men were up, standing, guarding. We quickly turned off our lights.

Quentin whispered, "Did you see Magnus?"

"No."

One of the men who was up and guarding called, "Who are you? We're armed," sounding not at all like a freaking alien, instead sounding totally like an American human.

I asked, under my breath, "Fuck, how is someone up guarding them?"

Quentin whispered, "I don't know, but we have one-second to decide what to do — I just decided. We have to kill them. Ready?"

I yell-whispered, "Kill them? We aren't supposed to interfere!"

"Yeah, but they all end up dead anyway, right? We just have to get through them for the vessel. Don't argue, we can't lose this. You guys get your weapons ready? Hayley, you got this?"

"Yeah, um of course, yeah..." I told Hayley where the buttons were for the ATV's weapons.

Quentin revved his motor. "Kill the guards, look for Magnus. Don't stop until one of us has a vessel."

We drove from the woods, our headlights blaring in their eyes, full speed, our guns firing. They fired back.

Hayley squealed and tried to stay lower than the glass that I hoped was bulletproof. I tried to hide behind her. It was dark, dangerous, loud, and terrifying.

But it was over really quickly and the four guards's bodies lay dead-still on top of the pile of sleeping, time-traveling aliens.

I jumped from the back of the ATV. "Keep an eye out for Magnus or the Scots."

Quentin climbed off his vehicle, and he and I picked our way across around the sleepers, to the dead guards, illuminated in the headlights of our ATVs.

I dug through an alien's coat: white and clean and looking very much like a human coat. My hand was covered in alien blood, red, not blue, like I might expect. A gurgling sound – he clutched my wrists, looked into my eyes, and tried to speak, as if he had something important to say.

I suppressed my need to scream. He was just a man, a human man, not alien at all, dying because I killed him...

Quentin behind me yelled, "I got a vessel!"

I dropped the man's coat and shook his hand off my arm and noticed the vessel beside him. "I got one too, just in case!" It was dripping wet with blood.

Quentin said, "These aren't aliens, this one looks like James's uncle Mike."

I nodded, "Yeah, they're humans." I wiped the blood on the dead man's coat and glanced around the wider circle. "We need to get out of here..."

The storm was dissipating; we had already been here too long. The man nearest my foot began to stir. He clutched at my skirts. I yanked them away.

Had we changed the course of history? I was still here, right?

But I wasn't even a question, the question was: did we just break this scene so now Magnus's kingdom wouldn't exist, or *Magnus*? What if killing one of these men was important to the history of the world? To my world?

They weren't aliens. They were human time travelers, maybe they were part of the story and – when would I know? Would midnight reset the clock and suddenly Magnus wasn't alive anymore?

I stood up in the pile of bodies. Hayley was about six feet away with the ATV humming. "Do you see Magnus?"

"No, I don't see any—"

Beaty called, "I hear horses, they be a'comin' this way!"

Quentin asked, "What direction?"

Beaty pointed toward the woods on the left.

Quentin yelled, "Leave your vehicle, run!"

I raced toward the right with Hayley's breathing in my ear as she raced right behind me.

FOURTEEN - MAGNUS

I had been thinking through this long night how I could get home tae Kaitlyn. I kent I could go back tae the fortress, but it seemed verra dangerous and once there I might nae have the chance tae escape again.

While considerin' it though, it came tae me: I could send Kaitlyn a message. I could tell her tae hide a vessel someplace where I could find it. Donnan told me he could set a tracking signal on a vessel, setting a storm above it. Then he could watch for storms tae find it. He also said it was dangerous tae do because once the tracking signal was set anyone through time could find it.

If Kaitlyn hid a vessel and set the tracking signal I could find a vessel. Then I could go home.

And I wouldna have to fight General Reyes tae do it.

This seemed tae be the best course forward. But where?

Amelia Island was close by, but twas far from Kaitlyn. How could I send her a message from there? General Reyes had Amelia Island under his control, I had tae assume he could watch it in any time, the 24th century, the 21st, and the 18th. I needed tae find out how and kill him tae turn it off but until then the island was off limits.

I wondered if I might find the vessels Kaitlyn and I hid in the waters of the spring here in Florida? Twas probably verra close tae this place, but I hadna any idea where.

I had memorized the map points tae the dock, but where was a map? I could walk through the swamp looking for it but how? And did it even make sense that they would be there in this time? I thought so, but did I really ken it, enough tae spend months lookin' for it?

But if I could get across the ocean tae Scotland, I could go tae Balloch castle. The ruins of Balloch were right beside Castle Dom in my kingdom. Kaitlyn was there now.

It made sense tae me that I could get a message tae her that way. She might think tae look there. I could get m'name on a registry of some kind, then she could look up the history of me. I dinna ken how but I kent it was my best chance tae reunite with her.

I said, "The port is ahead."

"Aye, tis morn and verra early still. If we find safe passage and daena draw attention tae ourselves we might be able tae leave well enough. We must guard against soldiers though, we would be safer with pirates."

"We will find a ship here tae take us tae Scotland?"

"Nae, we need a ship tae take us north tae Savannah, there we will find a ship tae passage us tae England."

The river opened ontae a large port. Docks lay tae the left of us, the mouth of the river tae our right, and the ocean beyond. We aimed our skiff for the dock and tied it off near a few others. A man walking the boards asked Fraoch, "What has become of the siege?"

Fraoch said, "Tis goin' verra well. I was sent ahead tae

arrange for a message tae be taken north tae Savannah. Is there a ship goin' there this morn?"

The man pointed down dock toward a ship. It was teeming with men as if twas about tae set sail. Fraoch waited until the man left and asked me, "Dost ye have any gold on ye, Og Maggy?"

"Nae, I was robbed when I was held prisoner. Dost ye?"

"I do, I daena have much."

While we walked in the direction of the ship, I bargained with Fraoch, "If ye will pay my passage, I will repay ye when we get tae Scotland. If I daena make it, I have family who will repay ye for yer trouble."

"Do ye? Even if the help has come from a MacDonald? If our fortunes were reversed, my family might shoot ye for askin'."

"Och, tis true," I laughed. "You must be a monster even if ye helped me tae cross the world. But my sister Lizbeth, or her children, would believe my life was worth more than our grudge. I am promisin' tae repay ye and I will. I am a man of my word."

He shrugged. "A Campbell who is a man of his word, I daena ken if such a thing has happened afore, but here we are a Donald and a Campbell travelin' taegether. I will trust ye tae follow through, besides I could use the company on the trip across. I am a deserter, ye art an escaped criminal, we may need each other for protection. Twill be a long two months."

"Och," I shook my head, "Tis a verra long time."

FIFTEEN - KAITLYN

When we got to the woods we kept running until we were sure we couldn't be seen. Then we crept back to the edge of the trees and crouched at the bottom of a tall pine, with a long view of the events unfolding.

Quentin pulled out his gun, the one he had picked from Hammond's arsenal, the one that would be best for shooting from a distance, a sniper's rifle to use on Reyes.

He checked the loading, then dropped to the ground, stretched out on his stomach, adjusted the weapon and looked for his target through the sights. He was as still as a part of the forest floor, focused, ready to fire. He just had to spot Reyes and the man was as good as dead.

The Scots rode into the scene and then it was a bare minute before they rode their horses in a circle around it, yelling in Gaelic, freaking out. The ATVs were there of course, their lights on, all those sleeping men and their futuristic gear, dead guards on top of the pile.

I supposed the Scots couldn't see very well either, probably blinded by the lights that were illuminating the morbid, frightening scene. The Scots yelled some more, their horses rearing, their voices panicked, and when the men lying on the ground began to stir the Scots drew their swords and began to kill.

I had been calling it a battle scene but it was definitely a massacre. Yelling, blades stabbing, horses circling, the men on the ground barely fought, and were killed as they were waking. It was horrific to watch, but I tried to rationalize my horror: Magnus and Tyler did this once, killing time jumpers before they awoke.

But I had slept through that one: this one I couldn't unsee, or un-hear: men screaming, horses whinnying, men waking up only to die. It was a frenzy of death. It also lasted for a lot longer than any of us could take — then there was General Reyes.

He was accompanied by two other men and they rode apart from the rest: darker, dressed differently, keeping to themselves, but watching intently. Their horses jostled and reared as they paced at the far end of the murder-pile.

I said under my breath, "Quentin."

He said, his eye on the sight, "I see him."

"Can you...?"

"Men in the way. Shhhhh."

So I quieted and watched and when that got too difficult, I stared at the ground and tried to think happy thoughts: Magnus, holding me in his arms, rocking me, telling me everything would be okay, while I waited for Quentin to kill the man who had taken Magnus away from—

Quentin fired.

My eyes jerked up and I watched as Reyes clutched his chest and fell backwards from his horse, but then something like ten men turned their horses in our direction and charged on us, their hooves thundering over the ground, fast.

I shoved Hayley and Beaty into a scrambled run, down a wooded hill in the dark, slipping and sliding, my skirts catching on brambles and branches down a slope. I shoved them into some low bushes and dove onto them through the scratching branches and lay across them, my arms out, my black parka covering us, acting like the shadow I hoped would hide them.

Hayley, under me, was breathing heavy, her heartbeat pounding. She was big and equal to me in size, but Beaty was diminutive, curled under my chest, as if she was used to going completely quiet until the bad shit went away.

I was mama bird, I held onto them, over them, stilled my body and prayed in my head that no one could hear us or see us in the darkened woods.

And we waited for a long long time, as hooves shifted leaves near us and men's voices called to each other as they searched for us.

I listened for Quentin, for sounds of the men finding Quentin, but it was just men on horses looking around and then they slowly moved on by and went somewhere else. As quiet as it got, we continued to lie there for a long time more.

My body began to ache from the tense stillness and Beaty was beginning to shift uncomfortably underneath me.

Hayley whispered, "Are they gone?"

"I think so." I crawled off them, sat up, and looked around. It was pitch black but the sky above was lightening with the very early thought of dawn, throwing the base of the trees into a deep dark by comparison. I listened for anything. I didn't hear any men, any horses, any sounds at all, but then again, it was the past, it was darker than it should be. All sounds were muffled.

Hayley and Beaty slowly got up, groaning and stretching from their sore muscles, the fear, the tension, the weight of me covering them. Beaty whispered, "Where is Quenny?"

We crawled up the slope moving cautiously, we crept to where we had been sitting before. Quentin wasn't there. I looked at the field where bodies were strewn across the ground. The ATVs were still there, their lights blaring, but as the sun rose the headlights weakened by comparison. *A bright new day always wins,* as my grandma liked to say.

There were a few men left picking through the dead men's clothes, searching for valuables. A man on the ground moved, struggling to get up. One of the Scots shoved him back to the ground.

A Scot was trying to touch the ATV but kept jumping away in fear.

I couldn't see Reyes anymore, but he had been on the far side of the circle, there wasn't a body there now, where he might have fallen.

And still no sign of Magnus.

"Pssst." A rustling in the pine tree above and Quentin dropped deftly to the ground beside me. He lowered down to his stomach and whispered, "Didn't see him."

Beaty crawled up. "I thought ye were gone."

"Nope, but I have never climbed a tree that fast in my life."

Hayley crawled beside me. "What about Nick, did you kill him?"

"I don't know, he was severely injured. If he stays here in the dark ages, I don't see how he survives it, but he's not dead yet."

"Shit, that sucks. Could we follow him, pretend to be a doctor and kill him again to make sure?"

"Nah, I think there are too many variables in that, too many things could go wrong..."

"I was kind of joking."

"As we like to say, in a shit storm this big there are no dumb ideas, just another idea that might be better."

"What's better?"

"I don't know. I know our main goal is 'get Magnus'. We should maybe focus on that and move to a better hiding place."

~

Fog rolled in and covered us. We were hidden, but also had no visibility. Occasionally Quentin crept closer to watch but couldn't tell us what was happening because our voices would travel. We had to sit, completely still and wait and hope no one tripped over us, but probably the Scots had to hunker down because of the fog, too.

~

The Scots were scrounging around the space, searching, I supposed they were trying to make sense of what they were finding. There wasn't much, the time-jumpers had traveled lightly. Quentin wondered if they were an advance party for reconnaissance which seemed plausible enough. They definitely weren't there to make war, they weren't carrying enough weapons.

Soon more Scots arrived and they loaded up what little plunder they found and left in the direction of Balloch castle.

They took two time-jumpers with them. The men looked mostly alive.

In Johnne Cambell's book there had been only one man left alive but here, now, there were *two.*

Again I hoped I hadn't changed anything, but at least there was someone left to teach Johnne Cambell how to use the vessels. It gave me a little hope that the timeline hadn't been changed too much.

But Magnus still wasn't here.

I was so sure he would be.

We walked further from the scene to discuss. "Where could he be, Quentin?"

He shook his head and looked away.

"I mean this was it, right? The moment Reyes would want to

dismantle — if he was going to interfere it would be during this battle, right?"

Beaty asked, "Mightn't he be inside the castle, Queen Kaitlyn?"

I stared in that direction. "I don't know." I added, "I would need to go check."

Beaty said, "I will go for ye, I can talk m'way intae any castle."

Quentin said, "That's my girl."

She giggled sweetly.

I rolled my eyes.

Then I agreed because she was definitely the one with the most skills in this situation.

SIXTEEN - MAGNUS

Fraoch gave me one of his belts and a leather pouch so I dinna look so sparse and desperate. As we walked down the main thoroughfare we kept our heads down and dinna speak, wantin' tae be unnoticed.

We passed a tavern, stepped inside, and after disagreein' on it, decided tae let me do the speakin'. I had studied for a time in London and had lived with Kaitlyn, my English was competent, whereas Fraoch sounded like a highlander and might cause onlookers to wonder why he wasna fightin' at the siege.

Of course I was wearin' a kilt, there was no doubt I was Scottish, but at least I wasna in a uniform like Fraoch.

I ordered us some ale and some meat and bread. We ate quickly savin' some for the beginning of our trip. Then we went tae the dock tae speak with the captain of the *Bellona* about passage North.

Fraoch told him he was carryin' a message from the siege tae the port of Savannah and after negotiatin' we were allowed on board.

As the ship slid from the dock, we went below deck, to sit on low benches, tryin' nae tae be noticed or talked tae until the port was well behind us.

~

An hour later I climbed up tae the deck and stood on the port side watching the long low barrier islands of northern Florida slip past. I was searching for the familiar one and soon found it, Amelia Island, here in the year 1740.

It was untouched, white gleaming sand, the morning sun glinting on its dunes. Twas verra beautiful and I couldna wait tae tell Kaitlyn of it, lyin' in wait for her almost two hundred years afore her birth.

I watched the ocean for the sharks that would be here, but found none, and laughed tae m'self that the sharks were too busy losin' their teeth.

I felt light for the first time in days. I hadna been recaptured and was almost away from General Reyes. I would make my way tae Savannah, then tae Scotland, I was already en route. It would take nothin' but time.

The north end of the island held a wooden fort.

Fraoch met me on the deck and I pointed toward it. "Dost ye ken the name of it?"

"Nae, has been held by the Spanish, but is now held by the English. I haena stayed there. Why are ye so interested in it?"

"Tis a beautiful island, see the grasses? They are sea oats, waving in the wind as we go by. I think the dunes would be full of turtles, have ye seen a turtle?"

"I haena until I came tae the colonies."

"I haena seen many wondrous things until I came here."

He shook his head. "Daena be goin' back. Daena be thinking on it long, Og Maggy, ye are headed north, tae home. From our ship deck the islands of the New World look safe and invitin', but daena forget the shores hold dangers."

I nodded. "The Spanish."

He added, "And the Timucua. Tis nae fit for a Highlander, too low." He chuckled. "I am hungry, Og Maggy, and verra tired. We needs be eatin' and settlin' in. I am told the trip will be another eight hours.

The trip up the coast tae the port in Savannah did take a verra long day. We left sight of land for most of it and there was nae much tae do. I used the travel day tae sleep as I hadna had much since I was last in Scotland at least a week afore.

When I thought on it, tryin' tae remember my last night sleepin' in a real bed, twas with Kaitlyn, at Balloch castle, the night that she let me take her on the high walls.

I remembered her glowin' against the night sky. She tried tae tell me she wasna important because of the stars above us, but what were they saying? 'I will light your way, I will take ye home again.' *Kaitlyn.* She might understand the future but I kent her importance in my present and I couldna think of anythin' else but gettin' tae her.

I thought about her, ridin' on me, wrapped in her blanket, the linen of her shift bunched in my hands as I directed her movements, these were my recollections as I fell asleep in the dark hold of a English ship, in northeast Florida, the year, 1740, runnin' from Reyes, the Spanish, and the English, all. But for now, I was in the lead.

SEVENTEEN - KAITLYN

In the dawn we walked toward Balloch castle, giving the Scots from the battlefield plenty of time to get there ahead of us with their spoils of war.

It made me cringe to think of the battlefield, all those men, jumping and not surviving. I wouldn't go back there. I didn't need to go back there. I had a vessel. Quentin had a vessel.

Though we needed to figure out what to do about the ATVs.

Balloch looked a lot the same, imposing and old, though smaller than it would be in a couple hundred years. Quentin joked, "That's odd, it's smaller than the castle I know, younger looking, and the walls are standing. It's almost like going back in time."

Beaty removed her parka saying, "I do like the warmth of it verra much, Quenny."

He said, "I'll keep it warm for you, Beaty."

I said, "You guys like each other so much, it's really sweet." I sighed. "But back to business, find out what you can of Reyes, is he dead, dying? Oh, and be careful of the Campbell men."

She said, "Och, I ken of the Campbell men, I have been wary of them since I was a verra young lass." Quentin groaned.

"Tis okay, Quenny, I will be back in a couple of hours. I will find out what I can of King Magnus."

And Hayley and Quentin and I stood in the forest and watched her walk up to the front gate of Balloch.

~

Quentin wouldn't move from watching the gate. Hayley and I were tired of standing so we leaned together under a tree and listened to Quentin as he fretted. "Why isn't she back yet? Do you think we should go for her?"

"I'm thinking about how many times, inside that castle, I was kept waiting for someone to come talk to me. She's well within that and maybe she's eating something, maybe she's waiting for the right person to speak to. Don't worry, she'll come out. She's a Campbell woman, it's not like she's an alien or anything."

"They weren't aliens." He said it without turning to me.

"I know, they were humans. Humans who were time-traveling and — do you think they're the ones who invented it?"

"I don't know, but their gear looked unfamiliar and futuristic and I've been three hundred years in the future, so it's beyond that."

I gulped. "Quentin, we killed four of them, their guards. If we hadn't done that, would they all have been killed? If the Scottish men came on them when the guards were alive, I think the guards would have held them off. Did we cause their death? Did we set this whole thing into motion, the kings in the future, the wars? I didn't show you the images of what the future looked like, but it was like a Mad Max movie but worse."

I was talking to his back because he couldn't take his eyes off the castle.

He groaned.

And then we were both quiet.

Finally he said, "I don't know. When you read the book before was there a mention of the ATV vehicles?"

"I don't think so, but I did skim the section of the battle because I'm a huge dumbass." I plucked some grass poking up through rocky ground. "We might have caused the humans from the future to die at the hands of these Scots and set this whole timeline into some weird disarray, and here we are, 21st century people, and our lives might have been determined by something we ourselves did in the 16th century. My head hurts."

Hayley said, "My head hurts and I'm barely following."

Quentin said, "You just said the 16th century, I'd also like to point out that you are terrible at keeping secrets."

"Crap." I slumped against the tree.

"Why isn't she back yet?"

"Quentin, what if Magnus isn't here?"

He turned, briefly, kindly, to say, "Then he isn't here. That's all it means. He's somewhere else. I know it. He isn't dead, Katie, General Reyes didn't want him dead, so Magnus is just somewhere else."

I thought for a moment then said, "Yeah, you're right, yeah. I mean, maybe we're wrong. Maybe this wasn't why General Reyes wanted him. Maybe it had nothing to do with this moment in time." I joked, "Back here in 100 BC..."

"Nice try," Quentin joked, "I don't see any dinosaurs."

I sighed dramatically.

"Where will I look next?"

Hayley said, "Maybe he's not the one who's lost. Maybe you're supposed to sit tight where he, by the way, knows you are supposed to be: that future house, taking care of his future affair-baby, and wait for him to come home. I mean, I know you don't like waiting, you want to be proactive, but there was a moment there where we were *really* lost in the past and we had to kill some aliens—"

"People, men and women, just people."

"Does it make you feel better to say that?"

"No, worse but—"

Quentin interrupted. "I gave the order. We had to get a vessel or we were going to die. So I gave the order. I'm the commander, I did that. You need to separate that from this. Those men were all dead anyway, hundreds of years before you were born. You just got them dead with bullets instead of swords. I think you should stop dwelling on it but if you can't, then blame me. I can take it."

"Thanks Quentin, I appreciate it, that makes me feel better."

"That's what commanding officers are for."

I scrounged for some food in my leather pouch and passed out something that was a little like a protein bar but wrapped in future-plastic and plainly marked because it was military-grade, provided by Hammond.

Hayley said, "Yeah, so my point is if Magnus isn't here, you need to wait for him. Do you guys have a plan in place for if you're separated?"

"Not really, usually there are too many variables to have a plan, but the last thing he said to me was to always know that he loved me and to be strong, to not go weak. Because he had to fight Reyes."

"Exactly, if he's not here you'll have to go back to the future and wait for him, and be strong. While he fights Nick, that total douchebag asshole motherfucking cocksucker."

I laughed a little.

Then added, "He wasn't fighting though."

Quentin said, "He couldn't. He couldn't fight with us there, one or all of us would have ended up dead. He could only submit until we got away to safety. Now he knows we're safe and he can fight. Hayley is right."

"Okay," I said, "If he's not here I'll go back and wait for him. Here's a protein bar." I passed one to Quentin and one to Hayley and we waited to hear what Beaty would find out.

EIGHTEEN - MAGNUS

Twas dawn when the ship was nearin' the Savannah port. I leaned against the rail with Fraoch and watched the coastline slide by. "Have ye been here afore?"

He said, "Aye, twas the port where I came in. The men on the boat were sick from the scurvy. Dost ye ken of it, Og Maggy?"

"Aye, I ken of it."

"Twill be the death of men tae nae see the land for a long time. I hope ye be strong enough. I wouldna want tae cross again but I ken now what lies here and tis naethin' but certain death. At the fort we had men sick and dyin' all around us, and from that misery we were tae get ourselves up and take arms against the Spanish."

I scowled.

"I ken ye daena understand my leavin' my men, but I tell ye, Og Maggy, I heard a commander say we had been brought tae the colonies because we were merciless and we could live through any deprivation havin' grown up in the highlands. He also said, I heard it with m'own ears, that we daena need tae be fed. We just had tae be told tae fight and we would kill. How is that tae be seen, Og Maggy?"

"I have been there, the last man tae rule over me had me fight for his entertainment."

"Aye, then ye ken what I speak of."

"I do."

"Did ye win?" He chuckled, his eyes lighting mischievously.

"Aye, daena I look like I won?"

"Ye are alive but ye daena look like much tae kill for sport."

I laughed. "You are the first tae think it of me. Aye, I killed every man he asked me tae kill. I was a verra good son for a time."

"Your father?"

"My father." I shook my head and joked, "He was nae a good father."

"Och, he sounds verra unlikable. My father, Auld Fraoch, died three years ago. Twas why I left. I daena like the idea of home without him in it, but now I have seen the world and I can return. I would rather be near a home that reminds me of him instead of a cruel land such as this."

"I have just lost the man who was most like a father tae me, Uncle Baldie. He was a good man."

"Did he raise arms against the MacDonalds?" We passed wide marshes as our ship slid up the river tae the Savannah port.

"Aye," I said, "and I think yer father battled a Campbell in his day as well."

Fraoch said, "That he did."

NINETEEN - KAITLYN

Beaty approached from behind, just about scaring the shit out of us.

After we recovered, Quentin hugged her gratefully. "Why didn't you come back directly?"

"I kent I was bein' followed."

"I have guns! I'm your husband!"

"Och," she batted him on the shoulder, "I ken how tae lose a Campbell man who is followin' me. I have been a maiden for many long years."

Quentin ran his hand around on his head frustrated and murmured under his breath about her not coming straight back, but I had more important questions. "Was he there?"

"Nae, the men in the castle haena seen any Campbell men that are strangers. There was a great deal goin' on and the men were discussin' everywhere what tae do. I found the woman who seemed tae ken a great deal and listened tae the story she told. She said there was a battle and she said there were two vile beasts that had been captured and were imprisoned under the castle."

"I wish we could rescue them, poor guys, this is kind of our fault—"

"Katie, it was my call."

"Right, it was kinda your fault. I still wish we could rescue them."

"We can't. One of them needs to be there to tell them how to work the vessels. We can't screw that up or we screw everything else."

"We might have already." My thumb freaking hurt from where I was chewing my nail to the quick. A little drop of angry blood on my tongue from it. "What about Reyes? Did you find out anything about him?"

"I asked if they had been visited by Spaniards and was told there had been one, an envoy tae the king, but she thought he was gone a'ready."

"No one else knew anything? He wasn't there injured somewhere?"

"Nae." She noticed my face was white and fearful. "Twill be a'right, Queen Kaitlyn, Quenny killed him, I am sure of it. Tis why he isna around the castle now. He is dead in the woods somewhere and we winna have trouble from him again."

"I hope you're right." I stared off at the distance. "And no Magnus?"

"Nae."

"Quentin what should we do? Wait for tomorrow? From the looks of it it's pretty late in the day."

Beaty said, "Aye, tis growin' verra dark..."

Hayley said, "It would be nice to get in a warm place with a —" She stopped herself. "You know, we need to find out about Magnus, if we go back now we won't know... we should stay another night at least."

Beaty asked, "Out here in the woods with the spirits and fae again, Quenny?"

"Aye, Beaty, one more night out here in the woods."

TWENTY - MAGNUS

The port of Savannah was busier than the one at St Johns. There were three ships anchored and wooden crates and barrels lined the shore. Fraoch and I spoke tae a few men, tried a first ship, and then found passage for us both on the second ship, the *Deptford*.

The crew was shorthanded. Men died comin' across and men planned tae stay ashore tae make their living. They needed men tae work the ship on the return tae England. In exchange we would have provisions and a bit of paltry earnings, so when we arrived in London, Fraoch and I would be able tae buy passage tae Scotland.

I was starin' down a road that would take a fair many months from my life. Without Kaitlyn. Without home. Without Chef Zach's cookin'. But I couldna think of a way back tae them without this stretch of road. I kent I was too weakened tae fight my way intae the fortress, and Reyes was likely gone a'ready anyways.

I tried nae tae dwell on my lack of strength as I embarked across the ocean for a far shore.

I had one thought, only tae work, only tae stay alive.

After a few hours helpin' prepare the *Deptford* tae set sail, we left the port, headed for Charleston.

Twas a warm day. I guessed twas near the summer solstice, hot and humid. The coastline looked much the same, low islands, sea grass wavin', then we left the shoreline for the open sea, and Fraoch and I took our places on deck, sailin' the vessel alongside the crew.

~

I passed Fraoch as I was coilin' line on the quarter deck. "Fraoch, ye have turned ruddy. You will be crisp as a summer sucklin' pig roast in a time."

"Aye, the sun has me on fire, but I would rather the warm sun beatin' down, than nothing but storm and darkness and us cowerin' in the holds under the ship."

"Och," I said, "daena speak of it."

"Tis why I am collectin' the sun. You will thank me later, during the storms, when the wind is howlin' and ye are prayin' tae God tae save ye, you will say, 'Thank the heavens my friend Fraoch has turned a red glow so he can light our way tae the English shore.'"

I laughed and continued with my work.

~

We had a moment tae rest at the end of the day and found some shade on the forecastle tae eat our provisions — a bit of salt pork cooked in beans, a small loaf of bread, and a shared mug of beer. Then we rested under the darkening sky.

"How do ye ken tae sail, Og Maggy?"

"Growin' on the shores of Loch Awe, the most beautiful loch

in all of the highlands, nestled under Ben Cruachan. Have ye ever seen it?"

"Nae."

"Tis a majestic day tae fish from a boat in the middle of it. What of ye, Fraoch?"

His eyes glinted. "I sailed the Loch Leven, the best loch, Og Maggy, everyone agrees on it. There are birds and fish there that ye haena ever seen. They winna go south tae see yer loch, they say, 'we are happiest here, on this grand loch.'"

"The birds say this?" I laughed, "Och, we will have tae disagree on it. Because Loch Awe has a beauty tae it unparalleled in all of Scotland and the New World. There is a place that comes close, tis called Maine. There is a loch by the name of Holden. It has a spectacular beauty tae it as well."

"I wish I could say I will see it someday but once we have our back tae this world I pray tae never set foot there again."

I lifted my mug, "Tae the wind at our back."

"Aye, Og Maggy, we hope for the best of the wind. Strong and sure and straight tae Scotland."

TWENTY-ONE - KAITLYN

It was freezing. Really really cold. Quentin said, his voice coming to me through the darkness, "I have to get Beaty somewhere warm, she's too cold."

I pulled myself all the way awake and my eyes adjusted to see she was shivering against his chest inside his parka. A shockingly sick sounding cough erupted from her. "God it's freezing out here – how long has she been coughing like that?"

"Started about an hour ago." She coughed again.

I sat up and took stock. I didn't want to leave. I needed to know if Magnus was here or coming here and I wasn't sure yet. But—

She coughed again.

"She needs to go back. We could send her with Hayley."

He said, "Neither of them knows anything about the future, at all, it's not safe."

We both thought for a moment. She coughed. I asked, "Does she have a fever?"

"She's hot and shivering, has been for about half an hour."

"Okay, take her. Me and Hayley will stay here for another

day or two. We have two vessels." I dug through my pack looking for one.

Hayley mumbled, "Beaty doesn't sound good."

"I know, Quentin is going to jump with her, you're going to stay with me..."

"In this fucking freezing-ass forest? Great, and by that I mean great because you owed me a trip to Scotland and this has been my plan all along."

He started to adjust Beaty to stand. "No, don't, just lay there. Quentin, the jump is really long, hold onto her, it's hard and she doesn't sound good." She coughed and my hands shook from fear. How did she go from sweetness and helpfulness to that sick that quickly? "I twisted the vessel. "When you get there, ask for Hammond, get her to a doctor. These are the numbers—" I said them.

He repeated them back messing up one halfway.

"Shit Quentin, stop, wait, don't — fuck, don't get the numbers wrong, okay? Promise me, she's counting on you."

"I know, I just got nervous."

"Don't, don't get nervous." I turned on my flashlight and dug through my bag for my pen. "Roll up your sleeve."

He pushed up his sleeve but his arm was too dark. The back of his hand, nothing. I started to write it on the palm of his hand but the stupid fucking ballpoint pen wouldn't write on his damp palm.

"Beaty, I'm writing something on your skin, bear with me." I pushed up her sleeve, her arm pale and dry and hot and fragile reminding me of my grandmother's arm in some weird way, like her body wasn't doing what it was supposed to do, pale and weak and terrifying. I wrote the numbers in a string down it while she whimpered because I was probably pushing too hard but I was totally freaking out.

"See it?"

Quentin said, "Aye," lapsing into a Scottish answer.

"Say the numbers just like that. Do you have your weapons?" He nodded.

"Hayley and I are going over there." I grabbed Hayley by the hand and dragged her far away and we watched through the darkness as Quentin held a flashlight, adjusted Beaty in his arms, and began mumbling the numbers. The storm built. Hayley and I clung to each other against the wind. Visibility went to zero in the storm and we cowered at the edge of the lightning, wind, and fury, until finally it was clear again and Quentin and Beaty were gone.

It was surreal to see the empty spot. I had rarely watched as someone else jumped before.

The storm was brutal. I never wanted to be inside it again.

When it finally ended Hayley and I kept our arms around each other because frankly it was cold as shit out here.

"Do you think she's going to be okay?"

"I hope so. Lady Mairead was really sick when she first jumped, she turned out okay."

"She turned out a bitch, hopefully that isn't a side effect. So it's just you and me? How long we staying at this swanky hotel?"

"I don't know. I've never been in the past by myself without Magnus or another Campbell to show me what to do and this is even farther in the past... Tomorrow we can watch the castle for signs of Magnus or Reyes."

"What do we do if we see Magnus?" Her voice was low and deep, beginning to go back to sleep.

"I run up and throw my arms around him and — yes, you can sleep. I'll take first watch."

Hayley yawned. "What if we see Nick?"

"If we see Nick, without a doubt he's a dead man."

"You are such a badass," she said.

"It doesn't feel like it most of the time. I spend half my life terrified about what will happen."

"Well, yeah sweetie, there's a lot of scary shit going on in your life." Her breathing slowed.

I asked, "Hayley, what was it Magnus said to you that made you forgive him?"

She opened one eye and looked at me then closed it again. She mumbled, "You can't let it go, huh?"

"I might never see him again."

She groaned. "Okay, fine. Remember that night when you were sitting in his kitchen, after you helped him take Lady Mairead to the hospital, right at the very beginning?"

"Of course."

"He said you were telling him about how to turn the lights off, and he had a feeling come over him — he knew right then you were going to be his wife. He said it was as if he glimpsed his future, all at once: you were in his arms and you were older and you were smiling up at him, and there were children around you. He said he knew then that the moment was important—"

"He did?"

"If I remember correctly, he said, 'The moment twas vastly important.'"

"He never told me that. That's really nice."

"But it's not really the part that did it for me. I mean, he says nice things all the time, am I right?"

I nodded in the cold darkness.

She said, "He told me that because the moment was so important, because he knew you were his future, he didn't know what to do. He said he prayed to God for the chance to prove himself worthy of you. And now that he had been given a chance he would spend his life trying to prove it. He said he failed all the time but he would keep trying to deserve you."

"Did he tell you he begged me for forgiveness and all of that?"

"Sure, and I knew it, I could see it in his eyes, he was so desperately sorry, but that wasn't the important part. The important part was that Magnus, that hot hunk of hotness, stood in front of me and told me that he never believed he was worthy of *you*."

I smiled at the thought. "He's delusional."

"No, he's a smart smart man. Smart and hot and he knows you're the better one of you both, so that was good enough for me."

"Thank you, Hayley."

"You're welcome. Now let me sleep, I might meet a Campbell man tomorrow, I need to look pretty."

"Campbell men are dangerous."

"So you tell me, but modern men are pretty dangerous too. Might as well be wearing a kilt." She snuggled down into her parka and went to sleep.

TWENTY-TWO - MAGNUS

After a few days at sea we landed in Charleston. It would take five days to empty the ship of its load and bring in more supplies. I was glad of the chance tae be on land, though the work was brutal and the day the hottest so far.

In the evening Fraoch and I went tae the tavern along with the crew. We were all exhausted from the heat and a frightful smell, and there were some men in our company that were the worst of men and I dinna want tae cross them.

After dinner Fraoch found a bed tae share with one of the women who worked the shipyards. "Do ye want a warm bed and a lass, Og Maggy?"

"Nae, I am nae wantin' tae spend the money on the bed and the woman daena interest me."

He laughed. "How can this be? You are healthy enough! Ye have a pump handle like the rest of us, daena ye?"

I chuckled. "I do."

"Then it makes nae sense tae hear ye say ye daena have the interest."

"I made a promise tae her."

Fraoch waved his hands at me. "Daena speak on promises, Og Maggy, a woman kens what a promise is. They canna blame ye for what happens in the New World. Ye could die and never have yer cock properly attended tae."

"Twill be a risk I have tae take, and will give me a reason nae tae die."

"I guess twill, I am thinkin' ye will be a different mind of it when we arrive in London, twill be a verra long time by then."

"Och, I daena ken how I will do it, but I mean tae keep my promise. I have broken her heart in the past, tis nae in my nature tae do it again."

Fraoch took his leave and went with a woman up the stairs tae the top floors of the tavern and I stayed down and drank some more and talked with the men about war and ships and the lands of the New World.

I wanted tae save the small pittance I earned for when I arrived in London. The fare tae Scotland would be expensive and I owed Fraoch for his help, so I slept on the main floor of the tavern with all the men who couldna afford tae bed a whore.

I woke up stiff. The sky was dark and by mid-day there was a torrential rain. We worked the full day again and again and again, for four long days.

Then, in the eerie darkness of the fifth day, it was time tae leave. The crew awoke in the tavern, full of good spirits, happy tae have the drudgery of carrying boxes behind us. We clambered aboard the *Deptford* and got her ready tae sail.

~

We had verra good weather. We were used tae our jobs and did them in a routine that exhausted our bodies but kept our minds busy. We needed tae swab the deck and polish brass tae keep our thoughts off our hunger and the relentless rockin' of the ship.

~

The day was bright and warm. The deck was steamin' as it dried from a three day rain. Men were turnin' their faces tae the sky for the warmth. We were many of us in good spirits after bein' soaked through. We could read the sky, the wind was behind us, pushin' us, there hadna been any big storms yet.

Fraoch walked by draggin' a bundle of sails.

I joked, "You have tae mend sails? I wish twere fishin', the only sustenance we've had has been the smell of flatulance for three days."

Fraoch joked, "Och, has been a dank and steaming cloud over our heads. I may never go below deck again."

I finished up my tasks and joined him on the main deck. I found a rip in the sail at one end and set tae the repair.

He asked, "What was the longest fish ye ever caught, Og Maggy? Mine was a bradan, this long." He held his hands out tae show me the length of it.

"Och, ye are making me hungry." He seemed proud of its size though, so I added, "Tis verra wee. I have caught breac that were twice that."

"You canna be tellin' the truth, Og Maggy. Ye have lived in London for too long, sharin' cakes with the king. You are a castle-dweller, always huggin' yer stomach, retchin' intae a bucket while the rest of us are tryin' tae sleep. The Campbells canna fish."

"Och! I daena need a boat tae find the fish. I could throw the net from the window of my Kilchurn nursery and the fish would leap intae my hands."

He laughed. "I will come see ye do that someday, Og Maggy,

but I wouldna want ye tae exert yerself. I will ask ye tae sit there idle and let a MacDonald feed ye."

I chuckled. "Did ye ken that I have eaten from a MacDonald many a day?"

"Really? Where?"

"In the New World. In my village there was a tavern run by a MacDonald. My wife liked tae eat there. Twas the MacDonald food that caused me tae fall in love with her."

"She liked the Macdonald food did she?" His eyes twinkled mischievously.

"Careful," I said.

"I winna tease ye on it since ye haena had her in a long time, ye are probably grown ornery. I reckon though the MacDonalds were nae aware ye were a Campbell when they fed ye."

"Probably nae, I kept m'family name quiet."

"For the best I would think."

"We are unlikely friends are we nae?"

"Aye."

He dragged the linen thread through the gash in the sail and pulled it tight tae close it.

I said, "I winna want my son tae do work like this."

He looked at me askance. "Do ye have a son, Og Maggy? I haena heard ye speak on him afore."

"Aye, he was born afore I left. Twas nae much bigger than..." I held my arms tae show the size of him.

"So wee for ye tae be out on a ship in the middle of a vast sea. When ye see him he winna remember ye are his father."

"He is still verra young."

"And your wife — what was her name?"

"Madame Kaitlyn Campbell."

"Madame Kaitlyn, you are fortunate she came through the birth a'right..."

"My Kaitlyn is nae the mother of my son..."

"Och, ye have broken a vow, now I ken the promise ye made."

"Aye..." We were quiet for a moment. Then I added, "My Kaitlyn has shewn a kindness tae my son, motherin' him as if he were her own. Tis a marvel she can love and forgive me as much as she does, so I have made a promise tae her and I winna break it, nae again."

"I see the truth of it now, Og Maggy."

"Dost ye have a bairn, Fraoch? I am surprised we haena spoken of it yet."

"Nae, my bonny lass died of the fever and the bairn went with her. Twas a son."

"Och, I am sorry."

"I lost my wife, my son, and my father in the same winter."

"Tis why ye went tae the New World."

"Aye, twas a terrible loss, I have been a verra broken soul for a time."

I clapped a hand on his shoulder. "And now ye are headed home."

"I canna imagine never seein' it again, the loch, hearin' the rowdy insults and mockery of my family—"

I laughed. "Nae one can insult like a blood relative."

"Aye." He smiled, "Tis tae toughen us for when the enemies attack."

I tossed out my line. "Like a Campbell."

He asked, "I have been meanin' tae ask ye, did ye take arms against the Donalds, Og Maggy?"

"Nae, I was scoutin' once, and found m'self and m'brother in a skirmish with three Donald men, just outside of Inverness. Twas a vicious fight, but we dinna finish anyone. We promised tae meet them on a field another day."

I stitched for a moment. "I lived for many years in London, so I dinna spend as much time fightin'..." I stared out at the still horizon for a few moments, then added, "but my brother Sean has fought and killed many a Donald. I daena hold it against him. If ye faulted him for it, Fraoch, I would protect him against ye. He has done what he needed tae do tae protect his family, and he is my brother."

"I would expect it of ye, tis right tae defend yer family."

"Have ye raised arms against the Campbells?"

"Aye, I have killed many Campbell men in defense of my family."

"Och," I said and then we sat in companionable silence, the unlikeliest of friends.

~

We had grown verra sick and tired of the relentless nature of the sea and had been at sea too long — then a storm rose on the thirty-sixth day. Twas a ferocious storm and it turned the sea an angry mood. Waves rocked us dangerously, salt water swept over the prow, the ship was climbin', then plunging down, hour after hour, the ship careened in the sea.

The crew worked in long shifts and returned tae the hold tae cower and try tae sleep. Our hammocks swung frightfully and men were moanin' from sickness. Twas verra hard tae keep your food down with the ship lurchin' us back and forth and risin' and descendin'.

Whenever a man wretched intae the bucket it would cause other men wretchin'. The stench under decks was terrible.

We couldna go above deck for fear the waves would wash us intae the swill.

We dinna speak, except in mumbled prayers to God. I begged his mercy for many long hours.

We barely moved except when drawn intae requirement then we tried tae finish the work needed tae return tae our hammock and moan and pray some more. I was thankful when I could sleep.

The storm lasted for three long days. Then there was a half day break and then another storm descended upon us for another five days.

TWENTY- THREE - KAITLYN

Magnus. Under me. We were face to face. I brushed my fingers down his cheek and looked into his eyes, up close, his pupils dilating, twinkling with pleasure as I adjusted my hips, straddling him.

He breathed deep, in and out.

I smiled. And brushed the edge of my lips against his. Pressing against his cheek, I breathed in the scent of him, woodsy, like a Scottish forest, fresh like a night sky. *I love you, Magnus.*

I love ye too, mo reul-iuil. His hands tightened on my ass, pulling me closer. His eyes closed, he whispered, *I dinna mean tae leave ye, but I have gone...*

Wha—?

There was nothing under me —just air and dirt and leaves and I patted frantically around for him — *Magnus, Magnus? Where are you? Tell me, please, Magnus, please, where did you go?*

"Kaitlyn?"

"Huh?"

Hayley groggily said from inside her zipped up parka. "You're having a nightmare, sweetie."

"Oh, yeah. Right." I thought back through it, it had been real and intense and like he was really there. I could hear his voice reverberating right inside my head, not like it came through my ears but like it came through my skin — *I have gone...*

Was it him?

My heart raced and I kept thinking about it, his hands had felt like pressure, his skin — it all felt so real. Had it been him telling me something? Was that a message?

—I have gone.

What did it mean?

I pulled the parka around me and zipped it even higher and tucked down into it. "Man, it's cold as shit out here."

But Hayley was already asleep...

TWENTY-FOUR - MAGNUS

'Twas a verra bleak time after this. We had some long days of the doldrums, nae wind tae push us, and many of the men were fallin' ill. The food was runnin' dangerously low. I was verra hungry. It pulled at my stomach and made me weak and angry.

Many fights broke out. We pulled the men apart, but sometimes we let them fight and watched for somethin' tae think on besides our growin' desperation.

Fraoch and I kent we would fight in defense of each other, but there were days when I hated the sight of him. We just sat beside each other mendin' sails and ropes, trying nae tae be noticed, tryin' nae tae argue, tryin' nae tae die in a fight on a ship deck.

I verra much wanted some spice on what little food I had left.

One night two men fought so hard they brought each other close tae death and the captain was so furious he sent them over the side to their end.

We were quiet as we watched them over the side and for a moment we could hear them still, beggin' tae return, but then the Captain stalked around the deck, bellowin' about how he could neither cure them nor keep them, and that he did it tae give the rest of us fair warnin'. He would drown us all if we were nae careful.

One thing was certain, as the days dragged on there was more work tae do, and fewer men tae do it.

By now we had lost twelve men.

That night Fraoch, in his hammock, in the dark, his voice low, asked, "How long do ye think we have left, Og Maggy?"

"I think two weeks yet."

"Och, If I get sick, would ye make sure he daena... I want tae see Scotland. I daena want tae go intae the sea."

"If ye get sick I winna let that happen."

"Thank ye, Og Maggy, I will do the same for ye." When I thought he had fallen asleep he said, "Ye talk tae her much when ye sleep."

"Och, I do?"

"Aye, ye say her name and tis like ye are tellin' her where ye are."

"Perhaps I am. I often dream on her; tis like she is verra close tae me some nights. I pray she is listenin'."

"Aye, I pray she is too, Og Maggy. I like tae think yer story will have a good endin'."

The next day the back side of the storm slammed intae our ship and we rode the waves and wind for five more days, past the point of bein' able tae work. Many of the men remained below decks, moanin' in their hammocks. Water sloshed around and the rats were in our hammocks with us, but the worst part was that men were dead and we couldna get them out and over the side; we were too exhausted from the daily battle with the winds and the sails. They remained in the hold rotting alongside us.

~

The final day of the storm Fraoch couldna help on deck.

I was verra worried for him as I battled the storms against the sideways rain, the surging ocean, and my relentless hunger.

TWENTY-FIVE - KAITLYN

I was grateful for the fog of dawn because it felt like it warmed by a couple of degrees. It was still cold as shit out here though. Birds were chirping like fucking little mad-men telling us and everyone else in the woods to wake up and Hayley and I were stiff and ornery. She did a lot of muttering about there not being any coffee.

We ate protein bars and then moved back to a location, up high, with a binocular view of the front gate of Balloch castle.

The trouble was there wasn't much going on. No one special went in or out except for the usual barbarians, most of them were heading through the woods in the direction of the massacre, to the east at Inchaiden.

I wanted to go there and see what they were doing.

I also didn't want to leave this spot in the woods and take my eyes off the gate. What if Magnus came through it, in or out, or what if I missed him? Hayley and I discussed the possibility of me going in there, but she couldn't stay out here by herself. And I had never gone into a castle without someone there to protect me. And I had seen some bad shit happen behind those walls.

But I was starting to get really cranky and irritated because why the fuck isn't anything easy with me? Why was this so hard?

I needed to go in there—

Hayley finally said, "He's not here. I know you think he is, that he might be, but he's not. I feel like you would know. He would have been there at the massacre, or near-by, he would've seen your ATVs. He would have heard about them. Or Beaty, he would have heard her or seen her or heard her name. He would be scouring the grounds, the woods, the *everything*, looking for you."

"I hadn't thought of that."

"Or maybe he is in there, he's dealing with shit, he's got young Nick, probably dying from a gunshot wound. He might have older Nick, forcing him to do things. He's got all these barbarians to deal with, a massacre, and trying to get home to you. Maybe he doesn't know you're here and he can't think about it right now."

"That could be true too."

"So that's two things that could be happening. Both of them mean you and I shouldn't be here in these woods anymore. I haven't even been introduced to the Loch Ness monster yet and you know what the worst part is?" She smiled sadly. "The very worst part of all of this?"

I shook my head.

She said, "I didn't download any songs to my Spotify. I was going to, before I left the Island with Nickwad, oooooh, that's a good name for him, Nickwad. I had a whole plan, all the romantic music I was going to play on our trip to Atlanta, but I didn't get to it and now this, a bleak forest, and no music." She added, "This whole thing," she waved her hand around, "really needs some Mumford and Sons, or maybe some Harry Styles, you know, the new stuff?"

"Yeah, I know the new stuff. It would sound really good right now. And it's impossible to be here without imagining Mumford and Sons playing." I took a deep breath. "Did you buy new clothes for your trip, too?"

"And a new suitcase. I really thought he was great. I was trying to impress him, a murderer. This might be a new low."

We were sitting at the base of a tree in the muck and mire of a medieval forest. "I'm so sorry about it, Hayley. I wish he had been great, you deserve it so much."

She threw her hands out to the side and dug her fingers into the dirt and wiped a little mud on both her cheeks. "I mean look at me," she crossed her eyes. "I'm finally getting my act together, why can't anyone love me?"

"Does it help to say that I love you? I have since we were five going to dance classes together."

"It does help, thank you, sweetie."

We both stared across the vast green forest toward the castle.

"And you're right. I can't go in there, I can't sit here forever and this is pretty damn dangerous. I wasn't kidding when I said you have to watch out for the Campbell men, they do have a propensity for violence..."

"Except Magnus."

"You haven't seen him kill someone."

She hugged me around my shoulders. "So we going back?"

"Yeah, we'll go back, but the more I think about it the more I think I need to get the ATVs first."

~

We crept to the edge of the clearing. Flies were swarming the bodies, the ATVS were parked, their lights still on. That had to be good right, it meant they had power? We watched the clearing for about ten minutes to be sure no one was there.

"Okay, we're going to run, straight for the pile of men."

"It's so freaking dark, like I'm partially blind."

"Yeah, I learned to stop struggling against it and just accept it, easier that way. I bring lots of flashlights. So we're going to check to see if there's anything in the pile we want. Check if someone is still alive and I don't know, just check. Fast. Then we go straight to the ATVs and drive them back here, don't head off in any crazy directions, stay close to me."

I pulled the vessel from my bag and checked the dials on it for placement. "I have the vessel at the ready, we'll twist it and fly if we see any danger. Got me?"

A voice right behind us yelled something loud which I guess was Gaelic for 'What the fuck are you doing here?'

"Shit!" I glanced over my shoulder, there was a man there on a horse. We scrambled up and ran stumbling over our feet and some logs. The man on the horse had to skirt some trees giving us a split-second lead.

I yelled, "To the ATVs!"

The horse was bounding over a log and bearing down on us, I leap-frogged onto the seat of one and Hayley jumped to the next. We both started the engines and with a jerk I set mine into motion and heard Hayley's pull in behind.

The man on the horse was swinging his sword and Hayley ducked as it went past. She pulled her ATV to my side and we sped away. My choice was flee into the woods, but he would probably be faster there and he was fast behind us. I whipped the ATV around in a tight circle, aiming right for his horse, causing it to rear and twist and lose its footing. The horse screamed, the man yelled, the ATVs were insanely loud.

I forced us into another loop as the man was still trying to control his horse. I pulled my ATV to a stop. Hayley did another loop around me, menacing toward the man on the horse, while I got the vessel out and twisted the ends.

I reached out my feet, keeping my butt on the ATV, my

hands on the vessel, "Hayley!" The storm began to rise above us, wind whipping the space, and from the edge of the clearing more men on horses riding through the trees headed toward us.

She revved her engine, causing the horse to turn and run the other way. Then she did a 360, revving, building a cloud of dust behind her wheels, and crashed her ATV right up to the side of mine, she slung her body across my seat, her feet on her own, and grabbed hold of my arm. "I'm here!"

I said all the numbers, fast, in the right order and headed us with a slam and terrible mind-scalding pain through eight centuries.

TWENTY-SIX - MAGNUS

Fraoch dinna rise the next day. I talked tae him of it, "Fraoch, I have yer rations," and placed the biscuit intae his sweaty hand, but he hadna the strength tae bite intae it.

He winced. "Hurts m'teeth."

"I ken, ye daena look like ye have the strength tae chew. Ye are a fright, Fraoch."

"Daena look on me if ye are goin' tae act a bairn about it."

I gave him some ale and then I went on deck tae do the work of two men.

I dinna ken how long I could work for us both, I was verra tired and this passage dinna look tae end with a shore.

That night Fraoch whimpered and moaned so much I had tae cover my ears tae get some sleep.

And then the followin' morn a man in the nest yelled, "Land!"

A great cheer went up from the crew. We rushed tae the rail and caught the most glorious sight — I dropped tae my knees, folded my hands, and thanked God for his divine goodness in bringin' us across the ocean and tae the shores of England, so close tae our home. I prayed he would keep Fraoch full of breaths for the next few hours so I could get him tae shore.

With land in sight the final day at sea was verra long.

The sky was covered in grey clouds, promisin' rain, but the wind was gustin', pushin' us closer and closer still. We worked at the sails and lines and all the while I kept up a steady prayer, keep Fraoch safe tae land, and thank ye, God, for seein' us safely home.

TWENTY-SEVEN - MAGNUS

The ship pulled tae a dock at the end of the day and the men swarmed from the ship. I fought the crowd the opposite direction headed down intae the dark hold, where seven men remained in hammocks, either gone from this earthly realm or nearin' it.

Fraoch said weakly, "We are at dock?"

"Aye, tis time tae rise, Fraoch. I am taking ye tae shore."

"I canna..."

"Och, ye can and ye will, tis too close for ye tae die in the hold of the ship. If ye are dyin' this day it has tae be on land."

He groaned.

I tried tae pull his shoulders up from the hammock but he was too big a burden. My same size afore, he was wastin' away in front of me, but I was grown small and weak as well. The hammock shifted against me and I couldna get ahold of him.

"Let me die here, Og Maggy."

"Nae, I winna." I yanked him hard and pushed the hammock away. I used my knife tae cut the hammock from the lumber and dumped him down with a splash intae the ankle-deep muck water below.

He yelped in pain.

I cut again at the hammock until I had a length tae tie in a long loop, and slung it across my shoulder. I pulled him up by the arm and got his shoulder across mine and lifted him tae my back.

His head lolled. "How ye goin'..."

"I am goin' tae carry ye, hold on if ye can, and keep yer cryin' down. I am tryin' tae concentrate." I pulled the loop around his side and pulled it tight tae mine so that much of his weight was carried with the rope. His feet dragged through the water as I hefted him tae the ladder.

I took three deep breaths. I was goin' tae get him up from this hold. He had saved m'life. I wasna goin' tae let him die alone down here and I wasna ready tae die with him.

One, two three, I adjusted him higher on my shoulder and with all my strength I put one foot in front of the other and climbed the ladder.

I crossed the deck and carried him down the gangplank tae the docks below.

~

On the shore of the Thames was a busy market just under the Westminster Bridge. There were some food sellers and beggars and a very crowded city street beyond. I asked a woman sellin' bread, "Mistress, dost ye ken a local physician?"

She shoved bread forward, "Half a penny."

I dug with my free hand in my leather purse and paid her for a hunk of bread. I tore off a bit and shoved it in my mouth. It was softer than the hard biscuits on the voyage but still I feared too hard for Fraoch tae chew. "I need a physician. Dost ye ken where one is, Mistress?"

She shrugged and began hagglin' with another sailor. I dragged Fraoch farther along the dock tae where a man was sellin' oysters from big barrels at a small table. Beside him stood a half-empty cart. "Mister, couldst ye spare yer cart?"

He grumbled and ignored me.

"I will pay ye for yer oysters and the cart. I need it tae travel my friend tae the hospital." We haggled over a fair price as a drizzling rain began tae fall.

I opened my purse and paid him six shillings for the cart and then I struggled Fraoch intae it. I asked the oyster seller, "Dost ye ken a physician?"

The man waved his hand in the direction of the main street and tae the right side.

The cart was terrible, poorly crafted and ill-used. It needed all my strength tae keep it righted and more strength than I had tae push it on the cobblestones. Fraoch looked near lifeless, wit a gaunt expression that was ghost-like and frightenin'.

I wove my way through the crowds searchin' up and down the street for the right door.

~

The sign was marked: St Thomas Hospital. Twas an imposin' building with a large courtyard. I crossed the open grounds and left the cart on the doorstep of the main entrance, heftin' Fraoch tae my shoulder, and draggin' him inside. We were led through to a back room with three rows of low beds. I dropped Fraoch down ontae the nearest empty one beside the wall.

The room smelled like death.

Fraoch was verra dirty and Kaitlyn had told me twas the dirt that was dangerous when there were wounds on a man. She told me I had tae wash m'self more than I might think.

I untied his leather boots and peeled them from his skin. His feet were wrinkled and pale gray, his legs bruised purple, twas then more than afore that I began tae really fear for my friend's life.

His clothes were filthy, the sheets were stained. Nae one had come tae see him yet, so I found a nurse tae ask for the physician.

I was told I would have tae wait.

So I sat on the ground beside Fraoch's hospital bed and waited for the doctor tae come.

The physician cleared his throat and I started. I must have been sleepin'. I clambered stiffly tae my feet. "Doctor, we have voyaged from the colonies, and my brother, Fraoch, has fallen ill."

The doctor said, "He is close tae death, twill be mercy on him."

"Nae, he canna die, I have tae get him home." I added, "I have money, I can pay for ye tae care for him. I—"

The doctor squinted his eyes at me. "We are a charitable hospital. We care for the indigent."

"He is nae, I have money for his care. We have family. I want ye tae care for him. My name is—"

His eyes traveled down my clothes. I was filthy. My beard was unkempt. I hadna bathed or changed clothes in two months except in the basest terms, the only shower I took was when I worked through a storm.

He said, "I have heard of a treatment for the ship sickness — a malt formula that will sometimes cure the affliction, but twill take effort tae procure it. It is expensive, and the treatment takes some time, if it works at all. You should save your money."

"I am Magnus Campbell, the nephew of the Earl of Breadalbane in Scotland, cousin tae the Lord of Argyll, that..." I wanted to add their names but this was 1740, forty-five years after I last saw them. "The Campbells that live at Ham House, here in London, dost ye ken of them?"

"I have heard of them, I—"

I dug through my purse. "I have six shillings now." I dug through Fraoch's purse. "I have another here." I passed him a pocket full of coins. "I will return in a few hours with more. But I want assurance ye will care for him and keep him alive until I return."

"Yes, Master Campbell." He pocketed the money, but I dinna trust he would give Fraoch the extra help he might require and now that I had been in a modern hospital this care felt verra inadequate.

I returned tae Fraoch's bedside. I couldna tell if he was awake; his eyes were closed and his face wore a deathly pallor. "I have paid the physician tae keep ye alive."

He groaned. Without openin' his eyes he said, "Tis nae matter in it. Save yer money."

"Nae. I winna." I patted his arm. "I have tae go Fraoch. I have tae get a message tae m'wife. She needs tae hear from me and must be verra worried. I will be gone for a time, but I will try tae send someone tae help ye. And if I canna, I will return in a few days. Then you and I will travel tae Scotland. I would like ye tae gain yer strength though because I daena ken if I can carry ye all the way there."

He moaned. "Ye are too weak tae do it, Og Maggy."

"Says the man lyin' in the hospital cryin' like a bairn."

"Everythin' hurts verra awful."

I squeezed his arm. "Well, ye look awful so I suspect it does. I will see ye in time."

"I pray ye get tae yer wife soon."

"Aye, I pray it as well, beannachd leibh, Fraoch."

"Beannachd leibh, Og Maggy."

. . .

I left the hospital and looked out over the main street. Twas a busy day, looked tae be evening, August, hot, and I was so hungry I wished I had eaten some of the oysters I paid for earlier. I would take the cart back tae the man I bought it from but twas now stolen from the courtyard.

I walked along the south bank of the Thames headed in the direction of Ham House considering what was left of my money. I needed food and a place tae sleep because by my guess twould be a three hour walk.

Twould be better tae arrive in the morn than in the deep night, so I found the closest tavern and procured the largest meal I could afford, a roast beef and cauliflower with celery and a pastry with raisins and almonds. I drank five mugs of ale, until I was verra full. I slept with my head on my arms at the table, grateful tae be on land again.

TWENTY-EIGHT - MAGNUS

I woke in the dark and began walkin' through city roads that were already busy with merchants and vendors setting up their shops and then as the day was upon us, hawking their wares.

I passed a bakery with bread in the window and though I needed tae save my last shilling for the trip north tae scotland, I was too hungry tae go without food.

I ate bread with some berry preserves while sitting on the road in front of the store, moaning with the happiness of a full stomach.

I was feelin' more energized from the food I had filled myself with, strengthened by the movement and the fresh air. As the sun rose, it was a clear sky and the day was beautiful. As I walked from town center the landscape sprawled greener and outside of town I filled my lungs with fresh air.

As I neared Ham House I pulled up to the river's edge, took off my shoes, washed my feet and legs of the sea salt, and then scrubbed water on my face and through my beard and hair. I longed for the mirror of our Amelia Island home, my toothbrush because my teeth were sore. I wished for the shampoo, bending forward with Kaitlyn rubbing it through my hair. I wanted a razor for m'beard, better clothes, and as I left the city behind, I wanted more than this small knife. I needed a dirk or sword, there were highwaymen about.

I was drippin' wet. I sat on the river bank and let the sun dry my skin. Then I strapped on my leather boots and resumed my walk following the Thames.

~

As I walked I thought about how happy I had been when I lived at Ham House. And remembered the day in my sixteenth year when Uncle Baldie sent for me tae come home.

Uncle John had read me Baldie's letter sayin' I was expected in Scotland and would be travelin' by myself. By then I had lived in London for six years. I thought of my cousins as m'own family and I verra much liked the luxury and comforts of Ham House and the excitement of living so close tae London.

I had missed Sean and especially Lizbeth, but she was already married and havin' bairns of her own. It pained me tae think it now, but I had grown used tae thinkin' of my older brother in Scotland as bein' uncivilized. Tae hear that I was now tae go live with my Scottish relations had left me heavy and worried.

I had been given a day tae prepare for my trip and then I had tae say goodbye tae my cousins in the formal living room. They curtseyed and bowed and we respectfully said our goodbyes under the watchful eye of my aunt and uncle.

As I had crossed the gravel drive though, for the coach that would convey me tae the carriage station, the cousins followed me from the house and there we hugged and said goodbye again, this time with laughs and tears.

Twas a verra difficult day tae leave them.

I kent I would be without them for a long time.

That had been the year 1697. Twas now forty-three years later. I was a ghost from the past and wasna sure how tae explain myself. I spent the next hour walking getting my story straight.

When I approached Ham House it looked much the same as I remembered even though close tae fifty years had gone by.

In my lifetime it had been only eight.

TWENTY-NINE - MAGNUS

I stood in front of the imposing door and rang the bell. The footman told me tae remove myself from the front steps and tae go around tae the back door.

"Pardon me, nae. Sir, I am Magnus Campbell, son of Magnus Campbell that once lived here, I..."

The man was dressed in an impressive uniform. He cleared his throat and looked me over.

I added, "I would like tae speak for a moment with the Lord Argyll or his descendents, Henry or Theodore..." I couldn't think of the right way to ask so I said, "I am wondering if there is a Master Henry Campbell at home?"

The man's eyes squinted. "The house is inhabited by the Duke of Lauderdale and the Duchess Mary, the daughter of the 3rd Duke of Argyll."

"Aye, Mary May, wouldst ye pardon my appearance and let the Duchess of Lauderdale ken that her cousin, Magnus Campbell, the son of her cousin, Magnus Archibald Caehlin Campbell, is here tae see her?"

He squinted his eyes some more and then stiffly turned and left me alone on the stoop.

~

About thirty minutes later, while I stood waiting, a woman came tae the door. She was dressed luxuriously in fine fabrics and lace, her skirt verra wide, a tilt tae her head, inquisitive, she was almost unrecognizable as the five-year-old I once kent, but she had a smile that reminded me of my aunt Elizabeth, her mother, and a twinkle in her eyes that I recognized as the little girl that once followed me around with a smile and a laugh.

"And you are?"

"I have explained tae yer man that I am Magnus Campbell, the son of—"

She waved her hand, "I have heard who you say you are, though I can barely believe it, we never heard from Magnus again in all these forty years and yet here you are, the same eyes, the same smile, clearly his son. Whatever has become of him? He must be verra auld now as I am well on in age and he was much grown when I thought him the most wondrous of men."

"He has passed tae his reward after living for many years in the New World. He spoke often of ye, Cousin May, and he wanted me tae travel here someday and see ye."

Her face fell. "I am so sorry about the loss of him. I suppose that as we age we have to get used to saying goodbye to our family and friends, but it is still very difficult. Well then cousin, I have a mind to tuck my arm in yours and take a turn in the gardens while you tell me all about your father. I would like this very much, but I see you have the countenance of someone who has traveled a grave distance..."

"I have, I have crossed the Atlantic from the Colonies. I have only arrived yesterday and came tae see ye first thing."

"Enter then, you have traveled far and have walked from London. We will not weary your feet with more walking, we will sit with our feet up and talk of my old friend."

She led me intae the house away from the sun that was beginnin' tae beat down upon my back.

I had forgotten how grand Ham House was, luxurious and sophisticated in a way nae other home I ever lived in was. The foyer was full of dark wood and black and white floor tiles. The ornate carving on the stair was exquisite, a familiar balcony stretched most of the way around on the first floor. I remembered the older cousins hanging over the rail the day I arrived. Cousin May had been born the following year.

She led me through the beautiful dark wood-paneled gallery to the parlor and though she offered me a damask covered chair, I tried tae sit on it without touchin' it.

"So tell me, Master Campbell, of your father."

"He has been living in—"

"The colonies? Tell me of it, did you grow up there?"

"I have lived there most of my life."

She stared off intae the distance. "I would have liked tae see it."

I shook my head, "Och, tis a verra long distance. I canna recommend the trip." I joked, "I am nae completely convinced I have survived it yet."

She laughed, "You have your father's sense of humor too. He was a legend among us for many long years."

"How are they? Henry and Theodore and—"

"Henry has been Lord Steward of the royal household. Is that not wondrous? Your father never would have thought our Henry would be so important."

I said, "I daena ken, he only had the highest words tae speak of Henry."

"Yes, well, Henry in his youth and your father, Magnus, were often at odds about what to do. Henry preferred to lounge, read, and ignore the rest of us, but Magnus wanted to create something of a day. I knew if I wanted attention I just had to find Magnus and within minutes the whole of us were outside with a game afoot." She stared off into space with a smile, then said, "I do not see Henry as often as I would like, but when I see him next I will tell him I met you. He will be very pleased. He often speaks of Magnus and misses him greatly. Archibald has been elected part of the Privy Council and they call him the most powerful man there. I have not seen him in many years, but hear he has been improving his estate, especially the gardens. The news is that he has been importing trees and his gardens are the talk of the kingdom. I really long to visit him sometime soon."

She added, "I am talking a great deal about people you do not know but you have made me feel nostalgic."

"I have heard my father speak of them so often I feel as if I ken them too, please go on. I am enjoyin' the stories. What of Mabel and Theodore, ye haena mentioned them?"

"Ah, yes," Her face fell. "We lost Teddy in the Battle of Sherrifmuir, it has been twenty-five years but I still feel the loss very much. And sweet Mabel, she lived with her husband, the Earl of Bute, and they were wonderful patrons of the arts but she has passed away now, five years ago."

"I am sorry tae hear of your losses, my father would have been greatly saddened."

"So tell me of their life there, and of your mother. She still lives?"

"She has passed as well, tis why I felt it permissible tae leave. I wanted tae see Scotland, and pay my respects tae my father's family."

"We are *your* family as well."

"Aye. He met her in the West Indies, they gained land and built a home in the colonies. They did very well."

"We get news from the colonies, I had not heard his name. I will be sure to pay closer attention now that I know he had land there. Was he growing tobacco? I hope he grew tobacco so you will have a fortune to live on."

"Aye," I said, because it seemed like I ought tae. "I have been doing verra well. I have come tae speak tae ye though, Cousin May, because I have had some difficulties on the crossin'..."

She leveled her eyes on me, now full of concern.

"I have a friend who came across with me on the ship from the colonies. He is a fellow Scotsman, and he has fallen ill. I have given the hospital the full rest of my purse tae keep him in health, and I have some pressin' business tae attend tae for a few days and... I canna return tae see tae him. I was wonderin' if ye could send someone tae the St Thomas Hospital tae look after him in my stead?"

"Oh, yes, of course, do you know what he is ailed by, is it the ship sickness?"

"Aye," I shifted in my seat. "The physician has said he is nae well, but I want tae get him home tae Scotland, if God wills it."

"I will help if I can. I will be going to London on the morrow, but I will send someone today to see to his care. He is a Campbell?"

"Nae, his is a MacDonald. His name is Fraoch."

"Is he a Jacobite, Magnus?"

I looked down at my hands. "He has saved my life three times. I vowed tae God I would try everything in my power tae save his. I hope ye understand, Cousin May, I am askin' only tae help him as a friend."

She sighed. "It has been a very long time since someone called me May and you have such a likeness to your father in your eyes. You are causing me to remember a great many happy days from our youth. Did your father tell you about the games we played in the gardens? He was always springing from the bushes and scarin' all the cousins, but he would never scare me. Instead he would rustle the leaves so I would know he was there and then he would wink at me and I would pretend to be afraid. He never wanted me to be left out of the games but he was always careful not to bring me to tears. The others though, he would promise not to scare them, and a minute later they were screaming because he had jumped at them again. We all loved the games and Magnus." Her eyes went very thoughtful.

"He told me about a secret stair?"

Her eyes regained their twinkle. "Yes! There is a stair for the servants, but we all called it our secret stair and had many a game running up and down it. I could only do it if Magnus held my hand."

I nodded, feelin' rather overwhelmed by the conversation.

She said, "Do you need a place to stay, young Magnus?"

"Nae, I have tae see tae some business. It will take me away for a couple of days, remind me of taeday's date?"

She laughed. "Long voyages have a way of causing one to forget the days. It is August 23."

I joked, "August 23, the year of our lord seventeen forty-seven? Because it feels that long."

She laughed again, "Your trip was not that long, Young Magnus, it is still seventeen forty by my count. The king is still George II. The last winter has been one of the coldest winters and I can still feel the frost in my bones, but I will go to London tomorrow. I will see tae your unlikely friend the one, Fraoch MacDonald. And have you enough money to see to your business? I do not want to tell you how to deport yourself, young Magnus, but as your elder, you need to adopt a better uniform for your status."

I chuckled. "I haena money for food or clothes. I do find myself in dire need of an elder's wisdom."

"Good, consider me your patron. I will take care of you and

your friend for the kindness your father showed me as a young child." She stood. "I will send a servant in to show you to a dressing room: new attire, some money, and then a meal before you go about your day. Will I see you again, I hope soon?"

"I plan to return after my business, to see to Fraoch and attend him home."

"Good, I will be expecting you here."

THIRTY - KAITLYN

I woke from the pain of the time-jump in the living room of the safe house. Every single muscle burned and ached. The long curtains were pulled over all the windows, throwing the room into a darkened-daytime feeling. A sliver of light coming from behind the edge of a curtain just about blinded me, which was good: it meant I was in the future.

I was on a Persian carpet. I must have been dragged in here while unconscious. Hayley was still asleep beside me. There were muffled sounds, but once I listened I could hear bombs, explosions, shooting, distant — but *still*.

I sat up and held my head with a groan. Zach's voice, "You're up, good."

I followed the sound — he was at the doorway of the living room, standing between the living room and the foyer, holding a gun. "Because we need to talk about what's going on."

Another explosion. Ben made a noise beside me. Emma was holding him in her lap, jiggling him with an anxious expression. "Where's Quentin?" I asked.

Quentin's voice from the far end of the room. "Here. Beaty is... not good."

"Shit." I moaned and stood and stumbled to where his voice came from, near the hospital bed, now on the inside edge of the room against the wall. Beaty was feverish, sleeping. "Where's the doctor?"

"We can't get one here, Roderick is attacking, we can't—"

"Yeah, no I get it. You can't stay here. This is— this is not good. Where's Archie?"

Emma said, "He's in Bella's wing. Lady Mairead has just been here looking for you."

And Hammond?"

"He's outside, at the barricades."

Hayley moaned and rolled to her side and began to sit up. The far wall had an overlarge projection of a nighttime war scene: red hot explosions, helicopters, military men running with weapons in hand, a town siren wailing. The volume was turned down low, but still felt alarming.

I said, "Hayley, to get you up to speed, there's a shit-storm here to deal with, so don't start asking a bunch of questions, thank you for jumping with me and all your help, but we have to get you guys out of here, pronto. So just listen up."

She groaned. "Everything about your life sucks."

"I have been telling you this for months and months. You just thought I was being overdramatic, now hush so I can think."

The house shook with an explosion outside.

"What the hell was that? Oops, sorry," she said.

Ben burst into tears.

I pushed the hair out of my eyes and stood.

"Do you think she will survive another jump?" I asked Quentin.

"Fuck Katie, I don't know, shit, you're freaking me out."

I was suddenly too hot. I unzipped the front of my parka and dropped it to the floor. "I'm sorry about that. *Really*. I don't know the answer to it but—" Through a back hallway Lady Mairead bustled in.

She nodded at me. "Where have ye been; where is Magnus? Explain tae me why ye were too incompetent tae rescue him."

I said, "I want to go over the parameters of our conversation first. One, you don't get to kill me or physically injure me in any way. As a matter of fact you stay across the room, over there."

One of our backpacks was on the ground near Beaty's hospital bed. I scrounged through it for a gun, found one, and held it aimed at Lady Mairead. "I will kill you in a red hot minute if you try anything."

Zach stalked over to the wall where he had leaned the shotgun he had been guarding us with earlier.

Hayley said, "Where's mine, if this lady is planning to threaten you again, I need to be armed too."

Lady Mairead glared at me. "Where is he?"

I took a deep breath. "He's still not here and I will talk to you about it in a few moments, but I need your advice first. You've jumped a lot, do you think it's safe for Beaty to do it in her condition?"

I followed her eyes to Beaty. There was a flash of concern then she said, "Well, you haena much choice do ye? She canna stay here and the only way out is tae jump."

"Is it?"

"Roderick has us surrounded, tis the only option at this point. They should go tae a time where there are good hospitals."

"Okay, sure. They should go home, but do you know if they can go? General Reyes has been tracking our movements in and out of Florida—"

"Och, he has a device that can sense the area of travelin'."

"Oh my God, we should have asked you in the first place."

"He was supposed tae be protecting Magnus not monitoring him—"

"He is not just 'monitoring' him, he's literally trying to kill Magnus, and he's been using it to—"

The look on her face was one of indignation.

Exasperated, I gestured with my gun and asked, "Tell me, is there some way around it?"

"Of course, they can jump intae another place and drive across tae Amelia Island. Tis simple tae do. And daena worry about Magnus, Reyes will be dead soon. Magnus will see his weakness and will easily best him in—"

"What do you mean, his weakness? Magnus hasn't found one."

"Reyes has a shoulder injury. He canna use his left arm verra well. It pains him and—"

Hayley asked, "What happened to his shoulder? He hasn't always had an injured shoulder — when did that happen?"

She looked at Hayley with her brow drawn. "He has always had it. He daena have the full use of his left arm. He is a good fighter but it — it happened when he was young. I have always kent him tae favor it."

Zach said, "When he was at dinner with us he kept rubbing his shoulder. He told me he injured it a long time ago. You don't remember the conversation, Hayley? He said the Florida weather bothered it. That's why he lives in the Greek Isles for the dry summers."

Hayley said, "I don't remember this at all."

Lady Mairead said, "I kent it from the beginning. I always learn of an adversary's weaknesses afore I do business with them."

I looked at Quentin. "Are you hearing this?"

"Yeah, I'm hearing it."

I said to Lady Mairead, "Well, you have Quentin to thank for

Reyes having a weakness. He used to not have an injured shoulder. He used to be very powerful and has almost killed Magnus many times, but Quentin and I went back in time and he shot Reyes. He did that. I was with him. We are responsible for Reyes being weaker. So yeah, you can thank us for that." I huffed and said under my breath, "...I always learn of an adversary's weakness..." I huffed again.

I said to Zach, "How about you jump into Savannah, rent a car and drive to Fernandina Beach, take Beaty to a hospital? Just lie low — don't make any new friends, that kind of thing." An explosion rocked the house. "But Beaty needs to be in a hospital and it should be close to our home, so... yeah, it's time for you to go back."

He shook his head, "Nah man, I'm not leaving you. I'll send Quentin with Beaty, Hayley, Emma and Ben. Emma will get them to Florida, but either Quentin or I need to be here in case you need us. You can't be alone."

Hayley said, "She won't be alone, I'm going to stay with her. I'll—"

I said, "Thank you Hayley, but I think I've risked your life enough, besides you're our go to person for everything. I need you on the ground in Fernandina."

"Last time I really screwed it up."

I put my hands on my hips. "You aren't going to screw up again. You get the stakes." I tried to smile. "You've been in the trenches."

"Yeah, but I'm still not leaving you, you'll need me."

Emma asked, "You're going to stay, Zach? I don't—"

"I'm going to stay and help. Quentin can't. Katie can't do this by herself."

She looked worried, jiggling Ben to keep him peaceful. "Sure, I get that Quentin can't, but are you sure you need to?"

"Magnus would do it for us. Lady Mairead says you'll be safe on the island, but Katie isn't safe here. If I can help I have to."

She shook her head, then thought a moment. "No, I get it. I understand, but don't be a hero. Just help, don't throw yourself in front of bullets or anything."

"Of course not. I'm like the least brave person you know."

She smiled sadly.

I said, "Okay. So we are going to jump some of you to Savannah, same place. Emma you'll go to the car rental place near the hotels and get a car. You and Quentin will get Beaty to Fernandina."

Hayley said, "What about Mags's baby? He can't stay here. Should he go with Emma?"

Lady Mairead said, "I will take Bella and Archie tae another time period and get them settled. I plan tae do that in just a moment."

Hayley asked, "Is that safe?"

"Tis how all the sons of kings have been protected, hiding them in the past. Yes, tis safe with some care and consideration."

I said, "Will you make sure I know where they are, so I can tell Magnus?"

"Of course Magnus must ken. I will make sure he always kens where his son is. My first priority is tae keep Magnus safe and keep his kingdom under his control, unlike you, with your galavantin' around—"

I said, "Don't forget I'm armed."

Lady Mairead waved a hand at me. "You winna kill me, ye need me tae help ye save Magnus. Ye dinna even ken that ye could go tae Florida. You daena have half the information ye need."

"Yeah, *whatever*, I suspected that I could go to Florida by car, I just didn't *know*. You know, whatever, *yes*, you have some information I need. I also have things you need. We are sadly very stuck with each other." I blew out air. "I will kill you if I have to. I will make up for my deficit of information by googling it if I need to."

"What is 'googling it'?"

"Exactly my point. And I wasn't galavanting around, I was trying to rescue Magnus. I thought you might be right about why Reyes has him. I went back to the day and year when your ancestors got the vessels, because I do have the book, by the way. I've had it the whole time, and guess what? Magnus wasn't there."

She looked furious.

I gulped. "So you were wrong about that." I powered on, "While we were there Quentin shot Reyes and injured him, but Magnus wasn't anywhere to be found and now I don't know where he is."

Her words were clipped and angry sounding. "I wasna wrong. I was right about it. If Magnus was nae there then Magnus has escaped."

"How do you know it?"

Her voice elevated. "Because I am never wrong and I am right in this. Reyes told me enough of his plan for me tae ken what he wanted tae do. If Magnus was nae there then he is not cooperatin' with Reyes."

I kept asking questions, apparently unable to stop myself. "So where is he now? Why isn't he here?"

She screeched, "I daena ken where he is, Kaitlyn! The reason he is nae here is because he daena have a vessel!"

My eyes went wide. "He doesn't have a — wait, what... oh my god, what are we going to do? How will we find him?"

She took a deep irritated breath, looking off into space for a moment. "I have some ideas how tae find him. Twould be best tae go tae him if he is injured. But how would we ken? It may be best tae set a vessel with a homing call. Dost ye ken how tae do this?"

"No, I don't. Let's do that, how?"

She shook her head as if I was being purposely dumb instead of just not knowing something. I said, "Just tell me how to do it and don't be such a judgey bitch about it."

She glared. "Twould have tae be in a place where he can locate it, but once we set the homing signal anyone can find the vessel; tis verra dangerous. You remember that once Donnan set a homing signal and you found it and ye were brought forward tae this time. Imagine how frightening it would be if—"

"It was plenty frightening."

"Imagine how frightening twould be if ye dinna ken of traveling through time?"

"I get it. Where would Magnus be?"

"Reyes spends some of his time in Florida—"

I said, "But we can't set it in Florida because Reyes would find it. Magnus wouldn't stay there. He's smarter than that. He knows I'm here, not very far from Balloch castle. That's where he would go. No matter what time period, he will go to Balloch."

"Then we have tae take a vessel tae Balloch and set the homing signal on it so he will find it." Beaty began to cough and looked wretched. It was enough to get us all moving as if the war outside wasn't enough already.

Quentin picked Beaty up and we all went out one of the back doors that overlooked a thin stripe of grass and some woods beyond. It was secluded. Zach looked left and right. No one had breached this side of the house, at least not yet.

I dialed Quentin's vessel and handed it to Emma, and went over the numbers with her. "Do you have your wallet, your phone?"

Emma held up her purse.

"Okay, then, take care of Beaty. Thank you, Quentin, for all your help back there and thank you, Emma. I'm so grateful, and we'll see you back in Amelia Island, soon, okay?"

Emma said, "Bring Zachary home safe."

"Definitely."

Zach hugged and kissed her. "Get some ice cream. I'll be there soon — same day."

"Sounds good." She looked up in his eyes. "I love you, don't be a hero, don't die."

He said, "This is me being a hero and I won't, I'm too fucking important."

Emma said, "That goes for you too, Katie, don't die. Magnus needs you."

"I won't."

The storm grew above them. Zach and Hayley and I backed up to the door and watched through the glass as our friends and family held onto each other and time-jumped back to our present lives.

~

A helicopter took off from the front of the house, loud and close. I ignored it and asked Lady Mairead, "Has Magnus's castle fallen to Roderick?"

"I daena ken, but this safe house will fall soon enough."

"Then I have to go fast."

"Come with me tae see Bella first. She will need convincing tae go tae the past. Bring your gun, Zachary." Lady Mairead looked grim. She handed me two vessels from a bag she had slung over her forearm.

"How many do you have?" I asked.

"I have enough."

She turned brusquely and we followed her through a small doorway at the back of the house and along a long, dark, windowless corridor to the west wing.

THIRTY-ONE - KAITLYN

The room was darkened like the main house with window coverings pulled tight and furniture pushed up against the front doors and over the windows, and the room was completely, totally, unequivocally empty of people.

Lady Mairead called, "Bella!" Then she yelled, "John Mitchell!"

I gasped for air.

She bustled down the hall looking in rooms and as soon as I got my wits about me I ran down the opposite hall slamming open doors and calling for Bella. It was scary though, so quiet and empty, when I opened doors I didn't really want to see. What if something happened?

What if something happened to Archie?

"Where are they?"

Lady Mairead's face drained of color. "I daena ken."

"Where is Archie?" I was more asking the universe because he was not here and none of us knew where he might be.

"You said that John guy works for you — where is he? Can you call him?"

"The last I spoke tae him he was verra angry. He wanted permission tae marry Bella and be the caretaker of the prince. I reminded him that he was only here because I allowed him tae be here."

"Well he's not here now!"

She looked furious.

I said, "Hayley, do you see the car seat, Archie's bottles?"

Hayley and Zach dug through piles of furniture and around in the other rooms.

"I don't see anything." Hayley called from the kitchen.

Lady Mairead said, "Did ye do something in the past tae change it?"

I did that slow turn thing. "Wait, what do you mean?"

"I mean, what did ye do, in the past? Since ye returned I have learned that Reyes's arm has been injured and now my grandson, who was here hours before, isna here. Tis nae trace of him, what did ye do?"

I opened and closed my mouth. "I don't know, I don't think we changed anything, I..." But my mind was reeling: We killed people. We messed with that whole entire time-travel scene, like really messed with it — death, mayhem, chaos.

Maybe Magnus wasn't around anymore.

Maybe Archie was gone.

It would be one big fucking ironic bullshit cosmic joke if I lost Magnus and Archie but had to keep Lady Mairead.

Just then Hayley rushed in holding a trash basket. "Diaper! There's a diaper in here! Archie was here, we didn't screw anything up!"

Relief rushed over me. Suddenly I felt idiotic to have even considered it. Of *course* Archie existed. He was a living breathing, albeit *missing,* baby. And there was a war outside.

Zach said, "That helicopter took off a little while ago, maybe they were in it."

I said, "Oh, that's right. Crap, how will we find them?"

Lady Mairead said, her voice clipped and even and scary as hell, "I have an idea. I will go get them."

"Okay, yes, where will you take them once you find them? I'll write it for Magnus." I crossed the room to a desk and found in the drawer a piece of paper and a pen.

Lady Mairead said, "First I will kill John Mitchell, and then I will take Bella and Archie tae the year 1890. In New York, the address is—"

"Why New York? "

Lady Mairead said, "Because I have decided it, without question."

"But I don't know my way around New York, Magnus doesn't know anything about it, how can you think of taking his son there?"

Lady Mairead's face turned red with fury. "Because I have friends—"

I said, "But we don't know anything about New York or that time or anything. To see Archie will be too difficult." Her face held a fury that scared the hell out of me. I asked, "Can we put him somewhere else?"

"And where exactly would ye want tae put your husband's mistress and son?"

Well, shit when she put it that way— nowhere, nowhere is where I wanted to put my husband's mistress, but Bella and Archie needed protection and I needed to be the hero who protects them.

Because my husband asked me to. He asked me to be a terrible arse through all this and hold his family together while he beat Reyes's ass and so far I had done a bang up job: Emma and Ben? Headed home. Quentin? Shot Reyes, injured him, now headed home and taking his wife to the hospital. Lady Mairead? I was holding a gun on her right as we fucking spoke.

I was the motherfucking matriarch and I was going to handle this. I needed to put Bella somewhere way way way back in the past so she would have to deal with some discomfort. My husband had been keeping her way too comfortable for way too long.

And I had to protect little Archie, but frankly, I was not cut out for it. Freaking danger was fast on my heels every moment. So I needed to make Bella uncomfortable, make Archie safe.

"Take them to Balloch in the year 1704. There's the castle, the high walls, they've dealt with future-danger before. It's not the best conditions for a baby, but we can make sure he's well provided for until it's safe to get him and there is no one else who would protect him better than Lizbeth and Sean."

"You are willing tae have your husband's mistress take his son tae live with Magnus's family? She has provided him an heir before ye have, twill look verra poorly for ye. Everyone will be discussing your failings—"

Hayley said, "Whoa lady, watch your mouth."

I raised the gun and aimed it at her fucking face. "Shut up. Stop talking about it like you're trying to advise me while you're really being a total bitch. You will find Bella and Archie and you will take them to Scotland, to Balloch Castle, the year 1704. You will tell Lizbeth that I sent them and that she is to take care of them. Do you understand?"

"You can put your weapon down. I daena understand, but I will do it. I do agree that Magnus would like them tae be there." Her eyes glinted mischievously.

I lowered the gun and wrote on the piece of paper a note for Lizbeth:

Dear Lizbeth,

Lady Mairead is bringing you Magnus's son, Archibald

Campbell, and Archibald's mother, Bella. They need protection, can you please watch over them?

Love, your Sister, Kaitlyn

I folded the paper and passed it to Lady Mairead. "For when you find them."

She said, "You are expecting a great deal of his family tae care for a bastard son..."

"If I remember correctly, you delivered a bastard to them to care for, and he turned out okay."

She huffed.

"That being said, please find Archie."

"Tis my grandson, of course I will find him. I will find him and I will kill the man who took him from this house." She turned to leave the wing.

I was in shock. I didn't get to see Archie. I didn't get to say goodbye and it frankly hurt my heart a lot.

The battle outside was frantic: explosions on the grounds and gunshots from the sky.

Then to make matters worse the power died, the whole house's hum stopped and it all went eerily quiet inside, while outside was complete mayhem and sure to be a crap-ton of carnage.

"How do we get back to the main house?"

Zach said, "Follow me."

Lady Mairead without even a 'goodbye' slipped through the back door to an enclosed patio and I watched her twist the ends of a vessel. Then the storm was raging, the noise of it drowning out the sounds of war ravaging the property, and—

I had to get back to the main house. I had to talk to Hammond.

I had to get through this battle to the ruins of Balloch.

THIRTY-TWO - MAGNUS

The last thing I wanted tae do was get on another ship so my other option was a coach tae take me tae Edinburgh. Twould be two weeks, they promised, if the weather was good. Twould be much longer if the weather wasna good.

I had money and clothes given tae me from Cousin May. I was attired in a pale gray coat with embroidery edging on the front and a ruffle at the neck. My hair held a bow. I joked with May, "Tis always a bow in my hair when I visit London."

She laughed and said, "When have you been to London before?"

I quickly added, "Tis what my father would always say."

She laughed.

My pants were short and there were tights and small shoes tae contend with, but I had a belt at my hip and she gave me a sword tae hang there, so I felt well-attired for a trip.

We had a nice dinner with talk of the news of the time: the king, the recent battles, the impending war, the banks, and a good night's sleep in a proper bed. I traveled with May the following morning tae London and met my seat on the coach.

There were six seats altogether, five were full of other passengers. My travel companions were a wealthy widow, Madame Fuller, and her son, Samuel, headed tae York; a young man who was a clockmaker's assistant, his name was Paul Hanley; and a young woman, a Mistress Brookes and her traveling companion.

Madame Fuller sat across from me and kept battin' her eyelashes, and smilin', and arrangin' herself tae be in my sight, accentuatin' her form in front of me. I found it hard tae ken where tae look when she kept leaning forward, dropping things tae the floor, and expectin' me tae collect them for her.

The clockmaker would have been a catch but she seemed bored as we all were by his opinin' on what he kent about clocks. He had a way of speakin' that was slow and endless much like the clock wheels he was ever describin'.

The Mistress Brooke, covered verra modestly, read from her bible, clearing her throat at the widow's offenses.

The days wore on. I was relieved I had been able tae clean myself and change clothes afore I came aboard, because the cabin seemed tae grow smaller and smaller. The conveyance rocked, the air was stuffy, the closeness dismayin'.

The trip was verra slow. There were many days I walked beside the carriage, climbing back in when it rained.

Sections of the route I had tae help push the coach through muddy passes, or climb off tae lighten the load during difficult terrain.

But I was grateful tae be movin' and every step took me closer tae Scotland, and unlike the ship, if I needed air I could climb out and take it. Many days I made it tae the next village afore the coach arrived.

I worried on all that needed tae be done. I was alone and

desperate, and nae closer tae killing Reyes, tae making my family safe. I prayed that Kaitlyn was protected in the future, and that she held Archie in her arms. That she kept Quentin and Zach and everyone close, and that she was being strong while she waited for me.

My only comfort was when I walked. It reminded me tae be patient. I hadna my Mustang and someone tae drive. I couldna fly through the skies. I had a need tae get tae Scotland and I was trapped in a different century. There was nothin' tae do tae help it. Except walk.

At night I stayed in hostels or taverns. Most nights I slept in the communal rooms, but a few nights tae get some peace and a deep sleep, I spent the extra shillings tae have a bed. For the most part twas all familiar: the people, the conveyance, the houses and the taverns. Twas the politics that had changed. I had tae listen a great deal, tae ken the truth of it all.

THIRTY-THREE - KAITLYN

We returned to the big house through the tiny, dark, hidden, secret hallway and burst out into the big powerless main foyer. Zach peeked out the windows. "Fucking bunch of war-shit going on out there still."

Then Hammond rushed in coming directly for me. "There were reports of storms here, I've been looking everywhere for you." He looked around. "Where is everyone else?"

"Do you know where Archie is?"

"He's not here, with you?"

I was wringing my hands. "He's not. Where do you think he could be? Bella's gone, the guy she was with and Archie — where could they go?"

"I don't know, I'll have my men scour the area, it's too dangerous to leave though, did they have a vessel?"

"I don't think so, but it's possible. I guess anything is possible. Also Quentin took Beaty, Emma, and Ben back home, to safety, Zach and Hayley are staying with me. Where's Mrs Johnstone?"

"We evacuated her a few hours ago, no one else would leave without seeing you first."

"That means Archie was removed within the last three hours? I mean, it might be possible to find them if they were on foot. Have there been any helicopters? How many storms did you see?"

"There are reports of storms happening for the last two hours. I do not know, Queen Kaitlyn, I wish I had better information for you, or better news, the safe house has been found. We're holding them off, but once I get you out of here we need to retreat, we are fighting in too many locations and are stretched thin."

"Are we going to lose the kingdom?"

"I can't say, it looks bleak but it's been bleak before. Do we have a king left to protect?"

I nodded but said, "The trouble is I don't think he has a vessel. I think he's stuck somewhere, but I know how to get him one, to set it so he can find it, but I have to get it to Balloch Castle—"

He shook his head. "You mean the ruins of Balloch Castle, and that's impossible. There's active fighting all over the ground—"

"I still have to go, even if it is impossible. I have to—"

"Helicopters are too dangerous. We would need a large military escort." He gestured at Hayley and Zach. "They aren't enough."

"That's okay, I'm not asking for a helicopter, just some weapons. We'll time jump there, to tomorrow morning."

"What about if you jumped back in time to before the war?"

I thought about that for a moment. "I can't. I can't loop back on my own life, right Zach?"

"Right."

"And if I go farther back I'll be in Donnan's time. I mean, if I thought on it long enough I could maybe come up with a time, but I don't have the luxury of thinking. I have to go. Tomorrow at Balloch is all I can—"

"I have a man I can send with you then. He's jumped before, as Donnan's guard. I trust him. I can't let you go without a guard."

"Okay, thank you."

He was in his fighting uniform and very dirty, his face covered in soot and black grease. Like he had been in a wildfire. Like he was tired. Like he had been through a war. "I'll send him in and notify my commanders that you're leaving and prepare the rest of us to retreat."

"Hayley and I will change out of our clothes."

"I can give you twenty minutes. Then we'll start clearing this place, you need to be out of here before that happens."

Hayley and I raced down the hall to the room that Magnus and I stayed in hoping there'd be something for us to wear.

I ripped open a drawer and tossed clothes around, while Hayley struggled out of her bodice and we both dropped our shifts and big skirts to the ground. I found a dark pair of pants. I tossed her another pair, plus a casual shirt with a jacket that belted at the waist for me, and a zip up one for her. I did some karate kicks to prove to myself that I could move in the pants if called upon, and felt light after taking off the past-century clothes.

Hammond was frazzled when he arrived with the new soldier. "Queen Kaitlyn, this is Captain Warren."

Captain Warren was big, ugly, and grumpy looking. With his shaved head and soldier uniform, he looked like the guy who would be cast in a movie as 'the big angry soldier who yells a lot.'

He nodded and grunted hello.

Hammond said, "He has been briefed. You'll need to leave now." He passed me a gun, a big one. "Have you shot one of these?"

"No."

He took it back and handed me a handgun. "How about this?"

"Yes, I have."

He gave one to Hayley. Zach was already armed.

Hammond had a bag beside him with four guns and some other weapons. He pilfered through it and pulled out a bullet-proof vest. He pulled it down over my head and strapped it around my chest. It was ridiculously heavy.

Hayley asked, "What about mine?"

He handed her one and passed one to Zach. They helped each other put them on.

Next Hammond brought out a helmet, planted it on my head, and latched the strap under my chin. He put helmets on Hayley and Zach and we all looked like military soldiers. Hayley looked like a 'scared as shit' military soldier. We stalked through the house to the backyard again.

Hayley and Zach climbed onto one of the ATVs and I climbed on behind Captain Warren. "What's the date today?" I asked Hammond. "I'm kind of freaking out and it's not easy to jump twice in one day. It's hard to concentrate on the numbers."

Hammond told me the date, and said goodbye and to be safe, and I added that date to the list of numbers I knew by heart: the numbers for Balloch castle, now a ruin.

THIRTY-FOUR - MAGNUS

After spending the night in the the Sheep Heid Inn in Edinburgh, I bought a horse and some supplies for my ride tae Balloch. Twould take two days, two nights of sleepin' in taverns tae get there.

I was verra exhausted from bein' always tryin' tae get there.

Until mid-day on the third day, I came tae it, finally.

The walls that had crumbled during the battle with the drones had been rebuilt. Another section of wall was being built, with scaffoldin' and workers around the base. There was glass in more of the windows. The gardens around the castle were planned and lavish. The stables were larger. The Earl and his descendants were doin' verra well for themselves.

I had been thinkin' long on who I would ken at Balloch, twas a question whether the Earl would be there, or Lizbeth, she would be close tae sixty years auld now and I had nae memory if she lived tae 1740. I wished I had a phone tae discover the history of them.

There would be my nephews and nieces and I could present

myself as their cousin, but I might be recognizable tae someone that had been living long. I decided twould be best tae be Magnus's son again.

Twas easy enough tae get through the gates, I asked after the Earl, but was told his son, the Lord Glenorchy resided there now. I inquired about seein' him and the guard explained he was off doin' parliamentary business in Edinburgh. So after inquirin' about some of the old folk around, it came tae me that Sean was gone, as was Lizbeth, and yet, there were many of their children there, and so I asked tae see my nephew, Gavin, Sean's son, who I guessed tae be about forty years auld.

Gavin Campbell strolled up with a confused expression. He was big like his father, ginger like his mother. I kent I looked out of place with m'fancy English clothes and wished I had bought a tartan in the city.

I introduced myself as cousin Magnus, son of Magnus Campbell, and that I had just arrived from the Colonies then laughed about havin' said, 'just arrived'. I told him I had been travelin' for weeks tae get tae Scotland from London.

He earnestly asked what the colonies were like and mentioned that his son, now eighteen years auld was dreaming of movin' tae the colonies soon.

"Nae, I daena recommend the trip. Twas far more likely tae kill a man than tae convey him."

"Where did ye live there?"

"I was near Savannah, dost ye ken of it?"

"Nae, tis near Virginia?"

"Aye, verra near."

"Dost yer family grow tobacco? I have heard tis a lucrative crop, we have been wantin' tae be in the business of it..."

He led me through the well-appointed courtyard, and tae the Great Hall. There were more tapestries than afore and more sculptures linin' the halls. I was brought close and introduced tae a group of men and we sat in a circle and talked of the colonies. They kent more than I thought. I was able tae tell them of the siege on St Augustine as well as the port of Charleston and then regaled them with stories about the crossing.

I considered it a service tae explain how bleak tis tae cross the ocean, as there were young men about who wanted verra much tae go. I warned them that the crossin' would take them from this life too soon, and told them of the monsters in the riverbeds and the mosquitos, like our midges but with a lastin' bite.

Then twas their turn tae tell me of the intrigues of the time, there had been riots and unrest. The French were involved with the clans and it seemed as if trouble was a brewin' on every front. Listenin' tae the men I learned many stories of the Highlands that confused me. I was seein' the future of my life, but also the past from Kaitlyn's and I had much tae ask her, much tae learn.

As I listened I wanted tae advise these descendants on how tae comport themselves. I was watching the faces and eyes and mannerisms of men who were much the same as Sean and Baldie and I wanted tae help them, tae take up arms with them, tae protect them. I wanted tae warn them about what was coming, but I couldna because I hadna asked the right questions in the future.

Across the way I saw a woman who looked exactly like Lizbeth, and I crossed the room tae introduce m'self. She was the embodiment of her grandmother, now young, now with a spirit verra like Lizbeth too.

She told me her name was Catherine but that everyone called her Cath. She was verra like seein' a ghost tae have her in front of me, a stranger in the place of Lizbeth of whom I was so fond.

I was offered the evenin' meal though twas still verra light out, just the end of August. We gathered at the big table, everythin' simple as the Lord of the castle wasna residin' there at this time.

There was a sense of unreality tae the day, so much was familiar, a great deal more was different. The faces were similar, the people strangers. There was enough of me tae remind them of a Campbell so they accepted me easily.

We were eatin' lamb with peas and cabbage and twas then that an older man by the name of Colin approached and introduced himself. "Ye are the spittin' image of yer father, Magnus, exactly as I remember him, though it has been thirty years — except the clothes, the Magnus I kent would rather have his gimcrack hangin' than be dressed in the clothes of an English jack-a-dandy."

I laughed. "My father and I are of a different mind on the way tae comport oneself when traveling, though I daena want tae look an English Jack-a-dandy. I much prefer tae look a highlander when in the highlands."

"Have ye been here afore?"

"Nae, but my father has told me so many stories I feel I have lived through it all."

"Your father was one tae tell a story. Twas many a night I listened tae him tell of fights and— I am sorry tae hear of his passin'."

I pushed my plate away. "I was thinkin' on taking a walk around the castle. My father told me a great deal. I was hopin' tae see it."

"Just daena go tae the west walls, they are being built and

there is a danger of having a chisel fall on yer head if ye get too close."

One of the other men complained. "I will be glad when the clangin' of the construction is over, it has been a racket for a verra long time."

THIRTY-FIVE - MAGNUS

I left the Great Hall and crossed the courtyard tae the west walls. Under some scaffolding I found piles of rocks and some tools strewn about, includin' a chisel and a hammer that I took for my own project.

I then skirted the courtyard tae the familiar stair. The one I would take with Kaitlyn, the route from the Great Hall tae the upper floors.

I remembered one of the last times I was there, our discussion as we climbed the steps —

You're looking around at everything thinking about having sex there? This is all so scandalous.

Aye, see that table? Your arse would look verra beautiful bent over it.

Master Magnus, I believe you are drunk!

See that corner? I could spread your legs there. I think ye wouldna argue on it.

She had pointed at the window, remembering a time with me

that I dinna ken and I had dismissed it as painful, but this was Kaitlyn, my Kaitlyn, remembering me. I longed for a chance tae tell her the joy it gave me tae ken she always wanted me in any year. I should have thanked her for it. I would, if I was ever able tae find my way tae her again.

~

I had seen Balloch Castle in the far off future and twas a ruin. Hammie had shewn me the images. I had studied them.

I had felt dismay at the time: Balloch was nae a home anymore. Once fortified and invincible, in the future twas only stone walls crumbling. Overtaken by trees and grass, the human endeavor dissolvin' intae the earth.

It had been hard tae look upon, but I had made myself look, tae see what the future held. Was good practice for me tae ken that I was mortal and would turn tae dust some day. I had long been thinkin' I could jump past m'own fate.

And my lookin' at the images had taught me something: that high wall, the one on the east side, the one that had taken the brunt of the damage from the weapons of the future, had been rebuilt and of the ruins twas the highest wall still standin' in the year 2382. Twas the wall that I had climbed with Kaitlyn the last night we had slept here taegether, and we had each other there.

We had laughed. She had been verra talkative, full of me and love and warmth, and losing her breath with it all and I had a view of her against the high starry sky and she had dazzled me more than the heavens that night.

I climbed the wooden steps, once a ladder, now built stronger, surer, but I kent that even these would nae last long. I arrived at the verra top of the highest wall.

Here, where we had once lain taegether, we had talked of the skies. I told her of the sureness of it. She told me of the vastness, and we decided taegether, whatever our view, whenever our location, twas always the same sky.

We found a comfort in that wherever we were we were both of us under it.

I found our spot, the exact point of that high wall and crouched there.

I love ye, I thought as I began tae strike chisel tae the stone.

THIRTY-SIX - KAITLYN

I woke slowly, the agony was familiar. The storm dissipated as I struggled to fully wake myself. After a time jump was the grogginess of a deep hangover, plus more, full body agony and wretchedness. If I had known my future would be full of it I probably wouldn't have been so flippant with my health all those party nights. That being said, just after a time jump, what I really needed was a stiff drink.

The hypocrisy was freaking real.

My head was on the foot rest of the ATV. My body lay in the dirt beside it. I wasn't a hundred percent sure where I was. Usually when I time-jumped to Balloch I landed in the woods to the east, but the world had probably changed a lot in 600 years. I guessed the forest was mostly gone.

I was in a grassy sort of plain and on first look didn't see anything familiar. Captain Warren was beside me. I jostled him with my knee. "Hey, Warren, get up."

He groaned and sort of pushed me away.

I said it again, "Captain Warren, get up. We're near the castle and it's probably dangerous and you're supposed to be protecting me."

He groaned again and sat up. "I forgot how awful it is."

I jiggled Hayley's foot and Zach's leg. "Guys, get up, we gotta move." They groaned and started sitting up.

"I know it sucks. Captain Warren, where did you go before?"

"Greece, Russia, mostly to gather antiquities."

"That sounds fun." I lurched to my feet and stiffly straightened in my heavy bullet-proof vest and helmet.

He looked around groggily. "Follow me." He and I jumped on an ATV, and took the lead, driving into the shade-cover of the closest trees.

We were somewhat hidden at the edge of the woods, but Captain Warren looked all around as we drove, keeping an eye out for trouble.

I asked, "Which way is Balloch Castle?"

"Tae the north, and Magnus's castle is that way." He thumbed the direction he had been watching. There was a far off rumble and the earth shook.

"Fighting over there. Follow me." He spun our ATV in a circle and Zach pulled his in behind ours. We raced through the woods, winding through trees and over brush. It wasn't far, but our engines made a racket, and now that I was looking I recognized the mountains and although the woods were thinner, more sparse, even the landscape seemed familiar.

THIRTY-SEVEN - KAITLYN

We pulled up at the edge of the forest and climbed off the vehicles. "Oh. I mean, wow, that is... so *ruined.*" My stomach hurt at the sight of Balloch. *Where are all the people? The family that we loved? Magnus? Where are the lives that made up the interior of this building?*

It was as if the living breathing people had held up the roof and firmed up the walls and when they were gone the monument to their lives had crumbled in their absence.

It wasn't just 'as if'. It was exactly that.

My family and friends had died and the building had mostly collapsed.

It was like seeing the ruins of Lord Delapointe's castle but so much more terrible, heart-wrenching, and weird.

This had been the Campbell stronghold. The seat of the clan. And Balloch Castle was left here derelict, trashed, all but forgotten.

Hayley asked, "Is that the same castle? The same one we were staring at for days? It looked so new, now it looks so old. It's freaking crazy how this works."

Captain Warren, not noticing my sadness, climbed off his ATV, and rifled through the bag. He passed out more guns, making sure we were all armed and ready, and then he slung the bag across his shoulder.

After looking in all directions, he decided it was clear and led us in a jog across the empty fields to the broken down wall that used to be the front gate.

It began to rain. The thick clouds overhead let loose in what could only be called a deluge. There was no getting out of it, because there was not really a roof left anywhere. The courtyard was stone with grass busting through, walls covered in ivy, like a temple in the rainforest, flourishing under this weather. This castle had been taken over by Mother Nature and was almost unrecognizable without the people, the attention and care — the shelter.

I stood under a half-roof near the gate and tried to figure out where to put the vessel to turn on the homing button, but logically the courtyard didn't make sense. It would be found out here in the open. The trouble was if I put it in the woods it might never be found.

I didn't know if it would work inside one of the rooms. We had always jumped from outside, except the one time when we jumped from the prison at Delapointe's castle, but what if I left the vessel in one of the rooms and it was found or it didn't work? I needed it to be somewhere outside.

Hayley said, "So where are you going to put it? I don't mean to pressure you but it's wet as hell out here."

"I don't know... now that I'm here this seems so..."

I took stock of the ruined building, walls dripping with rain, all that was left were the two tower staircases on the east side with the high walls, the ones where Magnus and I made love up there, at the top, that night.

It was sort of awesome that those were the high walls on the half of the building that was still standing and—

wait.

I pointed. "That's where we need to go, up there."

THIRTY-EIGHT - MAGNUS

There was a flat pale gray stone. I judged it for the length of what I intended tae write. I began with the letter I, chiselin' the line straight and sure and deep, with a clink, clink, clank, though when I was done twas just a line, nae a message. I gave it a space and began on the letter N. When I got tae the letter E, a night watch came and asked what I was about. I explained that I was tae write words in the wall and since he couldna read, he left me alone about it.

I had the D and the next E in nae time. Below it I wrote A. And then I began the next word with a V.... So that after about an hour I finished. I sat back on my heels and took stock of it. It was there and I wondered if I should also put it in another place. What next? Waiting? For how long would I have tae wait? I had a cloth with me, I rubbed it along the cuts, then spent a few more moments carvin' deeper for the V, smoothin' the S. Until finally I kent that was the best it would be and I prayed tae God it was enough.

THIRTY-NINE - KAITLYN

We climbed the steps covered in dark-stained stones with moss in the cracks. I passed the window seat where my husband, as old Magnus, had taken me on the sill, 600 years ago. My ass had been here. I sighed, it was so odd to think of it from here, now, so ancient.

The circular tower stair was crumbled at the top and there was no cover and rain poured down on us. We passed the floor that had our bedroom on it. For a half minute I thought, *I could put a vessel there, maybe under the bed, that would be* — but as I stepped out onto the half-gone floor, the rest of the floor clinging to one wall because the other wall was completely gone, there was a crumbling noise and a brick near my foot loosened.

Hayley gasped.

Captain Warren grabbed my arm and yanked me back to the safe stair. "Too dangerous, Queen Kaitlyn."

I peered through the rain. Our doorway would have been down the hall and around the corner; it looked like it wasn't there anymore.

"Yeah, you're right, okay, yeah, we'll go to the top."

We climbed another floor and came out on the very top of the walls.

I said, "See all of that wall? That had to be rebuilt after Samuel sent an army to the past and fought us." I pointed. "This whole wall was crumbled. Drones attacked, the Campbells were fighting back with their old-time weapons. Funny that now it's the one wall that's left standing..." I trailed off.

Zach said, "That's so crazy to think about. Right here?"

"Yep, and I guess that's probably why it's still standing, because it had to be rebuilt, because of us." I looked to the right, the wooden ladder that we had climbed to the highest walls was, of course, gone, but now there was a stone stairway, built after Magnus and I, but now so old.

I led them to the steps, so steep and dangerous they made my vertigo kick in just thinking about stepping on them, and we climbed, and then at the top of the walls, the view was crazy, big, wide, and very very wet.

He said, "Stay down, Queen Kaitlyn." I ducked, though the surrounding area looked quiet, wet, primordial, like an ancient wet forest.

He said to Hayley and Zach, "You two stay here behind this wall, you have a view down the stairs and behind us to the front gate. Shoot first, ask questions later."

Zach nodded. "Let's all remember that I'm a chef, not sure what I'm doing here with weapons in some ruined castle in the future. But I will do my best to be a soldier. Even though I'm just a chef."

Hayley joked, "I'm literally just a bestie who likes CrossFit. You and your brother taught me how to shoot and ride ATVS and that's literally the only skills I've needed so far, so you'll be fine."

Captain Warren and I left them behind and headed further down the wall. There were long distances with nothing to hide behind so we hurried to a place with protection about halfway across the expanse.

I peeked over the parapet. "Is that Magnus's castle over there?" I pointed past the trees. "Shit there's smoke and helicopters and a—" An explosion blew up in woods past the castle, the ground vibrated.

"Yes, that's Castle Don..." He checked his weapon, watching the fighting in the distance, a tank riding along a road, drones swooping.

He said, "I need to contact — give me a minute." He used a two-way radio to make a call. I sat quietly waiting for him, but he kept talking longer, then put a finger up for more time, and I got bored.

I hand-gestured to Hayley and Zach that I was going farther down the wall.

I crouch-crawled a distance away, toward the place where Magnus and I made love.

I put my hand there on that spot. In real time it wasn't all that long ago, weeks maybe? But in the timeline of history 600 years of sun and storm had washed any traces of us away.

This would be a good place. I could leave a vessel here. It would create a storm overhead and no one would come up to check for it.

Magnus, if he was at Balloch Castle, if he noticed the storm, and he would — he would probably—

That's when I saw it: carved letters on the stone. A stone that was mossy green, but with chisel marks like it was an old gravestone or a historic marker. The first thing I noticed was a deep arrow pointing down. I rubbed my finger on it. These hadn't been there the night we made love here, they would've been within my field of vision.

They weren't there.

There were letters to the left and right of the V. And below it...

An M.

My heart raced as I used my sleeve to rub the dirt and wet off the stone to make out the letters that had been carved there until I made it out...

I NEDE
A VESEL
M

Oh my god.

Magnus.

I held my fingers there and then I pressed my hand against them. He had touched this. He chiseled this.

Oh my god.

These letters had been there through all these years to reach me, here and — oh my god.

I couldn't go fast enough. I rifled through my pack for one of the vessels. I glanced over at Captain Warren, still on the radio, his head hanging, the news must not be good.

Hayley called through the rain, her voice muffled from distance and weather, way down at the far end of the wall. "What did you find?"

"A message! From Magnus!"

I found one of the vessels and — I wasn't sure this was the

best place, but Magnus left me the message here. He needed one and I had one. I needed to stop thinking, stop trying to decide, and do this thing.

I twisted the ends of the vessel and set it ready to jump and then, like Lady Mairead had told me, added two numbers to the sequence and set the dial's status to 'homing', pushed the button, and put it on the –

There was a loud gunshot from the direction of the trees. I threw myself down and looked over at Captain Warren as he slumped forward over his knees then rolled to the side, a bloom of red blood flowing from him.

Oh no no nnnnnnnnoooooo oh no oh no. I scrambled to the low parapet wall and clung hidden behind it.

He was ten feet away, laying still. "Captain Warren? Are you okay?"

Zach called, "Is Captain Warren okay?"

"I don't think so!"

He said, "Stay down then! Shit, let me think!"

I got out my gun and held it in both hands, clutched to my chest.

The vessel was lying about five feet in the other direction. If I tried to retrieve it I would be exposed.

The markings around the middle glowed and there was vibration from the energy of it. It was warming up, the storm was coming. I wanted to race to the stairwell before it hit. I needed to get out of here, but I couldn't.

There was no way I could crawl all the way to the stairs, part of the way there wasn't a wall to hide behind. I didn't know who was out there and where they were and I couldn't get to Captain Warren to see if he was hurt or please don't be – *dead.*

A bank of clouds built above us, wind whipped my hair and made it impossible to see. It was loud as shit.

All I could do was just hunker down. Zach's voice a fair distance away, "Katie! Can you crawl here?"

"I can't it's too unprotected!"

A giant storm surged directly on top of me whipping and roaring. It made it impossible to hear, to see, to even think.

FORTY - MAGNUS

It was beginnin' tae get dark. I had been sitting beside my message watchin' on it but twas just idle. What was I goin' tae do, wait for 600 years while starin' at it?

Now that I had done it I dinna ken what came next...

And nothin' changed while I stared at it.

I dusted off my breeches, stood, climbed down the stairs and returned the chisel tae the area where the men were buildin' the west walls.

I stopped in at the Great Hall and gratefully took a whisky that was offered. I could use a drink tae keep my mind from waiting. I had tae reconcile myself, now that this task was over, tae the possibility that I might be waitin' for a verra long time, perhaps forever. I had been told by Donnan that there was a way to set a homing signal on the vessels, that one could be put in a place and found in a different time by someone else, but I dinna ken if Kaitlyn kent this. And I dinna ken how tae explain it tae her. I might need tae add tae the message, directions, but I wasna sure of them myself. I only kent that it could happen, nae the strategy of it.

I joined a rowdy group of men and we drank a great deal. Two men had just returned from visitin' Stirling and had news from their travels. This was clan business that sounded much the same as always, but with new worries and different names. I listened, enjoyed my drink, and tried tae keep my focus on the room and nae the roof of the castle.

The man Murty had consumed too much drink and was standin' on a chair tae have the height of the room and was loud-tellin' a story about one of the young men. The young man had turned beet red from the embarrassment of it and was hidin' his face from a young woman across the way. Murty kent this and it only made him yell louder.

The young man was tryin' tae explain his side of it and we were all laughin' at the part where he woke at dawn in the kitchen garden with his buttocks exposed and a rooster crowin' above him and—

Thunder boomed outside the windows on the east side of the great hall. Then lighting sparked and lit up the room.

The men all turned tae the windows. Murty asked, "Were we expectin' a storm?"

The beat of my heart sped.

A few of the men rose tae go attend tae the stables.

Someone said, "Murty, continue!"

He waved them away and stumbled down from his chair. "Tis too loud tae continue, I canna hear myself think." Wind whipped against the windows and there was a howl from it coming through cracks in the walls.

I drained m'whisky, slammed my glass tae the table, and raced from the room.

. . .

I took the stairs two at a time. There were men comin' down, runnin' for cover, takin' shelter in the stairwell. I was pushin' upwards against their downward race.

As I reached the upper floor one of the guards was in under the roof. "Ye daena want tae go in it."

"Och aye, I daena, but I left somethin' on the roof, I need tae find it."

I looked out first.

The bank of clouds above the castle was gigantic and terrible. Lightning arced, focused on the upper east wall. The wind roared around us and twas hard tae imagine keepin' on my feet through it.

I held tight tae the stone wall and raced, crouchin' as low as I could, until I got tae the open roof stair. I hunkered down at the bottom and waited for the wind tae switch so it would hold me against the wall, instead of pushin' me out and off.

The wind switched.

I leaned intae it and fought tae climb the steps, a verra slow one at a time while the wind whipped and yanked, until I made it tae the top and collapsed against the stone. I held ontae the parapet and braced m'self as the wind switched and tried tae gust me flyin' out over the edge.

I lay down and held on, through the violent wind surge, m'eyes closed, prayin' that I would find the vessel. That it would be here, that I wasna just out on the high walls of the castle durin' a storm.

Lightning struck a few feet away, sparkin' the sky and settin' my teeth on edge. My hair raised and I pressed my fingers tae rough edges of the stone and tried tae keep the wind from rushin' me away from the castle.

The gust turned. Pushing my shoulders tae the parapet wall, it gave me a moment tae open my eyes—

A vessel.

Layin' on its own, twas nae twenty feet away. I used my arms tae drag myself across the stone with the wind rollin' over me. Gusts were pushin' against me. One threatened tae shove me tae standin' and throw me over the wall, but I braced my feet, pressed my back tae the stone, and held with all my strength until with another blast the wind switched again.

I took my chance and dove ontae the vessel. I held it against m'chest and held on as the wind slammed against me and though I hadna expected it — I was ripped through time.

FORTY-ONE - KAITLYN

Lightning crashed against the wall nearby. To call me terribly frightened would be an understatement. Wind shoved me, scraping across the stone, then gusts dragged me back. I tried to hold on to the stone edges but the wind was too powerful. The weight of the vest was the only thing keeping me from being tossed off the wall like a frisbee.

I held onto my helmet, my eyes closed as dirt pummeled my skin, the — I peeled my eyes open to see Captain Warren buffeted across the stone walkway and up against the parapet. He didn't look good, like he hadn't survived this, and the air was roaring. I slammed my eyes shut again, holding my gun, braced against the wall, *shit, when would this be over? It had to end soon, please, please, please end soon.*

When I had found the vessel in Scotland, the homing signal had been set every day for a couple of weeks before I got there. I knew this was just the first moment of a long process. And this was definitely the only time I would do it here on this wall — this was bullshit.

I needed to do it downstairs on the grass where there wasn't this much — except someone just shot and killed Captain Warren. Someone was down there, the only reason why they weren't here, right now, was because the storm was keeping them away. And they had to go through Hayley and Zach.

My friends were my armed guards. How was I going to protect them?

How was I going to get us off this wall?

Just then there was a loud shot from near Zach and Hayley. I peered over to see Zach aiming down the wall. He yelled at someone, "Fuck you, don't you come up. I'll shoot—" The rest of his words were lost on the wind.

We would have to jump out of here using the other vessel.

Lightning sparked, the air sizzled, chunks of wall exploded. I was going to get killed if I didn't get us out of here. I had to get to Zach and Hayley at the end of the wall. The wind switched, I shoved my feet against the wall and braced my back against the stone.

"I'm going to try and crawl to you!" I screamed but the words were faint even to my own ears.

Hayley's voice from far away. "What?"

I started to crawl but the freaking wind switched, gusted, and yanked the helmet from my head spinning it end over end off the wall and careening away. Noonnonononononno.

Fuck. I was unprotected. Whoever shot Captain Warren, whoever Zach was shooting at, they could shoot me now too.

Captain Warren had a radio.

I drag-crawled to him. He was lifeless, his two-way radio under him. "Captain Warren? Help me, I don't know what to do." I pressed my fingers to the side of his neck. "Captain Warren?" There was no pulse. I checked his wrist. Nothing.

I pushed his body off the radio, braced myself against him, and spoke, "Hello? Hello?"

A voice returned: "Who — — —?" It was all roaring wind and static and barely any sound out of it.

I burst into tears. "This is Queen Kaitlyn, I need to speak to Hammond. I don't — Captain Warren's been shot. I don't know— someone is shooting at us and—"

The radio was static and — I said, "Are you there?"

"— — are you in the ... ?"

"I can't hear you. Please, I'm at Balloch castle—"

I pressed my ear to the radio and tried to concentrate on what was coming from it, but I couldn't hear anything.

I looked up and — visibility was low, but — where I had been lying a few moments before — was a foot. Wind whipping and a foot, tights, breeches, a body laying on the wall. "Magnus?"

I elbow crawled toward —

Magnus.

"Magnus, are you...?" He was still and completely out, the wind subsiding, the howl gone, the gusts — over.

The roiling clouds were blooming above us and rolling in the other direction, like a wave pulling from the shore.

I threw my back across Magnus's body. Holding the gun in one hand, the radio in the other, I stared at the sky.

I had Magnus.

— I raised my head, thirty feet away, the far end, Zach and Hayley were hugging each other, happy, but also trapped there, I was trapped here.

There was someone shooting at us, if that person was coming up the stairwell they might hurt Zach and Hayley, but from the sound of it — helicopters were on the way.

I breathed and thought it through,

Magnus... I had rescued Magnus.

The soldier protecting us was gone.

Helicopters were coming.

But then it dawned, I didn't know if the helicopter was friend or foe.

I scrambled to my hands and knees. I put the gun in my belt. *Please please please wake up, please.* The weight of the bullet proof vest weighed me down. I shook him, but he was totally still. It sucked.

He needed to wake up so I could get him out of here.

The helicopter sounded closer.

Hayley and Zach were waving their arms at it.

I yelled, "I need you guys to come out here! We have to jump."

I watched as they scramble-crawled to me, Zach way too tall to be this exposed.

Another gun shot, Zach and Hayley dropped to the stone, their hands on their helmets. *please please please please let them get here, safe, please. Please oh please.*

The helicopter drew closer, there was no way to tell if it was on my side or not, and it was headed straight for us.

"Hurry! I don't think it's on our side!"

I twisted the ends of the vessel, lying across my husband, trying to protect his wide chest with my protective bullet-proof shield. Zach reached me, he leaned across Magnus's head, Hayley lay across his stomach and I said the numbers watching the helicopter in the sky as it gained on us.

The helicopter started shooting the walls of the ruins of Balloch castle — Blasts bashing the stone, beginning low but climbing up, rubble and rock breaking apart, stone spraying, the castle wall being ruined even more.

One thing I knew: Magnus's kingdom was gone.

There was no way Hammond was in control anymore.

Roderick would be king.

And that was fine, we could forget the future, ignore it, who gave a shit anyway...?

Except Archie was out in it.

The time jump ripped us from the year 2382.

FORTY-TWO - KAITLYN

I was super sick and tired of landing in these freaking bushes. I would guess the people here at the Botanical Gardens would be sick and tired of these storms by now too.

I looked around me. No one else was awake yet.

Just me. I tried to sit, but it was like climbing against gravity, and I didn't have the energy.

But then I remembered I was wearing a bulletproof vest. I unstrapped the Velcro on the sides, wiggled it off over my head, and sat up. Magnus was beside me, still, completely quiet. Hayley was curled on her side, moaning. Zach threw an arm over his face.

They were waking up, we just needed Magnus. I pulled his hand up, pushed back his coat sleeve, and took his pulse at his wrist. It was there, faint but there.

I wrapped my hand around his and then held his hand with both of mine and concentrated on it.

Magnus.

I had his hand. He was home.

A tear slid down my face. That had been so scary.

I kissed his fingers and rubbed my tear-stained face on his hand and then I just rested there, my face on his very fancily embroidered coat trying to breathe.

Zach got up, "You cool, Katie?"

"Yeah."

His voice was low and deferential since Hayley and Magnus were still sleeping. "We got him back, huh? I mean, that was some scary shit. I killed one of the men, he was coming up the stairs and I shot him, I can't believe I did that—"

"I'm sorry you had to. Was he in uniform? Could you tell?"

"I couldn't tell, it was all so, awful." He shook his head. "The important part is we got him back."

Hayley moaned, looked around, and clamped her eyes shut. Then she squiggled her head over and put it against Magnus's shoulder and wrapped around his arm. She smiled up at me and whispered, "Katie, you got your man back."

"I did, he's back. Thank you guys, I couldn't have done any of that alone. Thank you so much."

Magnus groaned and began to move and shift.

"Hey honey, it's me, Katie. I got you back."

He chuckled and opened an eye and scrutinized my face. "Why are ye cryin' then, mo ghradh?"

I wailed, "I'm just so freakin' happy."

"And who is this?" He raised his head to look down at Hayley. "Och, Madame Hayley, ye have survived the time-jumps and the murderous Reyes?"

She nodded.

He pushed the hair from her forehead and said, "Ye have a scratch there I think."

"Yeah, I do."

He joked, "But ye can cover it perhaps with a big bow, or one of those hats, what are those hats called, Chef Zach, the ones with the front gate that James likes tae wear?"

"A baseball cap."

"Aye, ye can wear a baseball cap, Hayley, and nae one will ken ye have the scar."

She giggled against his coat.

"And how are ye, Chef Zach, ye are here, where is your family?"

"They jumped earlier. They should be headed to Amelia Island already, or there now, Beaty needed to be taken to the hospital."

"Beaty?" He looked at me.

I nodded. "She has a really bad cough. Quentin and Emma brought her here to get her medical care."

"But Ben is okay?"

Zach nodded, sitting in the grass in Savannah, a cool breezy day. "Ben is good. He's probably going to be pissed about the jump again, but he's good."

"And where is Archie?"

"He's in the future," I shook my head. "There's a whole lot to tell you about..."

His hand went up to my cheek. "Your eyes are sad, mo reul-iuil, but you have survived it? You have rescued me again?"

I nodded, unable to speak without ugly-crying.

He dragged himself up to sitting. "Och, I am nae in the future, tis the gardens of the city of Savannah I think." He rubbed his hand through his hair. "We must be near the barrel of crackers where this whole thing started."

I curled up under his arm. Hayley leaned on his shoulder. I said, "I can't believe you're back."

"I canna either. We are safe here?"

"You tell me. Is Reyes dead?"

"Nae, not yet."

"Okay, then, well, Lady Mairead told me we could drive in as long as we didn't jump in to Florida."

"Och, we should have asked her from the beginnin'."

"As you know she isn't always easy to find."

Zach said, "And what's up with your costume, Magnus. It looks like you're going to sign the Declaration of Independence after a stop-over at your Ren-faire-themed prom."

Magnus chuckled. "I haena any idea what ye are speakin' on, but these are the clothes of a English gentleman in the year 1740."

A man stalked toward us from the gazebo at the gardens. He looked red-faced and irritated. "I'm sick and tired of you hippies sleeping in the bushes back here, move along, this is private property, get out."

We all stood as quickly as we could considering we were not ready to get up yet, dusted ourselves off, and allowed him to shoo us away from the gardens.

A few moments later, after helping to smooth down each other's wind-pummeled hair, and dusting our clothes for real, and spit-wiping smudges off each other's faces, we were walking along the familiar road headed in the direction of the hotels and restaurants.

Magnus and I sat on a bench outside the rental car company while tourists and locals gaped at his outfit. This was even more fanciful than the former kilt, this was bows and laces and clearly historical. If he had been wearing this the first time I met him surely I would have known something was up.

I was glad the rest of us were in a more casual kind of clothes.

It helped lend to his 'costumed' effect. But passersby still stared like crazy.

Twenty minutes later Hayley walked out holding a car key. Zach had a phone to his ear. He said, "They're at the hospital, Beaty is checked in. We should head straight there."

FORTY-THREE - KAITLYN

Hayley rented a Lincoln Navigator. She said we deserved it after what we had been through and it was Mags's money anyway. Zach wanted to drive because it was nicer than any car he had ever driven in his life, so we let him.

Then we drove through McDonalds and bought bags of food. I ordered Magnus an extra large Coke and gestured for him to put it in the cup holder. He pointed at another cup holder, and said, "This is one as well? It will need another drink."

I said, "By my count there's eight cup holders and we need a drink in every one of them." So we ordered more.

Zach passed them back, joking, "It's hard to argue with someone who looks like Thomas Jefferson."

Magnus asked, "Does Thomas Jefferson like tae order McDonalds?"

I groaned while I unwrapped a quarter pounder with cheese, "So much history you don't know about, my love, so much."

Magnus laughed. "I daena need tae ken it, I have been living it." He unwrapped a Big Mac and took a bite so big he ate almost half at once.

Zach pulled the car out of the parking lot and up the entrance to I-95.

Magnus took another big bite, chewed and swallowed. Hayley spread the meal out for Zach while he drove and arranged it nicely for him, and we were all quiet for a bit while we ate.

Then Magnus, after eating a second sandwich, moaned happily, leaned his head back on the headrest, and closed his eyes. He repeated, "I have been living it."

"Us too," I said, "Hayley and Quentin and I went to the way past. We thought you were going to be there at the beginning of the vessels. So we went."

Magnus looked at me and squinted his eyes. "Och, twas a risk."

"Your mother agreed with me, we thought that was where you were going to be."

"You were speakin' tae Lady Mairead on it?"

"Yes, she helped a little this time. Well, at least she didn't try to kill me. With Roderick fighting for your throne I guess she felt like we should all work together..."

"Roderick was still tryin' tae take my kingdom?"

I took a deep breath. "I think you might have to consider your kingdom lost. Hammond is trying to hold it together, I think, but it's not looking good. Roderick has the safe house. He probably has the castle too, it's..." I shook my head.

He groaned. "And Archie, where is he?"

"We don't know. I had him in the safe house, with Bella. Lady Mairead was going to take them to Balloch and ask Lizbeth to watch over them but then they were just gone. Someone removed him from the house. I don't know who."

"Archie is out there in it? Dost Hammond ken he is missing?"

I nodded. "Yeah, he knows they're missing."

Magnus scowled. "Archie is gone, the kingdom is falling, tis a mess. I will kill Reyes for takin' my attention away from it. Then I will kill Roderick for raising an army against me."

Hayley turned all the way around in her seat and joked, "Mags, you're giving me chills. You're all Fast and Furious sounding like you're about to get in your race car and speed off through the desert after them."

"Och, I canna drive, but I can ride a horse verra fast." He stuffed some French fries in his mouth, chewed them, and chased them down with some Coke.

I said, "I'm so sorry I didn't keep everyone safe. I know I promised, but I — I thought you were going to be in the past. I thought I could find you there. In hindsight I should have been watching over Archie."

"Nae. Daena worry on it, Kaitlyn. Ye canna always be responsible for everyone against men that are tryin' tae kill us. Ye had Archie safe and ye were goin' tae send him tae Lizbeth, ye arna at fault for him being removed from the house."

"Thank you for seeing it that way, but still, I'm sorry he's not here."

I took a sip of Coke and watched the trees slide by on the side of the highway. "The good news though is that when we were in the way, way past, Quentin shot Reyes, and now he has an injured shoulder."

Magnus looked at me dumbfounded.

"An injured shoulder?"

"Lady Mairead called him weak, like he is not as powerful."

"Och, which one?"

"The left. Did I do good?"

"Ye did verra good."

"How did you get away?"

"Now there is a story. Dost ye ken of the fort in Saint Augustine?"

"Yes?"

"I was taken there, and I was put intae a prison. Twas a verra small, dank dungeon. Reyes told me he was goin' tae force me tae the past tae get the vessels."

"See, I was right! Why didn't you have to go? We were there waiting for you."

Hayley said, "You should have seen me, Magnus, I was kicking some highlander ass."

"M'ancestors?"

"Sure, but like your great-great-great grandpa so you don't care and frankly he was a dick to those people, who weren't aliens, not at all, they were humans and we need to talk about that someday and figure out how they got the vessels."

Magnus looked confused.

I said, "Just ignore what she's saying. We need to not go there ever again. It's too easy to screw something up and I'm glad we didn't. We shot Reyes, hurt his shoulder. He's different, but everything else is the same. You're here, we're here."

"Aye, and we are goin' home. I dinna think twould happen."

"So tell us about it."

"I was in the prison. The fortress was held by the Spanish but then verra soon after I arrived the English, led by General Oglethorpe, tried tae seize it. There were ships in the harbor, cannons and guns firin'. In the ensuing battle I must have been forgotten. There wasna a guard stationed outside the hole they put me intae so I pushed the stones away from the door and escaped."

"You escaped?"

"Aye, the year was 1740. Twas June. I made it tae the postern door and out tae the harbor. Guns were firing from the ships and so I had tae jump intae the water with cannon shot crashing all around me."

My eyes were wide. "You could have died!"

Zach's eyes kept looking in the rearview at us. "Did you swim north or south?"

"I swam north, and am glad I did because the Spanish had all of the south. The English would eventually be beaten back."

He clasped my hand. "When I pulled myself from the water I was verra bedraggled and close tae starved. I needed a drink desperately. I hid myself in a clump of trees believin' I would die on that shore alone, but then within the trees was another man seeking cover from the battle. His name was Fraoch. He ended up saving my life."

Hayley tried to say it. "Frouick?"

Magnus chuckled. "Tis close, but ye have tae say it from your gut, such as this — Fraoch."

Hayley tried it two more times before I said, "Hayley you're missing the point. I get that it's a fun name to say but I would like to hear more about this man that saved Magnus's life please."

"Sure of course." She took a big noisy sip of Coke and batted her eyes pretending to be quiet and listening.

"Fraoch shared his water and food with me—"

"So he did save your life."

"Aye, he was a good friend, and here he is still feedin' me. This is his family's recipe." He put a small handful of French fries in his mouth.

"What do you mean—?"

"This food, he was a clan Donald." Magnus grinned.

"Clan Donald! But your family feuds with the MacDonalds."

"Aye, twas verra tense in the beginnin'. We were nae sure if we were goin' tae kill each other as we slept, but we soon came tae an understandin' on it."

He smiled. "I promised nae tae kill him as a thank ye for savin' my life, he had proven he wasna goin' tae kill me as he had already shared his last food with me. After that we became verra good friends. I told him I often ate food that was cooked by a

MacDonald in a tavern in the New World and he thought twas quite a marvel that I did."

"Jesus Christ I wish I had a video of that conversation. A freaking highlander born in the 1600s explaining to a highlander born in the 1700s about how fast food in the 21st century works."

Zach and Hayley laughed along with me.

Magnus laughed too. "Twas nae easy tae explain it, when I daena understand the half of it."

"That's what's so funny, my love. We should take a tour of the restaurant kitchen sometime and blow your mind. So tell me more."

"Fraoch led me tae a riverbank — did ye ken, that there are... what do ye call them, the monsters that swim in the ponds, we saw them when we went tae the place with the rides?"

My mind tried to wrap around what he was talking about, then I said, "Disney World, the...? Oh, we saw alligators in that lake!"

"Och, they are terrifyin'. I had tae sleep near one on the banks of the river."

Zach said, "Fuck, that's an eighteenth century one too. They're probably extra ornery."

"There was a monstrous beast in the river with me too, twas different though, nae scaled. Twas smooth. I was forgettin' tae breathe and afraid and unable tae keep goin', ready tae die, and it swam tae me and bumped me up tae the surface. That beast wasna frightening."

My eyes went wide. "I bet that was a manatee. Magnus, that's good luck. I think you had a moment with a manatee."

He tightened his hold on my hand.

I added, "I'll show you a picture of them. They're very gentle. The others, the gators, not so much. So you were on the banks of a river in St Augustine, was it near the fort?"

"Aye, fairly close."

"It was the St Johns, I would think..."

"Fraoch warned me against returnin' tae the fort tae kill Reyes for a vessel."

"So you didn't go back to kill Reyes?" I asked. "I mean, we are driving into Florida as if he was still a threat, but I hadn't really gotten the whole story yet."

"He is still a threat. I couldna go back. The fort was under siege and I was sure that he wasna there any longer but I have a plan and twill be easy now he is injured."

Zach said, "So how the fuck *did* you get from St Augustine to Scotland?"

"Oh," I said, "good point, how did you get from St Augustine to Scotland in 1740?"

"First Fraoch and I stole a skiff and paddled it up river tae the port. Then Fraoch lent me a fare tae get on a ship. We traveled up the coast tae a port named Savannah, the same place we just went tae. Then we found a ship that would give us passage in exchange for labor. That ship, the *Deptford*, went up the coast tae Charleston, have ye heard of it?" He looked down at my face, I had tucked my head onto his shoulder, my forearm along his, our hands wrapped together on the armrest.

"I've heard of Charleston."

"Aye. We loaded the ship with supplies and then set across the sea for London, twas..." he shook his head. "Twas a verra verra long trip."

I looked up at his face. "How long?"

He tilted up my chin with a strong hand and kissed my lips. "It took two verra long months, mo reul-iuil." He smoothed my hair back from my face. "Then two weeks more in a carriage that was bound from London tae Edinburgh, twas about the size of..." He looked around the inside of the Lincoln Navigator. "The entire carriage would be about the size of this seat. Twas verra uncomfortable."

Zach said, "Go back for a moment, how long to cross the ocean?"

"Two months, Chef Zach and do ye ken what we had tae eat? Twas a salted meat, a mystery of the kind, that ye had tae yank apart with yer teeth and then a bread that ye couldna get yer teeth tae settle intae."

"That's why you're so thin?" I asked.

Magnus nodded down at me and his eyes were so very sad. I nestled against his shoulder, wrapping my arm around his, and we sat quietly.

Until finally, as if he had been thinking on it more, he spoke. "Then I had tae ride tae Balloch. It took another few days. But once I arrived I went tae carve my message intae the rocks. And twas just an hour later that the vessel was there."

"It's like magic." I yawned big and wide. I was so tired.

He pressed his jaw to my head, then kissed my hair and pressed against me again. "Aye, tis like magic, though sometimes twas verra slow."

I took a deep breath so happy to have him again, here beside me.

He said, "Good night, mo reul-iuil."

"How do you know I'm going to sleep?"

"I can hear it in yer breaths."

"I'm really tired..."

Hayley snuggled down in her seat. "You cool to drive Zachary?"

"Yep."

And soon enough it was just a quiet ride, a sleeping family, heading home.

FORTY-FOUR - KAITLYN

Emma with Ben on her hip met us in front of the hospital and after tearful hugs and grateful happiness led us through to the intensive care unit.

We sadly were not dressed well enough, or clean enough, and so we couldn't go into a room to see Beaty, we would have to come back, but we watched through a window. She had a mask over her face, frail and small looking in the hospital bed. Quentin sat bedside clutching her hand.

He came to meet us when he heard we were there. His eyes full of fear and emotion. Magnus's eyes full of fear and emotion. They hugged and then Quentin filled us in. "She has pneumonia. We don't know what's up yet. It doesn't—" He broke down and so we all kind of held onto him in a circle for a while, not speaking, just holding his shoulders and then finally after like ten minutes, I asked, "Do you want to go for a walk around, get some air?"

"Nah, I need to get back in there."

Emma said, "We're all leaving, but I'm ten minutes away if you need anything."

"Yeah, thanks."

He left us to go back to Beaty alone.

~

In the parking lot we were trying to decide which house to go back to, the octagonal house that we still had a contract on until the end of the month, or our last home, the one we loved, on the north end, the one with Magnus's stable underneath, the big ass kitchen. It would be dusty and closed up and not ready for us and might possibly be on Reyes's radar, but the octagonal house was definitely on Reyes's radar: he had gone there for dinner one night.

Hayley wondered if we needed a new house altogether, but then Magnus said, "I want tae go tae our home, Kaitlyn. I daena care if it is dusty or — I have traveled a long time tae get here and I want tae go home."

I looked him in the eyes and said, "We're decided then. We go home."

~

Hayley drove. I sat in the passenger seat. Magnus sat in the back. From the backseat he asked, "Dost ye think we should take Beaty back tae her time? Perhaps takin' her from home is what caused her tae be sick? Would she get better in her own air?"

I turned around and shook my head sadly, "No, we've got better medical care now by far. We have antibiotics and surgical teams and — no, if she was sick like this in the 18th century she wouldn't make it, there'd be no way. They just aren't equipped to care for patients in your time. A lot of people wouldn't make it. No, this is best, it's just... I really regret taking her to the 16th century. I didn't know she was going to get sick, but I shouldn't have risked her life like that. I wonder if Quentin will forgive me."

Hayley said, "Quentin would never blame you, Katie, but I'm worried if something happens to her that he'll blame himself. He was such a wreck when his mama died, remember?"

"I do, yeah, I really hope he doesn't go through that again."

"Me too."

I reached back and held hands with Magnus for the drive.

~

We pulled up at the house and Zach pulled up right behind us. Emma got out and unstrapped Ben from the back seat.

Zach said, "We were going to stop at the grocery store but then I remembered delivery. If it's not necessary to have groceries delivered right now when would it be necessary? We ordered some stuff it should be here in an hour."

"Perfect." I said and looked up at the house. "Last time I was here I was screeching at Braden in the driveway. That seems like a long time ago. Now suddenly I'm wondering if there's going to be any issues with that video?"

Zach said, "Most people have probably forgotten it by now because you haven't responded or reacted. I'm sure they've lost interest under the deluge of all the other crazy stuff that's going on. Have you heard what's going on with politics lately?"

"No," I groaned. "Please don't tell me, I want to eat and drink and just wait for news of Beaty."

Zach pulled the garage door up and let us into the house.

FORTY-FIVE - MAGNUS

I was finally home. I couldna believe how long it had taken, how much of my spirit and health, and I was verra tired. I hadna been able tae explain it tae Kaitlyn, nae well enough, how I wasna fully myself yet, and there was still so much tae do.

We all took tae openin' windows and lookin' through our closets. And then Kaitlyn said, "Do you want to take a shower with me?" She unbelted her jacket and dropped it tae the side and then pulled her shirt off over her head.

"I do verra much."

"When was your last shower, Mister Fancy Pants?"

I unbuckled my breeches and dropped them tae the ground and stepped from them. I joked, "I am nae fancy pants, I am Mister Naked Man."

She giggled. "Your shirt is pretty ruffled for a naked man, it goes from your thighs to your jaw."

I pulled my shirt off over m'head and from my arms.

"Jesus Magnus, your chest, I haven't seen it in a while and—" she came tae press against me and kissed my chest and then pulled her pants down to the floor and kicked them away. She was naked and I was verra glad tae see the length of her skin.

She took me by the hand, led me intae the bathroom, and bent over tae turn on the shower. I took that moment tae stand behind her and press tae her. She turned in my hands, a warm smile spread across her face. Then she brought her arms around my neck, and ran her lips down my neck. She pulled me in under the water.

I couldna help but moan.

Her voice breathy against my ear, "Does that feel good?"

"Aye, mo reul-iuil. It has been a verra long time without any comfort."

She ran her lips down my chest and I was feeling verra interested in bein' inside of her. She put some soap in her hand and I leaned forward dutifully. She massaged the soap through my hair, around and around, with much care and attention. I was so incredibly spent.

With a groan, I dropped down to my knees. I wrapped m'arms around her legs and pressed my forehead to her stomach. Rivulets of water ran down my face. Her hand faltered. "Are you okay, my love?"

"Aye, now."

She held the back of my head pulling me closer in. I held tighter around her hips. "Would ye wash m'hair some more, mo real-iuil?"

She stood firmly and bore my weight as I clung tae her. She poured soap intae her hands and slowly rubbed it intae my hair, in and down; pulling it along the strands. She massaged the sweet-smelling soap intae my scalp in a circular pattern and then down the back of my neck and firmly across my shoulders. I pressed my cheek tae her stomach, my lips, and moaned from the feel of it.

I clutched her arse, pullin' her in closer. "I love ye, Kaitlyn."

Twas like bein' in a rainfall, the water rushin' down me, washin' away the soil and hopelessness of the months of tryin' tae find my way back tae her.

Her hands clutched me closer, her voice a sweetness above me. She whispered, "I know you do."

I spoke intae the flesh of her stomach tasting the water rolling down. "How dost ye ken?"

"Because you will always do anything to come home to me."

"And I will come again, my love, though it were ten thousand mile."

"You remember the poem I read you?"

"I canna forget that line, ye read it tae me with a bonny Scottish lilt tae yer voice, I winna forget it."

She held me tighter still. "I love you too."

In answer I lumbered tae my feet, picked her up under her arms so she would wrap her legs around me, and pressed her against the wall. Her arse in my hands, I brought her close and pushed inside her with a rush, warm rivers of water running down our bodies. We pressed and moved against each other, my chest against hers with small splashes as we rocked. She directed the water over our heads so that there was clear water and floral-scented soap and wet slippery liquid over us as I pushed and pulled against her.

"Ye smell like roses," I said, "I had forgotten ye tae smell like roses."

In answer she kissed me, tongue and lips and sweet breaths, and after the heaviness of my life these last weeks, the burden of it all, her weight in my hands was comfortin'. She was the burden I wanted. The lightness of her was refreshin' after months of nothin' but heavy toil. I pushed against her harder and she took me willingly and we ended with moans, their sounds muffled by the cascade of water around us. I pressed my forehead tae the cool tile wall. "Twas too fast, but I needed ye so desperately."

She nibbled my earlobe. "It's usually about enjoying the race, but sometimes the finish line is all we want. That felt good. Let's just promise the next time we'll linger.

"I like verra much the sound of that."

I slid from her and dropped her gently tae the tiles.

She ran soap around on her own head, and through her hair. I watched for a moment, the expression on her face, pleased, relieved, satisfied, happy, my wife. It struck me at that moment that I was fully home with her, finally together, and safe.

I hadn't had time to exhale and now I did and when I did she opened her eyes and smiled up at me. Her head wet and covered in soap, her skin glistening and clean and fresh.

I had almost lost her but here we were, married, together, in our own bathroom. Nae longer a king and a queen but instead Magnus and Kaitlyn, the Campbells, living on Amelia Island, Florida, smilin' at each other because here was another day of happiness for us.

She said, her voice like her own sigh of comfort and relief, "Welcome home, Magnus."

"Thank ye for the welcome." I ran a palm down her stomach, there was nae a swell. "Dost ye ken?"

"No." She wrapped around me and tucked her head against my chest. "No, I don't know, but it's only been a few days for me. The funny thing is I used to keep track of time by my pill. Now I can't remember what day it is."

She ran her hand down my chest. "I'm worried though. I've jumped five times in a few days. It's been nothing but drama and danger and I — what if... I'm just nervous about it."

"Me as well, mo reul-iuil, but I daena think we should let our fear stop us from livin'. I love ye too much tae cause ye tae live in fear or pain—"

She said, "I know. I know you want me to feel nothing but joy, and you worry over it, but you'll need to accept it — even

Magnus, the great and awesome, Master Magnus, even he can't protect me from every fear, from every worry."

I smiled and joked back, "Och, ye are questionin' my manhood while I am standin' afore ye with my sword..." I looked down and shook my head.

She teased me, "Your sword is not as unsheathed as usual."

"Sometimes even great warriors need tae put their swords away."

She kissed me, slow and sweet. "I missed you. I love you. I feel safe with you. I want you. You're my husband and I'm very glad you're home."

"I missed ye, mo real-iuil. Every night on the ship I would think on gettin' home tae ye, like ye were a prize that I might be lucky enough tae win again. I kept looking up at the sky and thinkin' tae myself, wherever I am she is there too. We are under the same sky, though we are in different folds of time. I wanted ye so much and tae have ye again is all I dreamed on and now here ye are. You are nae a prize tae dream on, you are mine, a part of me. You are my home and my family, waiting here, and it means everythin' tae me."

She said, "You're going to make me cry and I just got you back and we don't want to cry. Not anymore." She folded her arms around me and we both held on.

FORTY-SIX - KAITLYN

For dinner we didn't even try to eat a normal meal. We ate some sliced meat for the protein of it and then went straight to ice cream sundaes because it was something we all really wanted. Magnus, because he had been without for so long, the rest of us because that had been some hard shit and hard shit sometimes requires lots of carbs.

We sat at the kitchen island on stools with Ben toddling around and we talked about what we had been through. Charlie, one of the regular security guys, was already stationed out on the deck.

I told Magnus all about Captain Warren and we all recounted what it was like that he had been the commander of our excursion and then was just gone. And we tried to reconcile it with what we knew: That the kingdom was falling. Hammond was fighting for it. Archie was out there somewhere. I didn't remember old Magnus or Tyler telling me that it got quite *this* bleak before.

We came to the conclusion that history had changed.

Magnus said, eating a big spoonful of ice cream with caramel sauce on it, "We daena ken what will happen next."

I said, "That's frightening."

"Tis, but tis also the same as for every other person in the world. We all must try tae understand what comes next, prayin' tae god that it goes in our favor, and if ye think on it, Kaitlyn, tis a comfort tae be the same as everyone else."

We all raised our glasses with a "Hear, hear!"

Magnus said, "Slainte!"

Then Hayley said, "To Beaty, I hope she pulls through because she is a true bad ass."

I said, "To Beaty, a terrible arse."

And we all laughed and Magnus hugged his arm around me, which was the best feeling in the world to have my 21st century husband back, in our 21st century house, looking out over the beach — a little windblown tonight, seagrass waving, but warm enough outside that the ac was humming inside to keep us a perfect temperature. Plus we had the back door slid wide open for the breeze, because we were from the 21st century and it was okay to waste a little in the name of comfort, and smell a little like rose-scented shampoo, and glow a little from sex and love, and laugh a lot from relief, and yet to feel very sad about his kingdom and the people we knew who were stuck there in it and so worried about Beaty and Archie.

All of that.

Plus the ice cream tasted really good.

As we talked and ate, Zach did a few things around the kitchen, opening up drawers and cupboards, throwing away old bread, tossing boxes of cereal. It had been over a month and we had left in a hurry.

Some of our stuff had been moved to the octagonal house; someone would go get it in the morning.

We would deal with a lot in the morning.

And soon Zach and Emma and Ben went to bed and Hayley went to sleep in the guest room because she didn't want to go home, she had shared nights there with Nick and—

I shuddered at the thought.

She would sleep here.

We might have to come up with a better plan for her, sell her house, or move her to India, or *something*.

I used the bathroom and that was when I realized I had started my period.

That super sucked.

I mean, it sucked because I really really wanted a baby, but also Magnus said he had a plan. He was going to kill Reyes. And how could I help if I was pregnant? He didn't want my help, but he would need it. I was kind of a terrible arse through all of this.

Plus the motherfucking matriarch.

I was just having a harder time being an actual mother.

I sighed and pulled open the drawer beside the toilet and pulled out a tampon and well, did what one does with those, and sighed again. That's fine. It just wasn't the right time.

It wasn't the right time when we decided it.

It wasn't the right time now. I would get my period behind me, kick Reyes's ass, then after that, when I was all ovulating and stuff, then I would get pregnant... definitely.

Except first... I had to tell Magnus.

FORTY-SEVEN - KAITLYN

When I returned downstairs he was out on the back porch, looking out over the dark dunes, the breeze rustling his hair. His broad back stretched across the slats of the wooden deck-chair. I paused for a moment with my hands on the sliding door to just watch him for a moment. The back of his hair with the curls ruffled against his taut muscular neck. I wanted to kiss him there. Everywhere.

The edge of his jaw, the eyes — they were pensive, worried.

I slid the door open and crossed the deck. I pulled a chair up beside him and took his hand on the side-by-side armrest. It was the same position we were in when we talked about Archie for the first time, and he told me about Bella, really told me about her and broke my heart a little, but healed it too. Because this was us. I tightened my fingers around his. "Hi love. I have news. I don't think you look like you want this kind of news, but I don't want to keep it from you — I started my period just now."

He nodded. "You told me twould be a few days, tis okay Kaitlyn, we will try again."

"Yeah..."

I watched the side of his face while he stared out at the ocean. "Whatcha thinking about? Your kingdom?"

"Aye, tis verra complicated that tis—"

He let go of my hand and leaned forward with his elbows on his knees. "Dost ye really think Roderick has the kingdom now?"

"I do. I mean, who else is in charge? You'll need — I don't know, it will take a lot to get it back."

"I have Lady Mairead." He chuckled weakly.

"Yeah, she is not going to let your kingdom fall. She probably raised an army already."

"When you spoke tae her, did she seem tae want tae protect Archie?"

"She did. She wanted to take him to New York she had a whole plan. I decided though that she should take them to Lizbeth. She didn't love the idea, but she agreed it would be the best for them. She was going to do it. It was the first time we agreed on anything except you." I ran a finger up and down his arm. "Yeah, I think she wants to protect him."

"Good, I winna worry on him right now."

"You have a lot to worry about, huh?"

"I do, tis a big thing tae need tae kill a man. Even one that deserves it.'"

"Once you told me that before a battle you would pack your gear and it would get your mind off the worry."

He chuckled. "Aye, packin' or I can watch the movin' pictures of the cats."

I smiled. "The cat videos? Yeah, they can get a mind off any worries. Some might say they are the entire reason the internet was invented."

His brow went up and he teased, "What is the internet?"

I teased him back, "I've explained it already. You'll have to trust me that it's really just cat videos." He leaned back in the chair again and gave me his hand, warm and securely wrapped around mine. "Do you want to talk about your plan to fight Reyes?"

"Not yet, I'll talk tae ye about it tomorrow."

He raised my hand to his lips and kissed the back of it.

"Is that all you're worried about? It seems like there's more. Something else..."

He looked at me for a moment. "Tis my friend, Fraoch. I am tryin' tae get used tae a world where he will die because he voyaged across the ocean. Dost it kill a man tae cross the ocean these days, Kaitlyn?"

"No, we can cross the Atlantic Ocean by plane, flying, and it will take about eight hours."

He shook his head. "It daena seem fair that he was born in a time where his life is cut short from it. How many men have been lost because of what we daena ken about the world? We dinna ken we could fly and so we died in the crossing."

"It's really bothering you?"

"Aye, he was in his hammock and he was ready tae die there, in the dark, horrible bottom of the ship with the vermin and — he wanted tae go home tae Scotland. Tae start a family. But then he wanted tae die from the pain of the death that was nearin'. He wanted me tae leave him there, Kaitlyn, and I refused. I carried him tae shore and got him tae the hospital. I paid all the money I had tae save him, but it wasna enough. I asked my cousin tae sit at his bedside, but I canna save him because of the time he was born."

Magnus looked at me with such sadness. "The truth is, I can save him, I could bring him here. I could bring everyone here, Lizbeth and Sean, and my nieces and nephews, but they might get sick like Beaty. Twould be cruel tae give them hope that they wouldna die in the dirt and vermin of a barbaric castle, that they could have ice cream and air blowing, but they might die anyway. I daena understand why tis like this. I am feelin' like I daena want the power tae decide who can live and who will die."

My heart broke hearing him talk like this so guiltily because of the time we were in. I put my arms around him, my head on his shoulder, and hugged him tightly.

"I'm sorry you're feeling this so much." I kissed the folds of fabric stretched across his shoulder. "I know this might not help much, but we all die. That's the truth. No matter what the time is. We have a lot of comforts now, but Lizbeth knew she could come here and she still chose to stay there. There are things that are worth living for in that time — family comes to mind."

He patted my hand that was wrapped around his arm. "I am just feeling the loss of my friend."

"I can hear it, and I wish I knew how to save you from it. I'm sorry."

"You daena need tae be sorry."

"Still, he saved your life. I would like to thank him."

We watched the sea grass wave on the dune top for a moment and then I thought to ask, not really wanting him to relive it, but wanting to know. "What happened to him?"

"He got verra ill on the crossing as many of the men did. Tis like he was wastin' away. He was weak and I saw his legs, Kaitlyn, they had turned black. His teeth were hurtin' him so he couldna eat and—"

"He has scurvy."

"Aye," he nodded. "Scurvy will kill a man for darin' tae think he can live on the seas."

"Magnus, there's a cure for scurvy."

His eyes rose to mine. "There is?"

I nodded, "Yes, there's a cure and it's actually an easy one. I mean, I would need to make sure the best way to — but do you know the date, when you left him?"

"I made sure of it afore I left. You could cure him, Kaitlyn?"

"I don't know. I never really thought about scurvy before, but I think so. I think it's vitamin C. I don't know how far is too far, but we can definitely try."

"We can try tae save him?" His face screwed up as if he was holding down his emotions. "Thank you, mo real-iuil, it means a great deal tae me that ye want tae try."

"Of course Magnus, anything for you." I grinned. "Plus, what if he's the great-grandfather of the man who invented McDonalds restaurants? Civilization might stand in the balance."

He chuckled.

"Feel better?"

"I do, but I am verra tired."

"I'm going to take some Midol, get a hot water bottle, and then let's go curl up in our bed together."

He kissed my fingers again.

I hugged him and then led him back into our house.

FORTY-EIGHT - KAITLYN

I woke up in the perfect place, sprawled across his chest. It went like this: sleep, comfortable, warm, slowly waking, and then with a rush, Magnus, love and more.

He looked down at me. "Good morning, mo reul-iuil."

"Good morning, Magnus."

"Dost ye have a list a'ready?"

I rubbed my palm down his bare chest and lingered around the gathered top of his plaid pajama pants. "You better believe I have a list. First, we have to go see Beaty and check in with Quentin. Then, we need you to detail your plan how you want to deal with Reyes."

"Tis a different plan now I ken he has an injury." His stomach growled. "I will tell ye over breakfast."

"Sounds good. Plus I need to go see my grandmother. I haven't seen her since Thanksgiving." I climbed off him to get dressed. I looked down into my underwear drawer full of my assortment of toys, my panties, the next drawer down, t-shirts, the bottom, yoga pants and more. It had been a long time of wearing weird shit that other people picked out for me: queenly clothes and 'I only barely escaped' outfits.

I picked out a thong, one in a sky-blue color, Magnus's favorite so I owned about five, and pulled it up my legs slowly because I realized Magnus was watching.

I ran my finger under the lace and wiggled for him.

He groaned.

He was sitting on the edge of the bed, stalled in mid-rise to watch me.

"Do you like my thong, Master Magnus?"

"Ye ken I do, verra much."

"You missed it while you were on your voyage?"

"Tae say I missed it is nae the truth of it. I dreamed of your arse, cried for it, longed for the weight of it in my hands. Why daena ye bring your cheeks closer so I can kiss them hello properly?"

I grinned and walked backwards toward him.

"Och aye." His eyes were big with desire. He reached out for my hips, drew me close, and kissed the triangle of fabric at the top of my cheeks. "Good morn, Kaitlyn's undergarment, tis me, Magnus. Have ye missed me as much as I have missed ye?"

I looked down my shoulder at him, talking to my thong, and giggled.

He said, "Have ye been lookin' after Queen Kaitlyn's little arse?"

I said, "I actually haven't seen these since we left."

"Wheesht," he joked. "Daena ruin the story of it, your undergarment is tellin' me of yer exploits while I was away."

I laughed and rolled my eyes.

He ran a hand up and down my thighs and around my cheek and kissed the triangle of cloth again. He pressed his forehead to the small of my back. "Och, now I have been reacquainted proper, I will allow ye tae dress for yer day, mo ghradh."

"You have a lot of self-control."

He chuckled. "Tis nae self-control so much as ye have the wee string comin' from inside yer pleasure garden, a reminder that takin' a stroll there today wouldna be as much fun."

FORTY-NINE - KAITLYN

Everyone was up and bustling. Zach made scrambled eggs, bacon, and toast, but was cleaning off the shelves in earnest, wearing rubber gloves, washing the counters, and making a list for a proper grocery trip. Emma had already left to take Ben to Zach's mother's house so she could go to the hospital to see Quentin and Beaty. Hayley was on the phone, hiring two young men and a truck to move the few things from the octagonal house back to this house.

The safe would need to be moved too, that was the big one. And we had to return the rental cars. We had to get back to a normal life.

We all drove together to the hospital, wishing for a normal life, but in the hospital life was standing still.

Quentin stood distraught at Beaty's bedside. The doctor had just passed through, checked the charts, and declared she 'still needed the ventilator.' Quentin told us they were keeping her sedated because whenever she woke up she acted crazy-scared ripping at the tubes. He said to me, "It's just like my..."

"I know, it's just — but it's different Quentin. Your mama was really sick and things were wrong with her, things she couldn't heal. Beaty is young, she can heal herself from this. The doctors will help her." I glanced at Magnus, gazing into the window of Beaty's room, intense worry on his face. My warrior husband could ride into battle with barely a thought, but hospitals and illness totally freaked him out.

We took Quentin for a walk outside. He made it in a distracted circle around the front sidewalk of the hospital and then wanted to return.

While he used the bathroom, I spoke to the sleeping Beaty. "Hey sweetie, you need to start breathing again, normal-like, because Quenny really needs you. There is a lot of great stuff we want to show you. You just got here. You just made it to the cool stuff. You should stick around to see it."

I stepped away from her side and Magnus patted her arm and then we left to the warm beautiful Florida day.

"I hate to say it but now we need to visit my grandmother."

"Aye, tis a complicated day. We should do it though, I am learnin' we should see the people we love when we have a chance tae tell them."

"Perfect, I'll drive."

FIFTY - KAITLYN

I wish I could have had one of those moments of incongruity where my grandmother would have been unchanged in the month that had passed. I had watched my friends get married and been to the 18th century and the 16th century and had all kinds of life and death shit happen as well as welcomed a stepson into my life and then lost him somewhere in the 24th century.

But this was...

Grandma was dealing with life and death too.

She was bedridden.

So frail.

Withered from when I saw her last.

I said, "Hi Grandma, how are you doing? You good?"

She glanced at me, then said, her voice not much more than a croak, "Where's Christina?"

I patted her arm. "Who's Christina, Grandma, maybe I can call for her?"

She looked frightened. "She should have been here by now,

we have plans to go..." her voice trailed off and she looked confused. "...ice skating."

"I'm sorry she's not here yet, I'll look for her. I know how much you love ice skating." I busied myself with adjusting the covers on her bed.

"Hey Barb," said Magnus. "Tis me."

She looked up in his face and there was a glimmer of recognition there.

Tears welled up in my eyes.

She asked, "How are you, dear?"

Magnus sat down beside her bed and took her hand. "I have been better, Barb, I am terrible worried on ye."

She raised a frail hand with paper thin skin to his cheek and held it there. They locked eyes for a moment. She drew her eyes away from his and smoothed her palms across the thick covers spread over her now diminutive body and grew calm, focused, and lucid. "You are a good boy. You shouldn't worry so. You carry too big a burden, dear. The world is not yours to save."

Magnus hung his head. "Aye, some days it feels like it is though."

She patted the back of his hand. "When you have shoulders like that you want to pick things up and carry them, but you aren't a god dear, you're celestial dust just like the rest of us."

He chuckled sadly. "Tis sad tae think of myself as dust."

"Well, that's just household dust. I'm not talking about that kind. I'm talking about celestial dust, the universe bursting open from a tiny speck of nothing and exploding into particles throughout everywhere, in every time, and becoming every *thing*. Those tiny specks find each other and glom on to each other within that explosion — they come together and form chains and finally people, you, and your..." Her voice faded. She turned to me and her brow drew down.

"I'm his wife, Katie."

"That's right. You're Katie, the love of his life. The celestial dust that combined with his celestial dust and here you are. Spinning around each other..."

I sat on the edge of the bed. "You once said it was like we are entangled."

"True. That does sound like me in my more sensible days." She sighed. "I remember what it was like to be sensible. Most days now I just stare at things forgetting how to make sense of them."

I had a lump in my throat that wouldn't swallow down.

Magnus said, "So I am celestial dust? What is it?"

She waved a hand. "Stars and other shiny rocks. Some people might say the stars are the amazing part of this story, but think about it this way: those stars are the same things that make up you, a living breathing man, strong-shouldered, cryin' at my bedside. Who is the amazing part of this story, the star?"

Magnus said, "The man."

She laughed, then coughed, and it took a moment for her to recover, then she smiled a withered smile. "No, the amazing part of this story is the little old lady being cried over by that handsome man." She tapped his cheek again. "I kid you, dear, your heart and soul are the amazing part. Katie's. That you found each other and entangled up your heart and family."

"I have changed the natural order of time. I brought sadnesses tae people I love. I think they might have been better if..."

"Bullshit, dear. I have just been telling you that the world came from an explosion and that we are all celestial dust hurling through space and that there is magic in the particles of dust finding each other. Does that sound like a natural order you should be worrying over, or does that sound like magic and destiny and mind-expanding craziness? As Jack used to say to anything we didn't know yet: 'It's a mystery today, tomorrow it will be a fact.' You are a fact, my dear. Your dust has affected all the other dust pushing it away and pulling it near." She sighed, "Imagine if I had never met you, what sadness would my celestial dust have felt that your celestial dust wasn't there?"

Magnus folded down over her hand and cried. I put my hand on his shoulder, my grandmother put her hand on the back of his head, and we held on.

"You cry it all out dear. The worry, the fear, you let it go."

And so he did.

~

When he recovered, he was sheepish. He straightened his shirt and excused himself to the bathroom leaving me and my grandmother alone.

I said, "Thank you Grandma for that, he really needed it. He was on a long journey and he's worried about..." I didn't need to say it because it was everything. He was worried about everything.

"Everyone needs their grandma sometimes."

"That is so true. Thank you for being mine. You may not remember me sometimes, but thank you for taking him into your heart."

"He loves my little Katie so much. It's easy to take him into my heart. How could I not when he wants to take care of you and make your life so much better?" Then it was my turn to burst into tears.

She said, "Now honey, you have to get stronger. You can't be crying like this. You need to buck up. He needs you. He needs you to be strong and to help him."

I laughed through my tears. "I thought we were both just celestial dust?"

"I wish it was easier for you. You've gone and fallen for a god.

I'm telling him he's dust to keep him calm, but you know he's got more to do than that. He can't do it alone."

"I keep telling him. I'm trying to help him."

"I know you are dear. I see it."

"You do?"

"I do, you have grown into an amazing woman. I am so proud of you. I see how you talk to him, you have wielded your power in the gentlest of ways. He loves you for it. I see it."

"It's really nice to be seen."

"Well, yes, yes it is." She extended her arm, groping for the water at her bedside. I held the cup for her and directed the straw to her mouth. She sipped and then lay back.

"It's easy for us women to become invisible, but I see you."

Magnus returned to the room and sat down.

She asked me, "You haven't been here for a time, where were you?"

"I went to the 24th century and met my stepson."

She said to Magnus, "You have a son? Now that explains some of your worry." She returned her glance to me. "What is my step-grandson's name?"

I said, "Archie."

"Like the comics." Her eyes shifted nervously around the room. It was as if now that she had stopped talking in big philosophical statements she couldn't stay focused on what was in front of her.

Magnus took my hand.

My grandmother said, "Do you know what time it is?"

I said, "It looks like it's 11:30, Grandma."

Her eyes drew downward. "Do you—" She stopped mid-sentence, then said, "I'm very tired. I think I need to go to sleep now."

And just like that, as if she was turning us off, she turned on her side and pulled the covers up to her chin.

We waited for a moment and then left to go home.

Driving home I said, "Grandma was a lot like her old self, huh?"

"Aye, she was verra helpful tae me."

"Good, me too. She said some things, that she loved me and was proud of me, it was pretty great. I'm going to miss her so much when she's gone, but I'm really so glad to have had that moment with her."

He kissed the back of my hand.

FIFTY-ONE - KAITLYN

When we got home there was a tree in the living room. Undecorated, but still a tree. Zach was full-blown manic. It was December 23rd after all. We took one look at him and realized we needed to get busy.

Magnus and I wrestled his shopping list away and went to the grocery store. Magnus was amazed by stuff still but we tried to remain focused — there was work to do. The cool thing was that the grocery store had a Christmas section, marked down, half-off. We bought a dancing Santa who sang *Jingle Bell Rock* and made Magnus's face light up with joy. Then I made a late lunch for all of us of sandwiches and chips on paper plates.

I jotted down lists. I made sure people were taken care of, and I listened to Magnus. He wanted to be here. He also needed to handle Reyes. Reyes had lived here for a time, he knew our behaviors. If he wanted Magnus he just had to come and get him.

Magnus held meetings with Hayley about what she might have told Nick and what Nick Reyes told her and they hired two more security men for the outside of the house. Magnus met the new guards on the deck and gave them long and detailed instructions. I watched through the sliding doors while I helped hold the space so that Zach and Emma could get our house to the level of Christmas they wanted for Ben — a little guilty that they had traumatized him with the time jump. They had a Christmas style that was too much, excessive, awesome, overblown. I did laundry.

Magnus was always armed and watchful, walking the decks of the house. He was certain in his plan. A basic plan really: Go back in time to St Augustine and kill Reyes there. The only reason why he hadn't done it yet was because he needed Quentin and Quentin was on family leave.

So my list of complicated things that Magnus needed to do was very long. It involved so much that was necessary but hard to accomplish. The list went like this:

Wait for Quentin.

Keep us safe.

Have a Merry Christmas.

Make everyone's life as normal as possible.

Go at first possible dawn to the past to fight Reyes before he came here.

Find Magnus's friend in the past and help him.

My own list included:

Help Magnus do everything, plus research cures for scurvy.

Under that, be grateful to be home.

. . .

Under that, 'buy Midol!' because I kept forgetting it at the store and my cramps were awful, not the worst, but pretty bad.

FIFTY-TWO - KAITLYN

Just before dinner we went back to the hospital. Beaty was groggy but awake and the best part — the tube was out of her mouth. The doctor had hopes that she had turned the corner.

We all came into her hospital room to say hello. She was weak. I asked, "Beaty can you smile for me? I never know if someone is okay until they smile and I need to know you're okay."

She smiled. "Aye, Queen Kaitlyn."

I said, "See, Magnus, she's going to be okay."

He nodded. "How are ye, Beaty?"

She said, "You told me, King Magnus, that cars were frightenin' but they are nothin' compared tae these ropes tyin' me down and inside my body."

"Aye, I have been in a hospital afore. Tis verra noisy and nae one bothers tae tell ye if ye will ever feel good again."

I said, "Well, at least you did feel good again, and it sounds like Beaty is going to feel good again. We'll have her home in no time. Right Beaty?"

"Where is my home?" She sweetly looked up at Quentin.

"I have an apartment nearby. It's got—"

Magnus said, "I think twould be best if you and Beaty lived at our house, Quentin. Emma and Kaitlyn and Chef Zach can take care of Beaty while ye help me with something I need tae do."

"Alright, that makes sense, boss."

Magnus squeezed my hand. The look of relief on his face was palpable. I said, "When does she get to come home?"

"Maybe tomorrow. If we can keep her comfortable and have oxygen for her."

I grinned wide. "Oh I have oxygen for her. I have an oxygen treatment machine that I've been carrying around for three hundred years. So yes, bring her home tomorrow. We'll be ready."

FIFTY-THREE - KAITLYN

When we made it home that night we ordered pizza, because Zach and Emma were still decorating. It was beautiful though. Candles on the mantle. Pine garland across the tops of the sliding doors and really just about every surface. The tv on, shifting images of the weather channel once more. Though we knew now that Reyes could arrive in any place and just drive here, Uber or something, so yeah, that was why Magnus was planning to go, fast, like Christmas day.

The Santa we had bought stood on the coffee table. We pushed the button every now and then to see his whack-a-doodle dance and to see little toddler Ben's excitement or Magnus's astonishment.

After dinner Magnus took a shift on the decks so the security guards could eat and rest and then he came to bed much later — his sword sliding across the floor under our bed, kept within reach, his sporran unbuckling and being placed on the end table. The room was dark with just a little moonlight coming from the upper windows over the sliding glass doors with the shades drawn across them.

"Are ye still awake, Kaitlyn?"

"Yes." I rolled onto my side to wait for him. "Is everything safe outside?"

"Aye, tis nae a sound or a person about."

"It's very peaceful here on the north end of the Island. I love it so much." I stretched my arms over my head as his kilt dropped to the ground and the unclothed muscular form of my husband slid into bed beside me.

His strong arm slid under my head, the other arm pulled my hips close to his. His mouth nuzzled into my neck. I loved this, being pulled close, the comfortableness of lying here waiting, the familiarity of him arriving and taking me. Because he could. Because I wanted. Because he was home.

He kissed me long and nuzzled against me pushing me onto my back, licking along my collar bone and up and down my breasts and my stomach and causing shivers and a great deal of involuntary writhing.

"Wait, hold on." I stopped him. "This is awesome and everything, but I'm kind of a crappy period-mess and—" I sighed, overdramatically. "I do want you so bad, like so so so so bad, but not really, not tonight. So get ye to your back, Master Magnus, I'll do you."

He asked. "Dost ye want your toys?"

"You are awesome, yes, the green one."

He got up and went across the room to my top drawer and by the light of the moon found my green sex toy, which was kind of awesome to watch. His wide shoulders, his perfect ass, as he gingerly sifted through my underwear looking for what I wanted.

Then he climbed back on the bed and handed it to me and I positioned the toy between my legs and turned it on so it could turn me on and pushed him to his back and hovered over him, my little vibrator making a whiiirrrrrring noise within my folds. I kissed across his wide chest and brushed my lips down his stomach, and gently, with kisses and licks along the firm mounds and dips of his muscles moved to the top of his thighs and then pulled all of him into my mouth and played there enjoying the length of him for a long while until I brought him to moans. My toy worked its magic too and I collapsed on him, spent.

I rested my cheek on his pelvis, my arms wrapped around his hips and smiled up at him. He smiled down, his brow lifted, and he chuckled.

"What are you laughing at, Master Magnus?"

"You are nae usually so quiet when we are at play."

I laughed. "My mouth was full."

His eyes sparkled. "There is that wit I love."

So I climbed him, kissing and licking, all the way up his body to his mouth where our tongues met and our lips. I wrapped around him and we rested for a few minutes until I raised my head to look at the time. "It's Christmas Eve."

"Och. We will have a busy day on the morrow makin' all of Chef Zach and Emma's dreams come true."

"They do have a lot of dreams tied up in Ben's first Christmas. Though truth be told, I have a lot of hopes and dreams in your first Christmas too."

"We will have tae make it verra special."

"Tomorrow morning we'll go get Ben a present?"

"Aye. Dost he want a horse too?"

"Oh." I raised my head. "I haven't actually had time to get you the horse I promised you, or learned to ride, and—"

He ran his fingers through my hair, twirled his fingers along an end, and watched it spring into a wave. "Tae me it daena matter that the horse is nae here. What matters is ye want tae give me a horse. Ye want tae learn tae ride. I winna hold ye tae the day, twould take the fun from it."

"Good, thank you for being understanding." I thought for a

moment. "So you'll be okay with a box that means I will learn to ride a horse and I will soon buy you a horse?"

"Aye. I am okay with a box that means all of the rest."

His voice was sleepy sounding, quieter, lower. "And I will give ye a box that has inside of it a promise — everything you will ever want, I will give tae ye."

"We can wrap them. I like that very much."

He kissed the top of my head, right at the hairline between my forehead and my hair. A kiss that lingered with an intake of breath as if he was breathing me in and then his hold on my shoulders tightened and then loosened as he fell asleep.

FIFTY-FOUR - KAITLYN

I woke up very early and forced Magnus awake and after a quick breakfast we went to Centre Street to go Christmas shopping. I raced through gift shops and clothing stores buying every single stocking stuffer I could find for Quentin, Beaty, Zach, Emma, Hayley, Me and Magnus, as well as big stockings for each of us, and a bag of oranges and so much candy and chocolate from the fudge store.

Magnus and I went into a toy store and he bought Ben a wooden push-toy that looked like a red hippo and made clacking noises when he pushed it with a little yellow bird that spun up and down on the top and then he found a beautiful silver teething ring and put it with the other on the counter.

"Is that for Ben?"

"Nae, for Archie."

"You're right, I am sure Lady Mairead will find him soon. We should be ready."

I bought a silk baby blanket for Archie and for Ben a little boy doll made of cloth that had removable overalls and embroidered features and then I sent Magnus to the car with it all, eight bags worth, to stuff it in the trunk of the Mustang.

I ran into a gift shop to buy some wrapping paper and some gift boxes for our gifts. Then, because I wanted Magnus to have something real to open, I went back to the toy store and bought some frisbees, a few balls, and six nerf guns so we could play family games out on the beach on Christmas Day.

When I got that load out to the car I made Magnus hide his eyes so I could sneak the newest bags into the back seat. "Don't look back there or you'll spoil Christmas."

"Och, I daena want tae be the one who spoils the most magical holiday in the world."

FIFTY-FIVE - KAITLYN

We wrapped presents and afterwards everyone needed to split up for activities with their own families. To call Zach and Emma harried and overly-excited would be an understatement. They were seriously on edge and when they got in the car to drive to Zach's family's house they really didn't want to go, but we helped them in the car and waved goodbye.

Then Magnus and I drove to the hospital to pick up Beaty and Quentin. I had cleaned the oxygen tank and it was charged up and ready to go. We gently helped Quentin get her from a wheelchair into the back of the Mustang and then drove them to our house and helped her up the stairs.

She said, a little breathless from the effort. "Tis much less grand than yer last castle, Queen Kaitlyn."

I chuckled at her bluntness. "True, it's smaller, but you'll like it, the couch is very comfortable, and we have a perfect place for you at one end of it."

In the house she was surprised by everything and Quentin

was so excited to show it to her. "Check out this refrigerator, Beaty."

I lowered her to the couch and wrapped a blanket around her legs. "What dost it do, Quenny?"

"Cold food, and wait, would you like some ice water?"

Without waiting for her to answer he filled a glass with ice and water and delivered it to her at the couch. She looked a little peaked by the traveling so we put the oxygen mask on her face for some extra breathing help and then we all sort of stopped and looked around. To blow her mind I pressed the button to set the Santa in motion and her eyes went wide watching him rock his hips back and forth, in that red suit, singing that song that I had heard already 175 times that day but was somehow still funny.

And then we set up a gift-wrapping station on the dining room table, Beaty napped and Quentin ran to his house to pack his bags and probably buy Beaty a Christmas present and I wrapped a box for Magnus showing him how and then he wrapped a box for me, with his fingers all stuck to the tape and the paper ripping down the middle and some funny fumbling. At one point he jokingly stuck a piece of paper to his head. "I daena think it is listenin' tae me on how tae lie flat."

I teased, "I see that, you're supposed to aim for the box instead of waving your hands around."

He tried to flick wrapping paper off. It was stuck to the back of his hand by a wad of tape.

"I could help, but I'm not going to. You'll have to figure this out. It's part of the present to suffer over the wrapping of it. The end result is supposed to show the person how much you love them."

"Och, tis a great deal of importance in it." He pulled off a very, very long strip of tape. "Tis why I am wrappin' around and around so ye will ken it is my feelin' on ye." The strip of tape was folded over, taped on itself, wadded in places, and yes, went around the box twice, holding paper in some places, completely useless in others and there were big folds of paper on one side all pointless and the other side there was barely any paper covering the box. Overall it looked like a four year old had done it.

Magnus gave me a sad look, with his usual good humor behind it.

I said, "I think with practice you would have it."

He held it up. "Tis like when I asked ye tae marry me, twas nae perfect but my heart was in it."

"Well now that you said that, it's more than perfect. Now we put it under the tree." I led him to the tree and we placed our gifts there.

There weren't many gifts until Quentin came with his suitcase and a stack of presents for Beaty and at around 7:00 pm Hayley arrived after a shopping extravaganza carrying twenty-nine presents. She piled them under the tree and we sat around in the living room eating cheese and crackers and drinking wine, telling Beaty all about Christmas and the house and the Island and really overwhelming her with information until finally Quentin carried her up to their room.

He returned a bit later after getting her settled. I asked, "How are you?"

He slumped back on the sofa. "This has been one helluva honeymoon. What the actual fuck?"

Hayley said, "How long have you been married now? Like a week?"

He groaned. "Yeah, and I've almost gotten her killed like ten times."

Magnus said, "I need ye tae come with me on the morrow tae fight Reyes."

"If it keeps him from coming here, I'm absolutely game. Let's finish this. We should get the weaponized ATVs out of storage and use them."

Magnus's brow furrowed, "I daena ken how tae drive it."

I said, "I can go. I'll drive you."

Magnus shook his head. "Nae Kaitlyn, you canna—"

"I can, I've been going to the past. I learned to shoot, I can jump, sometimes I'm the first person up when we do. I've driven the ATVs and I've outrun men on horses and I—"

"Nae Kaitlyn, tis a man's job—"

"Nopety nope, nope, nope, that's not the correct answer—" I sat up on the couch.

"I ken what is correct, Kaitlyn, daena argue with me."

I asked, "Quentin, what do you think?"

Quentin looked nervously from me to Magnus, "Not sure how to answer."

Magnus said, "I daaena think Kaitlyn should come, but I would be willin' tae listen tae your opinion on it."

Hayley was chewing her lips, keeping herself from blurting her opinion too.

Quentin said, "I think it would help if we had two ATVs. Katie has proven herself capable of thinking under pressure and she's been able to keep people around her out of harm's way. I think she would be an asset."

Hayley held up her wine glass, "Holy shit Quentin, I did not think that was what you were going to say. You're usually a total misogynist."

He shrugged. "I don't know what the hell that is, but Katie can handle herself, and we might need someone extra who can handle herself."

"See," I pleaded with Magnus, "let me come. I can help."

Magnus glowered and took a deep breath then said, "I am nae agreein', but I will think on it."

"Good, thank you."

Quentin said, "Tomorrow when I gather the weapons in storage I'll bring two of the ATVs, just in case."

Magnus took a big sip of ale.

Zach and Emma and baby Ben came in through the front door carrying more packages and some aluminum foil topped leftovers from their Christmas Eve meal. We all rushed around putting everything away and then Magnus and Quentin went to take a turn guarding the house while Emma put Ben to bed.

I followed Magnus to the deck and wrapped my arms around his shoulders. "I'm sorry I argued with you in front of Quentin and Hayley. I get things in my head and just want you to agree with me..."

"I ken it, but sometimes, mo reul-iuil, I need time tae consider a thing. Ye have tae give me time afore ye try tae force your will on me. I will always try tae be fair, but ye have tae respect me enough tae listen tae my opinion on it as well. I am your husband, ye need tae listen tae me."

"As you know, that's really hard for me, to keep quiet while you think, but I do know you're fair and I do respect you. You've always taken my opinion in things, thank you for that."

He nodded then took a deep breath. "Tis nae that I daena want ye tae come. I am havin' trouble with the decision of it. You have been with me tae the past, ye are verra capable, but this will be dangerous. Tis difficult tae decide tae bring ye, tae plan tae put ye in danger. What if somethin' happened tae ye? Twould be my fault. I couldna live with it."

"I understand. I'm just sorry about the argument. Okay?"

"Okay, Kaitlyn."

"We're about to put out presents, promise me you won't look in the living room when you come back in?"

He joked, "Did Santa come a'ready? I have been keepin' guard and haena seen him."

"He's magical, but don't look."

"I winna."

I returned to the living room as Emma came downstairs. "Ben's asleep, you ready Zachary?"

They began to put Santa presents out. Emma said, "Katie, this is for you and Magnus." She put a small stocking in my lap. "It's for Archie. I know he probably won't be here, but maybe Lady Mairead will find him in time and... Zach and I don't want to make you sad, if you want to keep it to the side, just in case, we understand. But we thought we might want to put it up and put some presents in it, because he's a part of the family too."

Tears welled up.

She said, "I knew it, I didn't mean to make you sad."

"No, that's okay." I gave her a sad smile. "Actually Magnus and I bought him presents too. Let's hang his stocking. I think hope is so much better than fear."

I began filling all of the stockings and we all drank and talked and laughed. It was pretty special and festive and we were tired but remained in good spirits though we were worried about what might come, who might show up.

We knew Santa was coming, that was enough.

FIFTY-SIX - KAITLYN

In the wee hours of the night the bed shifted as Magnus climbed into it. "Are we safe?" I asked. It was becoming my habit to ask it.

"Aye."

He curled up against me, the skin of his face and the back of his hands were cool from the breeze outside. His breath and chest warm against me. "I am verra tired."

"I imagine. Me too." I wrapped my arms around his head and he nestled into my neck. "Do you think Archie is okay? I'm so worried about him."

"I am as well, mo reul-iuil."

"He should be here, a part of our Christmas. Instead he's out, what, in some war-torn world?"

Magnus nodded against my shoulder, his face scratchy. "Twas supposed tae be my kingdom. I was goin' tae keep him safe there."

"Well, Reyes got in the way of that."

"Tis why he is a dead man and if Lady Mairead is incapable of locatin' Archie, I will find him."

"Do you think you'll have to fight Roderick to win your kingdom back, does it matter?"

He thought for a moment. "It matters. If Roderick is king he will have tae imprison me or kill me. I would never ken when he was comin' tae finish me."

"God, that's scary."

He raised up and put his hands on both sides of my face and looked down into my eyes. "I will find Archie and I will keep ye safe. You have my word on it, Kaitlyn. Tomorrow is Christmas. Quentin and I have been speakin' about my plan, and we will leave tomorrow night after the presents and—"

"Who will leave?"

"All of us. Quentin, myself, and ye. If you are a part of the battle though ye have tae follow my orders, promise me."

"I do. I promise. Thank you."

He lay his head beside mine on the pillows. "I wanted tae practice your defenses again afore we left."

"That's okay, I remember enough. I'll fill my backpack with chocolate from my stocking and then I'll be savage protecting it."

"Twill be chocolate that ye protect? Good." He nestled down onto his stomach, under the covers, his face turned toward me, and just before he fell asleep, he asked, "How dost ye ken that Santa put chocolate in yer stocking... have ye been peekin' inside?"

I chuckled and curled up beside him. Almost nose to nose and watched him sleep for a moment before I fell asleep too.

FIFTY-SEVEN - KAITLYN

"Wake up Magnus. Wake up, it's Christmas, Santa came!" I said it as soon as my eyes opened. I was sprawled across his chest, and when I looked up at him he was already smiling.

"How dost ye ken he came? Ye have been snorin'."

I pushed him playfully and leapt from the bed. "I have not been snoring. I don't on principle. How can I snore when I have such a hot man in my bed? It would be unseemly."

I pulled on a pajama top and bottoms and raced down the hall to the bathroom where I peed, squeezed toothpaste onto my toothbrush, and returned with the electric toothbrush whirring on my teeth and paste lathering my lips. "What is taking you so long, Magnus? Up up, the sun is up, Santa came, up!"

"Och, ye are full of excitement this morn for someone who kens what is inside all the packages."

I ran down the hall, spit in the sink, and came back wiping my mouth with a towel. "I do know and I'm still so excited. Up!"

He tossed his covers to the side and dutifully stood. As he

passed me he pulled my hips tae his front. "We daena have time for a verra quick moment together?"

"No. Magnus, there is a literal baby out there, about to have his first Christmas and we might miss it having sex. It would either be a scandalous tragedy or a tragic scandal, one or the other, I don't know, but we can't."

He laughed as he headed to the toilet. "We canna make a baby because of the baby that lives here."

"I'm going to go put on the coffee, you have three minutes to get out there."

~

It took five minutes before everyone in the house came downstairs. The pot of coffee was on. The tree was lit up and sparkly which was a good thing because we needed the light to see by because it was really possibly too early. In hindsight, having woken Ben to open his presents might not have been the best idea, because he was in a mood, alternately laughing happily and then being overwhelmed by something and crying his head off. He was staggering up to shiny packages and beating them with his hand and then staggering to the next box and because he was teething stuffing everything that wasn't larger than his head into his mouth.

Stockings full of presents were out on all the furniture because there were so many presents inside they couldn't hang without ripping the nails from the wall. Quentin carried Beaty down and she sat on the couch under a blanket with a stocking full of presents in her lap.

Zach began making breakfast and Emma hugged me, "Thank you Katie for helping us make this so perfect."

"What did I do? This was totally Santa, there's no way we mere mortals got this done in a day."

And that's what we did all morning, as the sun rose on the beach, we drank coffee and ate some egg and sausage casserole, and pressured Hayley to get out of bed already, and we slowly one by one opened our presents and delighted in Magnus and Beaty's delight.

The only melancholy part was Archie's stocking with a present from Santa and presents from me and Magnus and an extra two from Hayley, because she was secretly a big softie, but it was the good kind of melancholy. We missed him. We wanted him here. We would fix this so that he was safe. This stocking was a promise.

We played with Ben and were in good spirits, allowing the house to get knee deep in wrapping paper and kissing and hugging each other and yes, it was everything I wanted and more.

And my present from Magnus, a box that was wrapped terribly, in paper printed with penguins in Santa hats. But I knew he had concentrated on it, had really tried to get it right. The tag read 'to Kaitlyn' in his swooping handwriting, and then underneath it 'love, Magnus'. I knew it was full of nothing but his intentions, both unspoken and spoken, but still, it really made me weepy when I opened it. I knew in every bit of fiber in my being, he loved me —that's what that box was. He wanted to love me forever. He wanted a family with me. To grow old with me.

I don't know if anyone in the history of time has ever been as happy as I was about an empty box for a present.

I also got a pair of sweatpants from Hayley with rainbow stripes on one asymmetrical leg that were so soft I might never take them off.

There was, if it was possible, too much chocolate.

Michael came over to see his big brother Zach and he brought Hayley a Christmas present and she seemed exasperated by it, but also happy, too. The two of them went out on the back porch and talked for a while. James dropped by. It felt like I hadn't seen him in a lifetime but it had only been a month. He, Magnus, Quentin and Zach played ball in the house with Ben, making an awesome dangerous racket, and then we all lounged, spent, jacked on caffeine, and crashing from the breakfast calories.

I loved having our house full. Zach was back in his element, feeding all of us. Hayley and Michael were not fighting. I curled up under Magnus's arm and we enjoyed the food and friends, with some music playing, and the lights twinkling. An epic day and it was only just now 11:30 am.

FIFTY-EIGHT - KAITLYN

Michael left to go to his parents' house for Christmas dinner, sad he had to leave our festivities. James went home to check on his dog.

Magnus and Quentin decided to get busy and loaded up in Quentin's truck to go to the storage unit to get the ATVs.

I guessed they had been gone for about thirty minutes when we saw the first sign of the storm.

The storm wasn't on the television's constantly running weather channel. This one was right outside. Zach and I both met at the sliding doors and a moment later Hayley met us there too.

To the south of us the sky was black. Storm clouds were banking up and rolling higher and higher. The wind was picking up and—

Emma came down the stairs with Ben on her hip. "Zachary do you see?"

"Yeah, honey, I see it. Can you get Ben back upstairs?"

He said to Hayley. "I'll go talk to the security guards, will you call Quentin?"

She already had her phone in her hand.

I said, "Shit, I hope that's just a storm," as the high storm clouds began to arc lightning strikes from the center of it down to the sand.

I heard Hayley's voice saying into the phone, "Yeah, it looks like it's centered over Main Beach. Yeah, how far away are you? Okay, I'll tell Katie."

She turned to me. "They're off the island and there's been an accident, traffic is backed up on the bridge, so it will be a while."

"Then that's too late. I can see someone under the storm."

I took the flight of stairs at a run to the second floor and went out on the deck to speak to the security guy. "Do you see that person?"

"Yes Ma'am." He was looking through his binoculars.

"Man or woman or...?"

His voice was a deep southern twang. "Well, ma'am it looks like a woman, do ya wanna give it a look?"

He passed me the binoculars. I aimed them toward the stretch of sand between the surf and the dunes, right in front of our house, and directly under the storm that was beginning to dissipate. There was someone lying in the sand, a woman. I passed him back the binoculars. "It's Lady Mairead, Magnus's mother, stay here, protect the house, I'll go out and see what she wants."

I raced back downstairs to the ground floor. "Zach, it's Lady Mairead."

"What the hell does she want? Doesn't she know she's supposed to jump into Savannah? She's directing Reyes right to our house."

"Yeah, We need to lock down this house. I don't know what she wants, but I'm going to go find out."

"What's the fucking protocol?"

Emma called from the stairs, "We used to turn everything off, go quiet, what do we do?"

I said, "Turn everything off, go quiet, hide in a closet. I'll be back."

Zach grabbed a handgun we kept in a drawer in the kitchen island and checked if it was loaded. "I'll walk out there with you."

Hayley said, "What should I do?"

Zach said, "Will you wait here?" Then he called up to Emma, "Emma! Will you show Hayley where our gun is?" He said to Hayley, "Use it to guard the inside door."

"Yes sir."

Then we were bolting out the door down the deck to the sand.

I was in my new Christmas sweatpants, with a crop top, also barefoot. I didn't need shoes because this was Christmas Day. We didn't need to go anywhere that required shoes. We jogged down the beach, the person we were racing toward moved and shifted in the sand.

Lady Mairead's face was pale and strained.

I pulled up in front of her with my hands on my hips. The storm was almost gone, the wind now just a high breeze, enough to whip my hair into my face and sand in our eyes.

"Lady Mairead, you're supposed to jump into Savannah, Reyes is going to—" Her eyes held mine, as she brushed sand off her big linen skirts and then straightened the deep green bodice from the 18th century with her Campbell tartan wrapped around her shoulders.

"What are you doing here?" I asked.

"I have come tae warn ye, Reyes is here, he is coming over the dunes at any moment. You will need tae tell Magnus tae be ready." She held up her hand for Zach to heave her to her feet.

"Magnus isn't here. He went to—"

"Why on earth isna he here?"

"He went to get a stockpile of weapons to go fight Reyes." More clouds banked above us. A second before, the clouds were parting, now they rolled back in, and I did not want to be under another fucking storm.

She looked up at the darkening sky and said, her voice flat and frightened. "We daena have time tae discuss it."

"Shit," I said, "We've got to get off the beach." I had to yell now over the storm, the whipping wind, my hair wild, the air sizzling with the electric charge of the lightning that was beginning to crash into the beach just behind us. I yelled, "Run, run, run!"

Lady Mairead hustled, I ran just behind her, sort of herding her faster, faster, please go faster, and Zach brought up the rear, turning around to look behind us. We hit the walkway and clomped down the boards. The security guard rushed out to help us in and I took one last look behind me. There were men under the storm, a grouping of them, still and quiet from the jump, not menacing at all beyond the storm, but from across the sand, over the dunes, were men on horseback, ten coming up from the south, another ten coming from the north. "Holy shit, he's got his freaking—"

"Run!"

Horses driven by soldiers covered in armor and carrying swords thundered across the dunes bearing down on us as we skidded to the sliding glass doors that Hayley was holding open for us. We raced in and slammed them shut behind us.

The security guard yelled, "Everyone down, behind the couch!"

He and Zach each had their back to the wall on either side of the door. I peeked over the back of the couch, my heart racing, my head spinning. Footsteps clomped down the boardwalk, steady and menacing in their pace, slow and sure, as if we were cornered, like we were — totally cornered in a freaking house full of my family that was knee deep in toys and excess and wrapping paper. That's what I had concentrated on for two days instead of getting the weapons out of storage. Buying gifts. Because I wanted some normalcy.

But I had forgotten that I don't get normal.

I get crazy bullshit-evil guys.

It came to me that Hayley was speaking into the phone. Her voice the voice of a person that was seriously freaking out. "What do you mean, *traffic*? Get on this fucking island, Quentin, there's a maniac with a —" She peeked over the couch. "A fucking army. He's got an army in Fernandina."

"Can I have the phone?"

She passed it to me as we locked eyes, both our hands shaking so much we barely got the phone from one to the other.

"Quentin what am I supposed to do?"

"Security called it in, the police will get there before we do, just hold tight. We're almost past the accident—"

Magnus's voice through the bluetooth of their phone. "Kaitlyn?"

I sobbed, "It's really scary Magnus. He has so many men and it's..."

"I ken, but he wants me, daena do anything. When I get there, I will kill him and twill be okay. Where are ye hidin'?"

"I'm behind the couch."

Quentin's voice, exasperated, "Get behind the kitchen island at least, Katie. You're exposed."

I whispered, "I can't, he's right here, right outside—"

There was banging on the glass door, loud.

Hayley and Zach and I went totally quiet.

I clamped my eyes shut and begged the universe for the police, anyone, a freaking horse — it could ride by the truck my husband was in and he could jump on and ride at a gallop up the side of the highway to get here. "I'm scared."

Quentin and Magnus discussed what to do. I looked over at Hayley, her eyes closed tight. Why were we doing that, did it make us hide better?

More banging.

The security guard commanded, "I've called the police. They're on their way, you have one minute to clear off this—"

The sliding glass door shattered.

Quentin's voice, "What the hell was that?! Is he in the house? Katie! Is he in the house?"

Reyes's voice, "I don't want any trouble with anyone, I want Magnus."

I squiggled down to the end of the couch and peeked around to see Zach, standing stiff and still, holding his gun, his eyes wild. I shook my head, *don't do it, there's too many men.*

The guard's voice, trying to sound dominating, said, "Magnus isn't here, so you can get the fuck out of here. The police are on the way."

From the distance sirens.

Reyes said, "What? Magnus is too scared to come out?"

"He's not here."

The man laughed. "Well, somebody better get out here and talk to me, I've got Archie and we—"

"He has Archie." I said it to the room, to anyone listening, as an explanation for what I was going to do, and then I stood from behind the couch with my hands up. "Where is Archie?"

From the phone I heard Quentin and Magnus's voices as they went ballistic. But I was already standing, locked eye to eye with Reyes. He was covered in gear, bullet proof vests, a helmet, full protection against our handguns and behind him, men with swords and other weapons. I couldn't even tell what most of them were. They all looked like some crazy Mad Max kind of scenario, like what you would get if a bunch of 17th century men just raided the arsenals of armies from a dozen different centuries.

I was facing them all down.

I had not thought this through.

Zach was in my line of vision, so was the security guard, but they were seriously outmanned. If they shot anyone, we would all go down.

I asked "Do you have him here, where is he?"

Reyes said, "Why would I bring a baby to a military exercise, Queen Kaitlyn? I'm a gentleman, not a terrorist."

"Fuck you," I said, "Do you have Bella too?"

"Your husband's mistress? No, I—"

"Why the fuck do people keep calling her that, you piece of shit. Where is Archie?"

His smile grew mischievous. His eyes held a glint I did not like.

It came to me that he might not have Archie, that he was bluffing, and I just basically surrendered to a maniacal monster without a back up plan.

But guess what?

He was in the house.

I really didn't have any other choice.

"I will take you to baby Archie, Queen Kaitlyn, you can comfort him while you wait for Magnus to run his errand for me."

The voices were muffled coming from the phone, but I could tell Quentin was trying to get me to stop. I pushed the phone over to Hayley so she could deal with it.

"Fine, but no one else gets hurt. Don't you touch a hair on anyone in this family's head. Not one. If you're a gentleman, prove it. Make a deal with me — you don't hurt anyone."

"Of course, Queen Kaitlyn, I wouldn't dream of injuring anyone else."

"And where are you taking me? To Archie? You promise?"

I stepped around the couch with my hands up, brushing near Zach who mouthed, "Be careful."

Reyes grabbed me by my arm. "Tell Magnus I will entertain the beautiful Queen Kaitlyn, while he travels to Inchaiden, the day of the dawn of the Tempus Omegas. Kaitlyn will be my incentive that he goes."

Then he said, "Did you hear that, Zach Greene? Will you tell Magnus where his wife will be? And tell him that if he does not go to Inchaiden, if his wife is not an enticement for him to fulfill my request, my men are going to jump to the beginning of the Tempus Omegas and start killing Campbells. There is a whole castle there, full of them — what would happen to the history of Magnus if my bloodthirsty men kill his great-great-grandfather, his great-great-great-grandmother?"

Zach said from behind the wall, "Yeah, um, can you repeat that? I had trouble hearing it over the asshole talking."

Reyes repeated it. "Tell him if he does not go to Scotland and do what he agreed to, then people start dying as soon as we land."

He yanked my arm and I stepped to the glass-covered deck in my bare feet.

FIFTY-NINE - KAITLYN

I was led between two men down the decking of my boardwalk, their feet clomping down the boards, to the waiting soldiers on horseback. A really terrifying uber-violent male-gaze happening and I seriously regretted my rainbow-striped sweatpants and cut off t-shirt. Like *seriously*.

Almost enough to ask if I could go back and change clothes, maybe get some tampons, though this had been a light period and was almost over, but *still*, I needed my stuff. More pressing though I needed to get this asshole away from my family.

One of the guards behind me said, "I want a piece of that."

Reyes laughed, unsheathed his knife, and with a yank cut the top triangle of the back of my thong off basically leaving me with no panties at all.

He sliced the small scrap in half and held them up. "First battalion, ready to go?"

"Yes, ready to go." Reyes handed him a scrap of my thong and the man gave me a disgusting-pig look. He twisted the ends of a vessel and the storm rose above us. That man left with three others.

"Battalion two?" Reyes handed another man a piece of my thong. I couldn't see or hear anything for the storm as groups of men and horses were all given directions to go to different places at different times and then Reyes twisted the ends of his own vessel. Our storm met the others to make a really big-ass storm and then with a slam I was kidnapped, hard.

SIXTY - MAGNUS

"I need a horse. I could get past this on a horse. Drive down the grass there, Quentin."

"I can't they'd arrest me. If you were driving, maybe — thing to remember: I'm a black man."

The policeman, directing traffic past the accident, waved us through, and the cars ahead of us set intae motion, verra slow. "They should go faster than this."

Quentin remained quiet. Then he began weavin' through the cars and I held ontae the verra convenient handle by the door. "We should have brought her, then he wouldna have her right now."

"Yeah, but who would he have? Hayley, Beaty, Zach or Emma? Katie is the only one equipped to handle it. I'm glad she was there to get him away from the house."

"He spoke of doin' terrible things tae her..."

"Yeah, the last mother fucker that did terrible things to Katie is a dead man. She's going to be fine."

"Och aye, and Reyes is a dead man already. I winna allow him tae breathe much longer."

Quentin took a corner and sped down 8th street. Hayley called again.

"The storms are done, they're completely gone."

"You've written down everything he said? We'll be there in twelve minutes."

"Zach and security guard are talking to the police. They have a whole story about a gang of teens, busting the glass, tripping the security alarms, trying to steal the Christmas presents. It seems to be working, but be ready to answer questions, Zach will probably call you in a few to get your story straight."

I asked, "How are Emma and Ben and Beaty?"

"They're all good, scared shitless, but good."

The rest of the ride we were quiet, I was prayin' tae God and willin' the car tae move faster.

~

When we made it upstairs and after the police left twas a verra worrisome look on everyone's face except Lady Mairead who began talkin' at once.

"He daena have Archie, I kent it. Twas foolhardy of her tae compromise with him on it. She should have more strength. I have been telling ye— and twas all for Bella's bairn. I am surprised she allows herself tae get so emotional about him. She should—"

I was packin' protein bars in my sporran tae take with me. I turned on her. "Kaitlyn was plenty strong enough tae stand up and go for this whole family. I daena want tae hear another word on—"

"You will hear me on it. She has put all of us in—"

I charged her and bowed over her, pressin' her back intae the counter. "Dost ye ken where Archie is?"

"Nae, but he isna with General Reyes. I believe Bella has

taken him tae Roderick tae join his court, as he is close tae being crowned king."

I scowled. "You were supposed tae find him afore that happened."

"I was distracted by trying tae help you." She shoved against my chest pushing me off. "Kaitlyn has greatly complicated things, *again*, and for what, the mistress's son?" She brushed off the front of her skirts and scoffed.

"She has opened her heart tae Archie and I winna fault her on it. You need tae be quiet on Kaitlyn or I will make ye quiet."

The security guard came intae the room. "James Cook is here to see you, sir."

James stormed in full of questions. "What the hell was that? That looked like that Nick guy, the one you were dating, Hayley? I ate dinner with him. I took him to a bar!" He was furious, wavin' his arms. "He had an army! Did he just take Katie? What the hell? What is happening?"

I shook my head. "Tis a great deal goin' on here Master Cook, ye canna understand and—"

"Damn right I don't understand. I was driving down Sadler and saw that big ass storm and then men on horseback, *again*." He glowered at me, his finger pointin' at my chest. "Explain it to me or I'm calling the police and telling them what I know."

Lady Mairead waved her hands at him. "What you ken? Ye daena ken anythin'!"

I stepped between them. "Master Cook, ye need tae ken that I am a time-traveler. Lady Mairead is also a time-traveler. We hail from the year 1702."

"What the hell? Quentin, you believe this bullshit?"

Quentin said, "Yeah, I believe it, I spent part of the year living in a castle in the 18th century. Hell, my wife is from the 18th century."

"Beaty is your wife? I thought she was your girl, and how the hell do you expect me to believe this — this is crazy. Zach, what is this shit?"

Chef Zach was leaned on the counter, a gun in his hand. "Welcome to my world. I just killed a man two days ago in the year 2380-something."

James looked incredulous. "Is this a meth house? Are you all on drugs?"

I said, "I ken there is a great deal tae explain, but I have tae figure out where that man has taken Kaitlyn and I must go and rescue—"

"Oh, I know where he's taking her. I parked my truck and snuck out on that dune over there and heard him tell his creep soldiers to meet him in Santa Reeni, wherever the hell that is, on May 20th."

Lady Mairead said, "Santorini! Did he say the year?"

"He said, '1840.' I thought it was an address or something. That was a year? He's taking Katie to a different century? What the hell?"

Lady Mairead turned tae me. "What is your plan?"

"I am goin' tae Santorini." I looked around the room. "Dost anyone ken where Santorini is?"

Lady Mairead said, "Tis in Greece, I have been there, tis where I spoke tae Reyes about joining me tae win the kingdom from Donnan."

I said, "An admission that tis always the fallible Lady Mairead who complicates everythin' with her conniving and dealing. I want ye tae remember twas your doings that brought Reyes here. You brought him tae our kingdom and now tis lost. Twas nae Kaitlyn, twas you that brought Nick Reyes."

She sighed. "I understand that."

"Good. Now tell me all ye ken of Santorini so I can get there and—"

"You have tae get there ahead of him. Tis how he travels. He sets men ahead, they recover and then guard the next men. He does it until he has a small squad—"

Master Cook said, "That's the way it sounded, he was sending men ahead."

"He dinna do that afore, tis a new tactic."

Lady Mairead said, "Nae, he told me of it. He learned it from the verra beginning."

Quentin was listening now too. "What do you mean he learned of it from the beginning?"

Lady Mariead said, "Reyes told me there were men left alive on the battlefield after the vessels were found. One of them had been part of a front guard. They had brought weapons for the time-period but were attacked with weapons that were more sophisticated than what they were expecting. They were outnumbered and then vanquished. That man and Reyes learned from each other."

Hayley said, "That was us totally blowing the mission. We left someone alive. We screwed up the timeline and now you know more about it. Cool, huh?"

I said, "Aye, cool, Mistress Hayley."

She smiled widely. "I am a terrible arse like Katie."

"Och, aye." I took in a deep breath at the thought of Kaitlyn doin' something as dangerous as this, going with Reyes. She was a terrible terrible arse. Twas true.

"What kind of weather can I expect in Santorini? Quentin, can ye gather me the firearms I will need? I will want a sword. I will go early and learn about the land. Chef Zach, can ye pack me food? And a great many vitamins? Kaitlyn told me I needed tae take vitamin C with me when I travel, can ye make sure I have it, Emma?"

"Of course," she said.

Quentin said, "As your security guy, I should go. Last I remember you were calling me your General or something."

"Twas my colonel, and nae, I daena need ye there, I need ye here, guardin' the house, making sure yer wife is well. I will do this myself."

James said, "What should I do?"

"Would ye help watch the house? I daena ken if the men are goin' tae come back." I buckled a belt over my kilt and said tae Lady Mairead, "I want ye tae find Archie and get him safe tae Balloch."

~

A few hours later I was at the south end of the Island with Quentin and Hayley sayin' goodbye afore my trip. "You will take care of everyone, Black Mac?"

"Aye," he joked and then became serious. "You'll find Katie, bring her home?"

"Or die tryin'."

Hayley groaned. "Don't die, don't not bring her home, just get her back here. She doesn't want to live in Greece or anywhere but with you."

I had bags of knives and guns. I considered bringing an ATV with me, but decided against it, tae blend better; twould be the year 1840 after all.

"Don't forget what we saw on Google Earth. You'll be on a wide plain, mostly grape vines and olive trees, tall cliffs, mountainside houses. Get the weapons to a hiding place. Then mix into the neighborhood. Ask for his house. Then wait for him."

I smiled. "Tis a perfect plan."

"Nah, it's a crazy plan, but it's all we got. And as we Campbells say before every battle...?"

"Cruachan."

"Yep, and me and Hayley will head over there to watch you go — safe travels."

He walked a few paces away, then turned, "You sure you don't need a front guard?"

"One of us would have tae go first, might as well be me."

I looked down at the gear and provisions leanin' around my leather boots. My kilt a deep blue and green, my sporran of black leather. The familiar weight of my broadsword across my shoulders and down my back. In my hands I held a vessel, itself a familiar weight, the size and markings meant tae take one from this world tae another. Twas painful, but necessary, in almost every instance, and never more so than this. I twisted the ends of the vessel and set it tae rip me tae another time and a distant land.

SIXTY-ONE - MAGNUS

I woke in the dust cloud of a diminishin' storm. Twas hot with a high blue sky. I looked around tae see I was alone and from the direction of the sun twas mid-day . An olive tree nearby was offerin' a bit of shade. I lumbered tae my feet and pulled my gear and supplies tae the base of it and sat and rested for my strength.

A while later I saw an older man dressed in simple pants tied at his waist and a loose shirt. He had on a shade hat and was carryin' a shovel. I stood and held up my hand hopin' twould be understood as friendly. He raised his hand as well and then began callin' tae me in a language I dinna understand.

He drew closer and I tried tae explain that I was restin' from a walk and had been caught in a storm. He waved me tae follow, lifted one of my bags tae his shoulder, and led me tae his home.

The dwelling was small, only one story, with white painted walls and a beautiful blue door. Twas Kaitlyn's favorite color and gave me a pain thinkin' on whether I would get a chance tae show it tae her.

His wife was friendly and made a great deal of fuss about my size and found good humor in my kilt, wavin' her skirt around as if we matched. She was plump and her voice sounded like a bird chirpin' and though I daena ken any of her language she made herself clear with her hands movin' tae express herself.

She had me understand that her name was Sophia and her husband's name was Christo and then she led me tae the table and offered me tea tae drink.

I rustled through a bag and found a bar of chocolate I had brought for Kaitlyn and offered it tae her. Sophia was thrilled and after it I could do nae wrong. She fed me some food, a fish broth with greens floatin' in it, and a white cheese that was verra tasty. I saw through an open window, Christo goin' tae work in his fields, so I excused myself tae go help him.

I spent the rest of the day pullin' weeds while Christo pruned, workin' side by side in comfortable silence. Without a common language tae tell him I needed a place tae stay, he and his wife took me in tae stay as long as I needed, givin' me a mat tae sleep on in a back room in their house.

On the second night they held a big dinner at long tables in the garden attended by Christo and Sophia's grown children and their grandchildren. They held wide smiles and laughed a great deal and most of them came tae the height of my chest. Being amongst them was much like bein' a giant.

At dinner I watched them closely and listened and soon learned a couple of phrases and gestures. I could tell when they were talking of fishin' and I shared the story of when I was thrown overboard. I stood and acted it out, having consumed so much wine I was quite drunk, and when I told of my Uncle Baldie tossin' me overboard they all laughed, even the bairn, and twas how I kent I had told the story well enough.

During the day I helped Christo and at night I slept in that back room, a clear view through the window, a starry sky. These were stars I dinna recognize, but they gave me comfort that

Kaitlyn would be here soon and we would again be in the same place and time.

She was probably verra afraid, but I had been given a place tae gain my strength and the time tae contemplate my actions. And though the language was a mystery, at the family dinner I had been able tae ascertain the whereabouts of Nicholas Reyes's house, a fair distance from here.

The next evenin' I walked tae see it, an unguarded house, nestled in the hills along the cliffs on the west side of Santorini. He had been absent from it for a long time. I watched the house for a couple of hours as the night grew dark and the stars unfurled above me and there wasna a soul around.

Through the windows I saw military-style barracks at the back of the house. I pried open a wooden shutter and slid inside, tae find a great deal of weapons and ammunition. I loaded a bag with all of it afore I walked back to Christo's home verra late that night.

The next day I watched and waited for a storm but there wasna one so I went and hid weapons: first, under a wooded vine near Reyes's home. A second, near a fence at the back of the house. I found a donkey cart and moved it near the back of the property. I loaded it with large rocks and a length of rope I found in a back shed.

I again waited as the day grew dark. I returned tae my perch and watched the house again.

A few nights passed and then one evenin' long after dinner, while sitting in the place where I had been sittin' for nights on end, a storm raised above me. Twas a furious wind that bent the trees and sent the roof tiles spinnin' intae the air.

My sword was across my back, a bag of weapons lay at my feet. I slung the bag over my shoulder and raced through the fields towards the center of the storm and ended at a far sheltered spot under a grove of olive trees. I armed myself as the sun went down and the storm was fadin'.

Under the storm lay four men, the front guard, the ones unlucky tae have tae time-jump first. I dropped my bag of weapons tae the ground, unsheathed my sword, and then I tried tae do the impossible work of convincin' myself tae kill them.

I was nae comfortable with killin' a man that I dinna have cause tae kill. These men were not at my walls. I wasna protecting my lands or my castle. I dinna ken them tae hate them. I went from man tae man relieving them of their weapons. I cut their leather pouches away and dug through them looking for valuables, all the while tryin' tae convince myself that these men deserved tae die.

Inside one pouch I found a finger, wrapped in cloth, the skin havin' turned tae leather. I dropped it tae the ground in disgust. In another man's pouch I found a lock of hair. They all had blood on their hands and I begged God that twas nae Kaitlyn's blood.

Then, in the last soldier's pouch, cut off and scrounged through, I found a scrap of cloth. Twas silk, the color blue of the sky, a favorite of Kaitlyn's, and verra much like her underwear, and — I broke down that she might nae have survived the ordeal.

My breathing was hard as I held that scrap of silk. I pulled in gaspin' breaths and found myself sayin' a prayer that God would forgive me for my sins as I raised my sword and walked from man tae man killing each where they lay, one by one by one.

Twas merciless of me tae do, I kent it.

But I kent too that I was never goin' tae be free of the fear of them. General Reyes wanted me dead. He dinna care tae keep my family safe, or my wife. He wouldna stop until I made him stop.

It was dark then, a full black clear sky with the guiding lights that once led the way for Trojan heroes circlin' the islands of the Mediterranean. They now led me as I brought the donkey cart near and loaded the bodies intae it and carted them tae the high cliffs.

I made a pile of them at the edge and one at a time I bound the legs of the soldiers with rope, tied them tae a boulder for the weight, and then shoved them over. I heard nothing of the fall until a faint splash carried them intae the murky depths of the sea.

The time was well past midnight when I finished the work, returned the cart, and returned tae Christo's home.

~

He had grown used tae me leavin' at night, so I did it again the next night just at evenin', and there was another storm, an hour after the one of the night afore. I kneeled on my sword, before their prostrate bodies and prayed for guidance about the deaths I was committing. I was protectin' my family, but I was havin' trouble reconcilin' that protection with the methodical killin' that I was made tae do.

This was another group of men, sent ahead tae guard over the arrival of Reyes, smaller, only three this time, I killed them as quickly as the others the night before. On checkin' their pockets I found another scrap of cloth in the same sky blue silk.

I carted them tae the edge of the cliff and brusquely pushed them over intae the sea below.

I was verra worried that she was lost tae me, tortured and killed. What if I was wrong tae come here? What if Reyes took Kaitlyn tae Inchaiden, or some other place and time? What if while I waited here with Christo and his family, I was allowin' Reyes tae have his way with her, tae finish her? What if I dinna protect her well enough?

My sleep was fitful as I waited for the followin' night.

. . .

Yet the followin' night there wasna a storm.

That night at Christo's home, with hand signals and guessin' at words, I asked him what was the date. It seemed sure tae be nearing May 20, and I worried she hadna arrived yet.

May 20 was in two days.

I worried that somehow Reyes kent that I had killed his guard and he was already exactin' his revenge.

The followin' night, again, there wasna a storm and I was greatly afraid for Kaitlyn's life.

SIXTY-TWO - MAGNUS

The next day twas the same as the others, a bright blue high sky, a lovely day that I kent I had tae get through tae deal with Reyes in the night, but Christo wanted tae shew me his boat. We had the closest thing tae a conversation on it, having spent days together learning tae read each other's expressions and basic words.

Twas the middle of the morning. The path down tae the shore was long and winding, along rocky cliffs tae the bottom. The beach was pebbled with boats pulled up all along the water's edge.

Christo's boat was nae much larger than the skiff Fraoch and I had stolen in Florida. Twas painted white and he proudly showed me the fishin' nets his sons were weavin'. His son, Marcos, was just returned from a fishin' trip so we helped him carry his baskets tae shore. Then we sat in a circle cleaning fish and repairing the nets. We were busy at our work when I caught Christo's eye as it traveled past me up the hill tae the sky.

My stomach dropped as I followed his gaze.

He and his son were talking, fast and energetically. I dinna understand their words but kent the meaning, they were talking about this, another storm of many, afflicting the island for the past few days.

And here was another.

And here I was, verra far away on the other side of the island.

I apologized tae Christo and Marcos for leaving and began my race across the shore and up the cliff-side trail tae the upper levels of land. By the time I reached the top, the storm was dissipating and I was running out of time.

I had missed my moment tae kill whoever was under the storm.

I sprinted along the footpath through fields and past small clusters of houses tae Christo's house. Sophia was at the market so I was able tae gather my things without conversin' first. I was breathin' hard and fast as I swung my sword intae its scabbard, and gathered my bag of weapons, tryin' tae ignore the pain that my achin' lungs were causing me and the fear that I might be too late.

I slammed out the front door, crossed the yard and sped through the vineyard, up and down the paths, tae the olive grove, through the trees, and intae, at long last, the wild fields and then farther I raced toward the spot that had been the center of the storm.

And there was Reyes, up, running for his home, holdin' Kaitlyn by the arm. She was being forced tae run, stumblin' beside him. There was only one soldier, my work of the last week had left him without enough protection, and if only I had been waitin' instead of fishin' I would have killed Reyes already.

I was furious with myself, but even more so with Reyes. My fury moved my feet though I had grown verra tired. I was close tae killing him. Twas all that was left tae do. I had spent weeks learning the lay of this land. I kent he was headed home, through his back gate, wonderin' about his soldiers —

His guard spotted me behind them and yelled, "Magnus Campbell, to our left flank."

I pulled a knife from the sheath on my belt. Without breaking stride I judged the heft of it, watched the soldier for his gait and speed, swung the knife behind me, counted, ran, concentrated, and aimed –

The knife flew, end over end over end, and slammed point first embeddin' intae the soldier's back. He flung his arms wide and collapsed to his stomach in the dirt.

Reyes shot a glance over his shoulder and pulled Kaitlyn closer tae his side, but I was gaining on him fast.

"Reyes! Let her go now!" I unsheathed my sword without breaking stride. "Dost ye hear me?"

He dragged Kaitlyn over the low wall and pulled her intae the open door of his house as I cleared the low wall and pulled in a few feet behind.

Instead of goin' through the door I jumped up tae the wide sill of a large window beside it and crouched there, taking the lay of the room.

"You dinna hear me, Reyes?"

He pulled Kaitlyn close in front of him, holdin' her by the neck.

"You let go of my wife. I winna ask ye again."

I held the window jamb. I felt calmed. I had become the hunter and Reyes was the hunted. He was more dangerous now, with his hands on Kaitlyn's neck, but I was watchin' him. He was shakin', and unsure what tae do next.

He said, "My men will be here—"

"Your men are dead. All of them. But right now, I have men comin' up from behind ye. I have been livin' here for a verra long time, waitin' for ye tae arrive. I have men. I have weapons. I have a deep and abidin' need tae finish ye."

I focused on him, the shift of his foot, the racing heartbeat evident in the pulse of his neck, near Kaitlyn's, his finger close tae her throat. It twitched ever so slightly. I had the exact spot that would end him, twas in my view, and he was a second away—"

He was looking left and right trying to discern whether I was tellin' the truth. "I don't think you have men with you or—"

"Are ye callin' me a liar? Remember when ye had me in the dirt at yer feet and ye were tellin' me what ye would do tae my wife? I wasna lyin' when I said I would kill ye for it. I am nae lyin' now."

I dragged my sword closer tae my side, remainin' crouched on the window sill, ready tae spring. I added, "How's your shoulder?" sure it would unsettle him.

"What about my shoulder?"

"My man, Quentin, fired the shot. I am proud of him for—" His fingers tightened on her throat.

Kaitlyn, her eyes wild with fear, whimpered.

I said, "Daena make one more move..." I locked eyes with her. Trying tae tell her *daena be afraid, I will protect ye, I am protectin' ye.*

I could see in her eyes, she was telling me — yes.

I answered her in my thoughts — *aye, mo reul-iuil, you move on my move.*

He said, "I think you're bluffing and—"

"I am nae bluffin', but I do like tae tell a story. You need tae decide if I—"

A chicken ran squawking past the open door behind him.

He turned tae look.

Kaitlyn twisted from his hands tae the ground and scrambled away.

He drew his sword as I leapt from the window sill and met his blade with my own, then I shifted feet, and swung my sword around and met his blade again from the other direction.

The room was too small for a fight. Reyes backed up, and I fought him out the open door tae the yard.

He wasna dead yet, but I had swung at him from both directions tae gain a feel for his weakness. He had a great many. He was surprised and unprotected.

I rested. I watched him as he shifted his sword from his left tae his right. His left arm was weak compared tae the other.

He said, "I will only make the deal to take care of your family once, Mags the Dust. You had your chance to—"

I brought my blade down in a wide curve, met his blade, and fought him, backing him from the house, blade tae blade with clangs of our steel. "Ye winna provide for my family. Tis for me tae take care of them."

The fight was longer than I wanted. Our swords met again and again. He fought me well and wouldna die easily. He swung his sword down, aimin' tae hit my right side, my fightin' arm, but I was able tae shift from his reach.

He was three steps away, breathin' heavy, his face held a fury and yet he wanted tae seem as if he was in control. He attempted a smile. "You think you are going to win this, but I am stronger than you know. I have built an army and what are you? A dethroned king, nothing but dust."

I swung my sword, testin' the heft of it, distraction' him from my intention, plannin' tae come from another direction. "I may be dethroned, but I am nae just dust, I am celestial dust."

His brow drew down. "What do you mean by that?"

I slashed at his left side, but he dodged my blade. Twas nae matter in it, I kent the fight had turned in my favor.

"I mean, I am goin' tae kill ye, Reyes the Dead."

I swung up as he arced his sword down and our blades locked taegether. I backed him tae the low wall. I was calm, focused, glarin' intae his eyes. I called, "Kaitlyn, daena look, turn away."

I heard her voice, from inside the house, *okay*.

I shoved him, stumblin', and with a roar, swung my sword high. I charged forward, two steps, one swing down and then with a fast change of motion up, before he saw it coming — a slice on his arm. For a grave second he lost focus, his eyes shifted from mine tae his arm. I swung my arm back, plunged it forward, and dropped General Nick Reyes tae the dirt of the garden of his home.

Blood poured from his chest, spilling out on the dirt around him, and our long feud was ended. I used my foot tae kick him free of my blade. I stood staring down at him, breathing heavy, trying tae get on top of the roar of fury still rushin' through my ears.

And then Kaitlyn was holding my arm and pulling me away and climbing my body, her legs around me her head against my chest. Her arms under mine, around my back. I was stuck, broken, a monument tae the man I was become: bringer of death, soulless, emotionless, as much like a stone as the wall and the house and the island I was standin' on —

But here was Kaitlyn — flesh and blood and life and warmth and she held ontae my whole body wrapped around me and she was tremblin' and sweatin' and holdin' me so tight that she brought me from stone cold hardness and warmed me back tae my life.

And brought breath back to my lungs.

And with my hands under her thighs, I held her up tae my waist. "Are you okay, Kaitlyn, did he hurt ye?"

"No. I'm just scared."

"Tuck in your head, mo ghradh, daena look on him." I turned us away from the dead man in the dirt.

We were holding on, tight. She was crying. I carried her intae the house and held her and stroked her hair. "He dinna hurt ye?"

"No, we didn't do anything but come here."

I dropped tae my knees, takin' us both tae the dirt floor. I collapsed on top of her, her legs around my waist, my elbows beside her ears. "I was worried, mo ghradh. Some of the men I killed, they had scraps of cloth from your..." I couldna finish it.

She sobbed. "He cut it off and offered it to his soldiers, first one who got here, got me, or some other horrible thing."

"Och. Tis horrible." I held on tighter. I buried my face in her shoulder, breathin' in the scent of her hair.

We sat wrapped around each other for a verra long time, breathin' and holdin' and comfortin' while she cried. Then she put her hands on the sides of my face, and looked into my eyes, her chin tremblin'. "Are you okay, my love?"

I searched her eyes, they were the familiar green I kent, that I got lost in. The color of the highlands held in the flecks of her eyes. *Tis why I fell in love with her,* I thought, that color seemed tae mean something as if she was meant tae be mine.

Her eyes were also unfamiliar tae me. Behind them were secrets and dreams that I dinna ken. I meant tae learn them in time, but I had come verra close tae losin' the moment tae ask her. "Magnus, answer me, are you okay?"

I kissed her cheek. "Aye."

"It wasn't too much fighting, too much killing? I promised you that you weren't going to have to do that anymore and—"

I rubbed my thumbs across her cheeks wiping her tears. "I ken ye meant it. But we have promises we can keep, mo reul-iuil, and there are promises that our hearts make that arna possible tae keep. You once said ye would marry me tae keep me alive and then ye married me. Tis the only promise I am holdin' ye tae. The others, the keepin' me safe, well-fed, and happy, ye will do your best on it and I will love ye for trying."

She laugh-cried, wrapped her arms around my neck and brought her forehead tae my lips. "Oh my god, Magnus, you scared me so much."

"I scared ye? What of the monster I just vanquished? He is dead, ye arna relieved?"

"I am so freaking relieved."

I felt her body relax in my arms. I said, "I verra much liked those..."

"What?"

"Your undergarment."

"My sky blue thong?"

I looked in her eyes. "Och aye, twas my favorite."

She said, her voice all serious and concern. "I have more."

"Och," I joked, "then everythin' will be okay."

"Yes, I think it will." She looked around the room of the dead man's house. "I gather Archie isn't here?"

"Nae, Lady Mairead went lookin' for him. This time she better find him."

"I hope he's okay."

"Me too, mo reul-iuil."

"Where are we?"

I rolled off her intae the dirt and we lay side by side. "We are midway through the 19th century and tis the month of May, mo reul-iuil. We are on an island called Santorini, and tis a beautiful place." I turned my head to face her. "I have made a friend, his name is Christo, his wife is Sophia, and they have let me stay with them. I help them in the fields during the day, then sit here at night watching and waiting for you."

She smiled a smile that held some sadness but promised happiness. "You are always making friends. Are you responsible for their health and well-being now too?"

"Nae." I chuckled. "Maybe a little bit. I do need tae help Christo bring in that load of fish as soon as I rid this farm of the bodies."

She groaned. "And Quentin isn't here?"

"Nae, he isna." I chuckled again. "I am a liar."

She laughed.

"Twas an excellent time for the chicken tae walk by."

She laughed more. I had really missed her laugh.

She asked, "And you've been here for how long?"

"Almost a month. I wanted tae make sure I made it here afore ye."

"Thank you for rescuing me with your epic sword-swinging thing you did there."

"You're welcome. Thank you, mo reul-iuil, for goin' with him, taking him away from the family."

"I knew you would follow. I was only a little terrified."

I kissed the top of her forehead. "Will ye stay here, in the house, while I clean up from the battle?"

"Do you need help?"

"Nae I daena want ye tae see."

SIXTY-THREE - KAITLYN

While Magnus cleaned up, I poked around in the closets. Reyes had been hoarding like Lady Mairead so I took the valuables, lots of gold, including some bricks, coins and paper money from many different places and times, very expensive and historical looking jewelry, and a few pieces that were small and mysterious but seemed to match the tech of the vessels. I dumped it all into a bag.

Then I looked for some clothes. I wasn't sure what the women here would wear, but I suspected my sweatpants and crop top weren't right for the 19th century. I called, "Magnus, what do the women wear?"

He had gone to take a trip to the edge of the cliffs so I kept looking. There was a stack of men's brocade jackets another stack of cloth. I wondered about togas but that seemed too far back in history.

This was yet another moment in a long line of moments that I wished I had paid attention in history class. But I was from the New World couldn't I be wearing anything? I decided to make something work.

Over my sweatpants I draped a long piece of white linen and belted it. I took a piece of brocade and crisscrossed it over my front and tucked it under the belt as well. Then I found a jacket to put on over it. My arms were bare so the jacket was probably necessary but it was also very hot.

I was still barefoot but found a pair of sandals that were probably Nick Reyes's and made me gag as I slid my feet into them. But I needed shoes to be presentable.

Magnus returned. I called, "Can I come out?"

"Aye, I have disposed of—"

I came to the door. "How do women wear their hair?"

"Och, ye look beautiful."

"I do?" I blushed and looked down at my clothes. "I just — thank you."

He came close. "They put their hair up high. Ye ken, like..." He pulled my hair up and put it on my head. "Och, I daena ken how tae..."

I smiled. I used a band off my wrist to put my hair up in a messy bun with some hair hanging to the side. "Will this do?"

"Aye, verra much."

He put the vessels and the valuables along with Reyes's sword and a knife into a bag. He said, "I am much lighter now. I have gotten rid of most of the guns I brought with me. I dinna need them."

"You threw them over with the...?"

"Aye."

That was enough. I was very glad he was keeping the details from me. I hated that he had to do it by himself, but also, I was feeling very fragile after all we had been through.

He slung the bag over his shoulder and we walked hand and hand through this strange land. Magnus pointed out things he had learned along the way. He knew some new words and phrases, one for olive trees and another for grapes, though it confused him slightly — was the word for the vine or the grape or the type of grape? Even if he wasn't sure, he seemed happy to know something new.

I asked, "Don't they wonder where you came from? What you're doing here?"

He said, "I think so. I was only tae stay a night, but Christo wanted help and I did my best. I think they would like tae ask me where I am from and what I am doin' here, but I canna tell them, so they just accept me. Tis the same in Scotland, travelers are often put up for a time, ye wouldna want them freezin' on yer doorstep."

We came to the low house, white walled, beautifully bright in the sun. It had a bright blue door, my favorite color.

He said, "You will like Sophia: ye canna understand a word but she sounds like a bird and is quite funny as she does it."

He wasn't wrong. Sophia bustled to the front door a very incredibly short older woman. A second later she had her rough-worked hands cradling my face, speaking very fast, then she held up my arms and made me spin. She spoke faster still and Magnus laughed and answered a word here and there because apparently she called me his big giant wife or something that I needed to take as a compliment.

Christo wasn't home yet so I walked with Magnus to the shore and there I met Christo and three of his sons. Magnus introduced me but then there were a few things said that only Magnus could understand and Magnus couldn't understand most of it.

Magnus slung two baskets of fish over his shoulders to carry up the hill to Christo's house and we realized there was going to be a very large family party that night.

SIXTY-FOUR - KAITLYN

Sophia found a linen shirt for me and so I added it under the criss-crossed brocade cloth. Apparently the rest of what I was wearing was good enough for her family.

Their daughters arrived and we stood at long tables and they mimed instructions for me and we cleaned fish and chopped vegetables and prepared dishes. I didn't know what I was doing for most of it but carried on anyway and while I worked I ate so many delicious cherry tomatoes listening to the cadence and odd sounds of their conversation and delighting in their banter. It sounded like the banter of women in any time or place. The oldest sister reminded me of Lizbeth without even one word of understanding between us.

As the cooking neared completion, the men showed up, and kids of all ages were in the gardens. Tables were constructed stretching across the yard at the front of the house and we decorated them with small vases full of flowers. There were ceramic plates and pitchers of wine and we soon had a big spread of a meal down the length of a table and the entire family, men and women, some of the older children, sitting along the length of it. Magnus sat midway and I sat beside him. My face tired from smiling, but it was also joyous — Magnus's deep laugh, the way he had assimilated himself here even though he had nothing in common but a deep generous spirit. I was so fucking proud of him.

We held hands and I brought his hand up to my lips and kissed his fingers and the women of the family rejoiced and clapped their hands and beamed at us. It was quite lovely to be in the midst of it all — outside, under a darkening sky, at the top of a crest of an island, the starry heavens unbroken by anything but the lowest trees and vines of the gardens. The wide deepness above it, sea to sea, us out in the middle of it, under the same sky together.

Christo was quite drunk, as were we all, truth be told, and he stood and held up a glass of wine and made a long rambling speech about Magnus from the looks of it, about me a little too, and then the whole family raised their mugs and said something that sounded like "Yiamas!"

And Magnus and I said, "Slainte!" our family's version of it.

This family.

Our family.

All families the same, with laughs and loves and joys and little children causing havoc, but even here there were parents that reminded me of Emma and a sister that reminded me of Lizbeth, and both were fun to watch. I imagined which one I would rather share a glass of wine with, which one I would rather attend a mommy-and-me playgroup with.

Before I knew it, most of the family went home leaving me and two of the sisters behind to clean up the food. And then very late, like one-in-the-morning late, Magnus and I went out to pee in the pit toilet. It had a small wooden bench inside a little hut. I went first and then heard him say from outside, "Och, I canna listen tae it without havin' tae..." The stream of his urine sounded outside.

He moaned and I giggled. I teased, "Well you were close, another five seconds and you would have relieved yourself like a civilized man."

We returned tae the house and he got comfortable on his back on a mattress that was no more than a bag of cloth, too short for our bodies, stuffed very lightly with hay, the ground right under it. There were a few rolled cloths for pillows. To call it an overly firm, bumpy, uncomfortable, scratchy, irritating mattress was an understatement. I was grateful for my fluffy sweatpants to save my hip bones.

Magnus said, "See that?" He pointed through the square window, a hole in the wall really, up at the sky.

I said, mimicking his voice, "Tis always the same sky."

He looked down at me his brow lifted. "Tis good that we are truly under it taegether." He shifted the pillow under his head and I nestled in further on his arm.

"I guess it would be too much to get busy right here?"

"Tae get busy, ye mean tae have me here on the reed mattress in the back room of Christo's house?" He grinned. "Ye canna be quiet enough."

"I can't? I'll have you know—"

Just then a very loud snore came from the room next to ours. "Oh," I said simply. "Yeah, that's really close. I can't be that quiet." I whispered, "He is asleep though, that's—"

Magnus's chest jiggled as he suppressed his laughs. He whispered very quietly. "Tis nae he, tis *she*, he haena fallen asleep yet. His snores will join her's eventually and then twill be a cacophony about our heads."

I giggled along with him. "I guess I'll have to just go to sleep then, huh?"

"Aye, if we can sleep through it we ought. We will go home on the morrow. Twill be time enough tae be with ye then."

SIXTY-FIVE - KAITLYN

The next morning we had a light breakfast and said our goodbyes to Christo and Sophia. We set out along the path through the gardens and I thought we were looking for a wide open spot but Magnus said, no, he had someplace he wanted to take me, a place Christo's son, Marcos, had drawn a map for. "He told me tae take ye here today," he explained. So we kept walking in the beautiful day, full of a high sky and the scents of the Mediterranean: sea salt and fish wafting on a breeze but also a warm smell that I—

I breathed it in. "What is it, Magnus? That wonderful smell?"

"Tis fig and olive and—" He breathed deep. "I will miss it when we go, tis the smell of this island. I like it verra – it keeps me hungry. Dost ye smell the lemon? And the basil? All of it on the breeze."

"I really love this place."

"Aye, me too."

We walked for hours, talking and resting occasionally, to walk some more. After some thinking I asked, "What are we going to do with it all?"

"With what?"

"All the gold and jewelry and the art that Lady Mairead is collecting and the antiques. It's theft and it freaks me out that we're the recipients. Heck, I just stole from Reyes's house."

Magnus grunted. "He was a thief and a murderer, we have taken what daena belong tae him."

"It doesn't really belong to us though either."

We walked quietly for a few moments, then Magnus said, "I ken it, Kaitlyn, but what would ye have me do?"

"I don't know. I think we should start giving it back."

"But if we daena ken who it belongs tae?"

My forehead was growing sweaty from the walk, I brushed my hair away. "Maybe a charity or something? I don't know." I thought for a second. "It's very complicated, having all this wealth from the centuries, but in our bags are a lot of Greek coins, we should have left them with Christo or—"

"I left a great deal of wealth for Christo and his sons and daughters."

"Good, that makes me happy." I grinned. "So what you're saying is you agree, and we'll think about how to disperse our wealth better?"

"Aye, I agree with ye on it. As long as my family is taken care of the rest of it does nae matter tae me."

"Perfect. We'll start a charity or something. As soon as we get home." I paused for a beat. "Speaking of getting home, will what we're walking toward be worth it?"

He chuckled. "I daena ken, but we have been doin' it for a long time a'ready, I believe we ought tae keep goin'.

We passed a small village and bought some crusty bread, a bit of goat cheese, and a bottle of the island's wine from a woman who had baskets out in front of her house. She also had bowls of cherry tomatoes, sun dried tomatoes, and a few dozen oranges.

Magnus asked, "Do these have the vitamin C in them, Kaitlyn?"

"Yes, do you — are you worried about scurvy?"

"Aye, I dinna like how Fraoch was dyin'. I daena want..."

I gestured to the woman that I wanted to buy the oranges. I also bought some cherry tomatoes and a pouch of sun-dried tomatoes. I held out a handful of greek coins and she took them and bundled our food in a cloth leaving a few out for us to eat with our lunch.

We sat in the grass further down the path and ate and had our bit of wine. Magnus ate all of his orange with a contented sigh.

I pointed out. "You know, I hate to be the kind of person who says I told you so, but I told you to take your vitamins."

With orange juice dripping down his chin he grinned. "I have learned that Kaitlyn Campbell was in the right on this."

"Good, I'm glad you see my point."

He added, "You are always wantin' me tae agree with ye and now it has been twice in a day. You are goin' tae have tae agree with me on somethin' so I daena feel so insignificant."

"And what would that be?"

"I daena ken, let me think." He ate the rest of his orange and said, "I ken it. I daena like the rose-scented soap ye use on me."

"The what — the rose...? Like the shampoo? And the conditioner and the soap and the — I thought you loved it!"

He grinned wide. "Tis nae my favorite and I daena like tae wear it."

My eyes went wide. "But you love it on me, right? It makes me smell like a rose garden!"

He scowled and shook his head.

"Magnus! All this time and you don't like rose-scented things?"

He laughed. "You are arguin' with me about it, ye are supposed tae be more agreeable than this. Tis your turn tae be."

"I'm just shocked. I don't know what — what do you like then, if not beautiful flowers?"

His eyes were lit mischievously. "I like the scent ye have in your undergarment drawer."

My eyes went even wider. "What is...?" I thought for a moment then remembered the sachet I had in there. It had hints of vanilla and a bit of clementine orange and blackberry — "Magnus do you like me best when I smell like food?"

"Aye." He breathed in deeply. "I like ye verra much when ye smell like somethin' tae eat."

I laughed so hard I fell back on the dirt and then when I was done laughing and was warm from the good humor of it all, I rolled on my side and sighed. "So you want me to smell like food instead of flowers?"

"Aye, tis my favorite. When ye smell like spices I want tae bed ye and I think ye should agree with me on it."

I giggled. "Okay, yes, if you put it that way, I agree, one hundred percent."

He grinned. "You should also agree that I am the verra best husband because I am so agreeable with ye on everythin'."

"That's the reason you're the very best husband? Okay, I agree, though I thought it was because you were so capable with your sword."

It was his turn to laugh heartily and then still chuckling we helped each other to standing and continued walking with a little bit of a buzz now, which was nice.

After a while our walk crested on an even higher hill. There was a small foot path that went down the cliff.

Magnus said, "There!" and pointed at a large volcanic rock with a hole through it and—

"It's shaped like a heart!"

"Aye, tis why we have been walkin' tae see it. Tis the most romantic and secluded spot in all the world."

"Wow." I dropped my bags, and sat down, completely speechless.

Magnus placed his bags beside mine and sat down too.

"Where did it come from? Did someone make it? It frames the island there, and that's got to be a volcano and..."

"I daena ken, Marcos told me twas the heart. He said I had tae go with ye, but twas all I understood of him."

"Wow," I said again for the lack of anything better to say. "It is sooooo beautiful." I looked all around: the land, the sea, the sky, a church beyond. "It's all so beautiful."

Magnus said, "Aye, tis."

I tucked my head to his shoulder and we sat in silence for a time looking through that heart to the sky and sea and volcano beyond. And then Magnus tilted my chin up and kissed me and then the kiss lingered, lips and breaths and nibbles and then we lay back in the volcanic dirt and ash of this ancient island, an island from before history. The kind of island that Trojans visited and multitudes of gods ruled over. It was so old but also timeless — because when were we here? The 19th century? It seemed like it could be the 14th or the 20th. Anytime, always the same.

Magnus's hand ran up my thigh and brought it around close to his, and his kisses were deep and mine were wanting. I pulled him closer and pulled his kilt higher. And we were fumbling intently on the wrapped fabric of my skirt rumpled between us until we had it cleared and we were finally pressed together.

Magnus chuckled, "I dinna think we could do it."

I joked, "I was wondering for a moment there too."

We slowed and looked into each other's eyes. I sighed a deep breath of Mediterranean air and my husband, exotic and familiar, both. His hand dipped and played between my legs, my view a deep blue sky, high above us, tufts of clouds blowing by, framing Magnus: his darkness, his brow sweaty with desire, the curl of his hair resting on the taut muscles of his neck. I pressed my lips to the spot where the thrum of his heart beat loudest and felt its steady rhythm.

I breathed in the scent of him, spice and heat mingled with the fragrances of this island, the fig and salt and olive. I held on around his head as he slid inside me and we adjusted our fabrics so we were not too exposed out on this open place in the fresh air — his face pressed to mine and his breath close to my ear, and mine, so close to his.

A bit of breeze picked up some dust and flung it past us into the sky and I didn't realize I spoke — *I love you so much, Magnus, my husband.*

I love ye too, Kaitlyn, my wife.

Making love to him here was slow and beautiful and necessary and I tried to be still and I tried for as much decorum as I could considering I was being taken to the edge: his fingers, his mouth, his kisses — and then *ogodogodogodogod...* I was flung — past caring about anything but him, want, more, Magnus, oh my god. I had been concentrating on the skin where his throat met his chest but now I held his hands above my head and watched the vibrant blue sky beyond and lost myself completely in the way he felt on me, in me, here, now. Always.

He raised up over me with my legs around his back and slammed against me, all skin slaps and wet sliding and intensity, until he was finished and collapsed down with an, "Och."

I wrapped around him tighter. "Was that good, Highlander?"

"Aye," he answered. "Twas good, mo reul-iuil?"

"Absolutely."

He teased, "I could tell, ye were speakin' tae god about me."

I giggled. "I want to make sure she knows how much you mean to me."

He laughed. "Last I heard of it God was a man."

"Don't let Athena hear you say that, this is one of her islands."

We kissed deep and slow and then he slid from me and rolled to his side and put his kilt to rights as I adjusted my skirts.

His brow lifted and he smiled. "We made a baby just then, I think."

"Don't get ahead of yourself, my love, I doubt the sperm have even had time to introduce themselves to my egg yet."

He chuckled. "Tis an egg? Like of a hen?"

"Kind of, like the inside, without a shell."

"Och, tis much that is a mystery." He shook his head. "But I daena need tae introduce m'self. I just vanquished m'enemy, rescued the maiden, and am takin' home the spoils of war. Your egg kens twas me."

"Oh it does, does it?"

"Aye, your egg said, 'Master Magnus, welcome home and...' How dost it work?"

"One of your sperms joins with my egg and... if a lot goes right, a baby happens."

"Your egg said, 'Welcome home, Master Magnus, and opened her legs for me. She is a verra good egg."

I giggled.

He kissed me on the edge of my throat and then leaned up on his elbow and watched the volcano. While I watched him — so fucking hot. That jawline, the small crinkles near his eyes, his intense expression that could break into a smile in a second. He was strength and power and love and fun all in one, and I sighed again thinking about how he was everything to me.

"I can't wait to go home with you."

He nodded, but there was a sadness to it.

"Are you okay?"

"I am just thinking of Fraoch, in the hospital. He may never get tae see a day like—"

"Oh." I watched his face searching for what it held inside. "What if we went?"

He looked down at me. "You want tae go home though and—"

"I do, I want to finish our Christmas and sleep in our bed and celebrate that Reyes won't be bothering us anymore and worry about Archie while also planning how to find him and maybe have a bath for once, a long bath, with that bath bomb that Hayley gave me and — all of that I want. But you, my husband, are worried about your friend, are you not?"

"Aye, he was verra close tae death."

"And so we must go see him." I ran a hand down his cheek. "We must." I added, "I have all of these oranges anyway."

He smiled, "And I have verra many vitamin packets."

"Perfect. Do you know how to get there? The numbers, the time, the date? We don't want to loop back too close to when you were there."

"I can get us tae the date a couple of days after I left for Edinburgh. I think twill be okay."

I sat up. I took a deep breath and said, "Then that's where we need to go."

SIXTY-SIX - KAITLYN

I woke up on a wide undulating field of grass, a tree here and there, but none over us. I shifted and moaned and felt the familiar hand of my husband on my hip. He was already up, watching.

As soon as I uttered the sound, he asked, "Are ye ready tae rise? We needs tae be away from this wide open land."

"Yes." I pushed the hair from my eyes and lumbered up to standing and tried to be ready for the world. What world? The 18th century world. Midcentury. This was London.

We gathered our things and headed south. Magnus said, "Toward the Thames." It was a cloudy day full of bluster and chill.

We headed toward the city center and as we neared it the streets filled with people bustling around. There were a great many very poor people. The scents of the city were smoke, and shit, and moldy food and desperation. But then there were the posh, their outfits like the one that Magnus had been wearing before, silk and taffeta with embroidered touches, breeches and shoes with buckles. The men wore wigs and the women looked—

The dresses were wide and beautiful. I looked down at what I was wearing.

"I'm not dressed well-enough."

Magnus agreed, "Nae, we are neither of us. We need better clothes but I am worried about him, what if he has passed on?"

I held his arm tighter. "I hope not, my love, I really hope not. But we should go see." So we headed toward St Thomas Hospital.

SIXTY-SEVEN - MAGNUS

A nurse led us through tae the beds.

She dinna mention if Fraoch was alive and as we were ushered in, I asked Kaitlyn, "Dost it sound like he is still...?"

"I think so, or they wouldn't—"

Fraoch's bed had more space around it. There was an empty chair pulled beside it. It looked as if he was much the same.

I gave her the chair and crouched beside Fraoch's bed. "Hello, friend, how are ye?"

Fraoch was weak, his eyes dark and sunken. He was verra thin. His beard was scraggly.

His eyes fluttered open. He weakly said, "Og Maggy, tis you? What does ye...?"

"Aye, I have brought my wife, Kaitlyn Campbell, tae see ye, and I have brought ye restoratives." Kaitlyn was pouring a packet of vitamin powder intae one of my bottles for filterin' water that Chef Zach packed for me. She shook it vigorously and passed it tae me with the top opened up. "I am going tae give ye a drink, Fraoch, tis nae beer. Ye will dislike it greatly, but twill begin tae work on ye."

He weakly said, "It hurts, Og Maggy."

I pulled his head up with my arm and tipped the bottle tae his mouth. I fretted that a great deal of it spilled from his lips. I said, "Ye needs tae drink like a highlander or ye will never have the taste of whisky again. Are ye good with nae whisky or dost ye want tae drink this medicinal and live tae drink more?"

"I am past savin', Og Maggy, daena worry on me—"

"Nae."

Kaitlyn peeled open one of the oranges and divided it intae small sections. She passed me the orange slices and I pushed one intae his mouth. "Ye arna past savin'. I have heard that this orange and this drink might cure ye. If it will, then my Kaitlyn and I will take ye home tae the highlands once ye are well enough tae travel."

Fraoch chewed and grimaced. "Och, you are relentless and ye have dragged this beautiful lassie intae it."

"Tis my wife, the Kaitlyn Campbell, I have told ye of her."

Fraoch coughed, looking very weak and near-death. "Og Maggy, if this is it for me, will ye tell my sister what—"

"Aye, I will tell her, but twill nae be necessary. Have another slice of orange." I pushed another slice of orange intae his mouth and made him chew it again.

Kaitlyn asked, "What does Og Maggy mean?"

"Young Magnus, he has been callin' me it since he met me."

Kaitlyn smiled and held the orange in her palm, passing me pieces one by one. I hated tae have her in this hospital, full of sickness and disease, but I was grateful she was attending with me.

Fraoch said, "Your cousin Lady May has been here."

"Good, was she a help tae ye?"

"Aye, I have more space because of it. She has told the physician that she will come every day, so he is verra careful with me."

"Have some more of this drink." I held the edge of the bottle up and had him drink a little more.

He groaned and scowled at the taste. He said, "Tis the thanks I get? Madame Kaitlyn, did Og Maggy tell ye I have saved his life?"

Kaitlyn answered, "He did. He said you were the best of men. That's why we're here to give you this terrible juice."

He lifted his hand and waved it a bit. I was grateful tae see the movement, twas the first sign of any life tae him. "Juice for a life. Twould have been a better trade for whisky."

I chuckled. "You get capable of sittin' on your own, Fraoch, and I will buy ye all the whisky ye want."

Kaitlyn said, "Perhaps we might need a bit more health and vigor than sitting up before we feed you whisky, but yes, get well is what we are saying."

"Och, ye are as irritatin' as Og Maggy, I see why he likes ye."

I said, "My wife has come with me tae sit at your bedside and ye are insultin' us. Tis your way as a MacDonald? Or have ye been livin' too long with the men at the fortress that ye forgot tae be polite?"

"I remember, friend, ye have come tae force me tae live. I remember. My apologies, Madame Kaitlyn."

"No offense taken Fraoch, you're allowed to say stupid shit when you're sick."

He laughed. "Tis the wit ye told me of, Og Maggy." He coughed and took a large draft of the orange drink and I began tae see that he would get better.

SIXTY-EIGHT - KAITLYN

Magnus left a note for his cousin May, explaining that we planned to get a room at the Bridge Inn.

We discussed it as we left Fraoch's bedside, we would stay until he was well. We wanted to go home, but when we went we wanted to be able to stay for a while. We also discussed that we couldn't remain in London dressed like this.

Magnus looked up and down the street. "Follow me."

He took my hand and led me over the bridge, through the crowds, down a brick road lined with quaint little shops with wooden signage hanging above.

He came to one with a sign that said, The Tailor, William Shudall. "My uncle used tae get our coats here, years ago. I will get dressed here and then..." He looked up and down the block. "A shop just there, Thomas Ravenscroft. My aunt used tae visit that dressmaker. We can get a dress for you."

We entered the tailor shop and waited for a few long minutes. Then Magnus explained his dilemma to the tailor: he needed to be dressed, he had plenty of money, he needed it to happen right now. The tailor finally relented. He had a suit that had been made for a wealthy client and it wasn't needed for another few weeks. There would be time to make it again.

I was given a chair to sit near the back of the store while Magnus was taken behind a long heavy curtain to be measured and fitted for the gentleman's coat. Magnus stuck his head out. "The coat is a blue one, dost ye—"

"I love you in blue, get that."

"He has tae sew me intae it, twill take a bit of time."

I waited and waited and tried to look demure and proper sitting in a tailor shop in 1740, watching all of 18th century humanity walk by outside: a pressing, bustling, street of shoppers and hawkers, and beggars and gentlemen and ladies. I really wished I had my phone to take a photo, because this was one of those moments. It was like watching a historical movie but with a horrific smell wafting about.

I admonished myself about how little I knew about history, and promised that I would start reading history, really studying, so when I ended in a place like this, I would know how to behave and dress. In lieu of reading history books, which on second thought sounded like a lot more effort than I could give it while all this drama was going on, I would definitely watch more historical movies, that might help.

An hour later Magnus emerged. His hair pulled back in a jaunty bow. A tricorn hat on his head. A high collar with a ruffle and lace under his jawline. A pale blue silk coat with embroidered edges down the front, breeches and white socks and little shoes. My eyes went wide.

"Dost ye like it?"

"Oh my, Magnus, that is so hot. You are so hot, that is..." I fanned myself. The tailor looked scandalized.

It came to me then that Magnus looked the gentleman and I was definitely looking like a woman of ill-repute.

"My turn?"

"Aye." Magnus paid for his clothes and a leather duffel-style bag that would carry his sword and some of our other smaller bags inside.

Out on the street people gawked at Magnus: his height, his new clothes, his hotness, though I'm sure there was a whole other word for it.

They looked confused by me, a little angry. I was in a Greek-style jacket with wrapped linen cloth skirts. Sandals. My feet were cold.

Magnus tugged at his cream-colored, embroidered vest and looked generally uncomfortable. "How does it feel?" I asked.

He tugged at his crotch and jiggled a leg. "Tis bindin' on my olive tree."

I laughed. "A Santorini Island metaphor, I like what you did there, Highlander."

Five doors down was the dressmaker. We entered and it was very crowded with women all waiting their turn. Magnus did not fit in the shop. He spoke to the man in charge and paid for my clothes, then said to me, "Lady Campbell, I am leavin' ye in the capable hands of Master Ravenscroft." He bowed and I curt-seyed, while everyone stared and my heart sank a little because he did literally have to leave me to step out to the street to wait.

He was on one side of the window, I was on the other. I waited and waited for my turn watching the young women as they were fitted and preened and modeled for each other.

I pretended like they were Kardashians and that amused me greatly. Occasionally I watched my husband outside, standing firm and erect, the taffeta stretched across his shoulders. He tipped his hat when people walked by. I tried to stand as still, as patient, as mannerly as he did.

Then it was my turn. I was taken to the area behind the curtain and shocked the staff with my odd layers of fabric over sweatpants. I told them I had just returned from a trip to Greece and they quieted because of the exotic nature of my recent trip, but there was a great deal of frowning as they undressed me.

They had three dresses that had been created for women who had never returned for them. I asked for blue to match my husband.

The dress was gorgeous, though not at all my size. They scowled when my shoulders wouldn't be as small as they needed them to be and they were irritated because my waist wouldn't go as small as it was expected to be. I hadn't been trained properly apparently, and when they tried to get it anywhere close enough, I acted like a big baby and couldn't breathe.

They gave up and got it tight enough, but seemed disappointed in me overall.

My bodice was brocade with a piece of stiff embroidered material that pinned on over it. The embroidery was exquisite. My skirt was so wide it was like three of me could fit inside. My cleavage was something to see and literally everyone could see it, just bosom galore, and there was delicate lace on the edges to accentuate it even more.

To top off my look I was given a weird straw hat, but I did truly need to cover my hair and we had been doing this now for hours, it was time to be finished already.

I was expected to stay inside until Magnus came in to retrieve me, because that's the kind of lady this dress made me. His eyes went as wide as mine had at the sight of him. "Och, Lady Campbell, ye are a beauty."

I beamed and almost cried.

And we went out to the street beyond. "I'm so terribly hungry."

He bought us some bread and cheese from a vendor and we ate standing together trying to keep the crowds from whisking us off away down the street.

I joked, "City life is exhausting, huh?"

"Aye, we are wantin' a carriage, but they are nae much better. Either we are jostled in the fresh air, or inside a wee box."

"This is fresh air?"

"Tis why m'lady has a handkerchief, tae cover her dainty nose."

He put his hand on the small of my back and directed me through the crowds.

I'm not going to lie, I freaking loved how his protectiveness made me feel.

London was beautiful, historical, quaint, amazing, and horribly disgusting. It was noisy, crowded, stinky, filthy, and freaking fascinating.

The only saving grace was that with the new very fancy clothes people deferred space to us and seemed generally afraid to get near Magnus, as if his wealth and power gave him a license to punish.

I was ignored. People stepped out of our way, looked askance, gave us room. It took about five minutes before our chins went higher, our backs straighter. It was all a part to play: ours was rich, landed gentry. Their's was the riffraff of the street.

But the mere act of walking was still tough. Despite what the women who dressed me thought, my bodice was very tight. There was also the air thing or lack of. The streets were cobblestone and I couldn't see my feet, and god only knows what my skirts were dragging through. Puddles were plentiful and what were they? The smell of feces was ripe. And coal smoke. And a rotting river.

We neared the bridge. The crowds were full of many more men, a port, workers, sailors. I swear to god most of them looked like pirates. There were a lot of filthy stinky people with menacing stares. I went quiet and clung to Magnus, while he led me up the bridge with a protective arm around me. When we got to the top, I was out of breath. "Can we stop for a moment?"

We clung to the rail looking out over a river so full of ships that it was a marvel, really, boats everywhere, docks, barrels and boxes, buckets, plus the smell of rot. It was pretty astonishing to be in this gorgeous dress looking down on it all.

I wrapped tighter around my husband's arm and kissed his shoulder. "So you were here before, just off a boat from coursing the ocean?"

"Aye, I pushed a cart, much like that one." He pointed at a small vendor cart. "With Fraoch inside tae the hospital. I was verra hungry and near sick with exhaustion."

"And then what did you do?"

"I gave all my money tae the doctor tae watch on him for me, twas five days ago by my calculations of this date, and then I walked tae see my Cousin May at Ham House."

"How far away was it?"

"From the hospital tae Ham House was over three hours tae walk. London is verra vast."

"Oh," I said, as the enormity of all that he had done truly hit me. Everything he had done. The scale of it all.

SIXTY-NINE - MAGNUS

We walked for a long time, each within our own thoughts. The streets here were less crowded. There was a park and fewer shops. It was evening and we were lookin' forward to the bed we would be fallin' intae even if it would be an uncomfortable 18th century bed.

Kaitlyn slowed and turned tae face me. She looked up at me with a tilt of her chin.

I asked, "What are ye about, mo reul-iuil?"

"I'm very impressed with you." She smoothed across the front of my coat. "I don't know if I tell you this enough, and I don't want you to feel embarrassed when I do, but I am very proud that you are the man you are. Really. You take my breath away."

"Och, either ye are verra romantic feelin' toward me or yer bodice is too tight on ye."

"I mean it. Both those things are also true, but I mean it. I love you. I'm so very proud of you. You're a good man, a patient man." Someone jostled by her and knocked her toward me. "And you are a kind man." She wrapped my hands in her own. "I love that so much about you. When you are feeling worried about the things you've done or need to do, remember that I love you because of your strength here." She placed a hand over my heart as her lower lids filled with tears. "And I just wanted you to know that's how I feel about you."

I pulled her intae my arms and kissed her, though the brim of our hats caused some difficulties. I said, "I am verra—"

"Don't. You say beautiful, wonderful, romantic things to me all the time. Let this one moment be me, in my big fancy dress, standing on a cobblestone street in a puddle of urine, let this be me, telling you how much you mean to me."

"Aye, tis a verra romantic moment." Someone jostled against me as they hurried past.

She said, "Well, what I'm learning is we have to take the moment when it comes, because we never know, right? So this is me telling you, I love that you're the kind of man who would push a cart through this muck and mire to get a friend to a hospital. You crossed the world in a ship to come home to me. You lived in Greece without me for weeks to rescue me. You're my hero."

"Thank ye, Kaitlyn." Then I added, "You winna allow me tae say anythin' in return? I am verra proud of—"

"See? You can't even help yourself. I'm going to make you keep that compliment in your back pocket."

I pulled at the front of my breeches. "I daena have room, my breeches are verra wee."

She laughed, "They are accentuating your cannon very nicely. It's making me quite warm." She fanned her face with her handkerchief.

"Okay, I winna tell ye how much I love ye and make a fuss on your beauty and your wit and wisdom. I will listen tae ye tell me I am a hero because I helped a friend and I rescued ye from an evil man. I will nae return your kindnesses with a compliment on you at all, except tae say that I verra much admire this wee bit of flesh here."

I leaned over and kissed her on the top edge of her cleavage, a bit of soft skin that was wonderfully exposed. The skin was delicate and rose and fell with her breaths. The movement was almost imperceptible unless I watched and I thought I might want tae press my lips tae that spot and linger there.

When I drew away, there was a glint in her eye, a smile at the edge of her mouth. "Oh you do? You admire that one little spot?"

"Aye, tis blindin' me with its beauty. I canna draw my eyes away from it."

That beautiful spot of skin rose with a sigh. "What else would you say to me?"

"I would say I would verra much like tae take ye tae bed, Madame Campbell, if ye would be willin'."

Her smile spread. "Oh I would be willing, Master Magnus, I would definitely be willing."

The end.

SERIES ORDER

Kaitlyn and the Highlander (book 1)
Time and Space Between Us (book 2)
A Warrior of My Own (book 3)
Begin Where We Are (book 4)
A Missing Entanglement (short, optional, between 4&5)
Entangled With You (book 5)
Magnus and a Love Beyond Words (book 6)
Under the Same Sky (book 7)
Nothing but Dust (book 8)

ALSO BY DIANA KNIGHTLEY

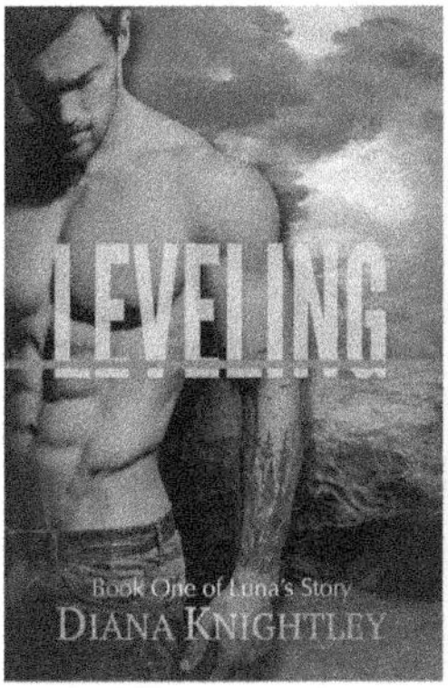

Can he see to the depths of her mystery before it's too late?

The oceans cover everything, the apocalypse is behind them. Before them is just water, leveling. And in the middle — they find each other.

On a desolate, military-run Outpost, Beckett is waiting.

Then Luna bumps her paddleboard up to the glass windows and disrupts his everything.

And soon Beckett has something and someone to live for. Finally. But their survival depends on discovering what she's hiding, what she won't tell him.

Because some things are too painful to speak out loud.

With the clock ticking, the water rising, and the storms growing, hang on while Beckett and Luna desperately try to rescue each other in Leveling, the epic, steamy, and suspenseful first book of the trilogy, Luna's Story:

Leveling: Book One of Luna's Story

Under: Book Two of Luna's Story

Deep: Book Three of Luna's Story

SOME THOUGHTS AND RESEARCH...

Characters:

Kaitlyn Maude Sheffield - born 1994

Magnus Archibald Caelhin Campbell - born 1681

Lady Mairead (Campbell) Delapointe she is the sister of the Earl of Breadalbane

Hayley Sherman

Quentin Peters

Beaty Peters

Zach Greene

Emma Garcia

Baby Ben Greene

Sean Campbell -Magnus's half-brother

Lizbeth Campbell - Magnus's half-sister

Sean and Lizbeth are the children born of Lady Mairead and her first husband.

Baby Archie Campbell - born July 9, 2382

Bella (?)

John Mitchell - Bella's guy

Colonel Hammond Donahoe

The Earl of Breadalbane - Lady Mairead's brother

Uncle Archibald (Baldie) Campbell - uncle to Sean and Lizbeth

Tyler Garrison Wilson - Archie's alter-ego

Grandma Barb

Fraoch MacDonald - born in 1714, is aged 26 in 1740 when he meets Magnus

Some **Scottish and Gaelic words** that appear within the book series:

Chan eil an t-sìde cho math an-diugh 's a bha e an-dé - The weather's not as good today as it was yesterday.

Tha droch shìde ann - The weather is bad.

Dreich - dull and miserable weather

Turadh - a break in the clouds between showers

Solasta - luminous shining (possible nickname)

Splang - flash, spark, sparkle

Mo reul-iuil - my North Star (nickname)

Tha thu a 'fàileadh mar ghaoith - you have the scent of a breeze.

Osna - a sigh

Rionnag - star

Sollier - bright

Ghrian - the sun

Mo ghradh - my own love

Tha thu breagha - you are beautiful

Mo chroi - my heart

Corrachag-cagail - dancing and flickering ember flames

Mo reul-iuil, is ann leatsa abhios mo chridhe gubrath - My North Star, my heart belongs to you forever

Dinna ken - didn't know

A h-uile là sona dhuibh 's gun là idir dona dhuib - May all your days be happy ones

May the best ye've ever seen
Be the warst ye'll ever see.
May the moose ne'er lea' yer aumrie
Wi' a tear-drap in his e'e.
May ye aye keep hail an' hertie
Till ye're auld eneuch tae dee.
May ye aye be jist as happy
As we wiss ye noo tae be.

Tae - to

Winna - won't or will not

Daena - don't

Tis - it is or there is. This is most often a contraction t'is, but it looked messy and hard to read on the page so I removed the apostrophe. For Magnus it's not a contraction, it's a word.

Och nae - Oh no.

Ken, kent, kens - know, knew, knows

iora rua - a squirrel. (Magnus compares Kaitlyn to this ;o)

scabby-boggin tarriwag - Ugly-foul smelling testicles

latha fada - long day

sùgh am gròiseid - juice in the gooseberry

Beinn Labhair - Ben Lawers, the highest mountain in the southern part of the Scottish Highlands. It lies to the north of Loch Tay.

"And I will come again, my love, though it were ten thousand mile." Is from the beautiful **Robert Burns** poem, *O my Luve's like a red, red rose,* written in 1794 after Magnus's time.

beannachd leibh - farewell or blessings be with you.

Locations:

Fernandina Beach on Amelia Island, Florida, 2017-2020

Magnus's home in Scotland - Balloch. Built in 1552. In early 1800s it was rebuilt as Taymouth Castle. (Maybe because of the breach in the walls caused by our siege from the future?) Situated on the south bank of the River Tay, in the heart of the Grampian Mountains. In 2382 it is a ruin.

Kilchurn Castle - Magnus's childhood home, favorite castle of his uncle Baldie. On an island at the northeastern end of Loch Awe. In the region Argyll.

The kingdom of Magnus the First is in Scotland, his Castle Dom (really needs to be renamed) is very near Balloch Castle.

Magnus and Kaitlyn's safe house is in a secret location.

The Cracker Barrel off I-95 in Savannah.

Castillo de San Marcos - St Augustine fort. It does have that sort of hold in a wall dungeon.

Ham House is a historic house with formal gardens set back 200 metres from the River Thames in Ham, south of Richmond in London. It is a three and a half hour walk from St Thomas Hospital.

Elizabeth (1659–1735), married Archibald Campbell, 1st Duke of Argyll in Edinburgh in 1678. Their first child, John Campbell, 2nd Duke of Argyll, was born at Ham House in 1680 and their second son, Archibald Campbell, 3rd Duke of Argyll was born in the same room a few years later. (Some names and dates have been changed in this story, but this family is Magnus's relations in London. He lived with them from when he was about 10 until he was about 16.)

St Thomas Hospital was described as ancient in 1215. Seriously. It is located on the opposite bank of the River Thames to the Houses of Parliament.

True things that happened:

The **Siege of St. Augustine** was a military engagement that took place during June–July 1740. It was a part of the much larger conflict known as the War of Jenkins' Ear, between Great Britain and Spain. Magnus was verra fortunate that the siege happened while he was in the dungeon.

During the Siege of St Augustine there were 14 deserters. One of those must have been our new friend, Fraoch MacDonald.

The War of Jenkins' Ear began in October 1739. In November, in response to **two Scots garrisoned on Amelia Island** being killed in an ambush by Spanish-allied Indians, the Darien settlers mobilized and, together with forces from South Carolina, captured some Spanish forts including Fort Mose, before attempting to lay siege to St. Augustine. Then the Spanish won the Battle of Fort Mose, resulting in the death or capture of 51 Darien settlers, most if not all of them were from Scotland.

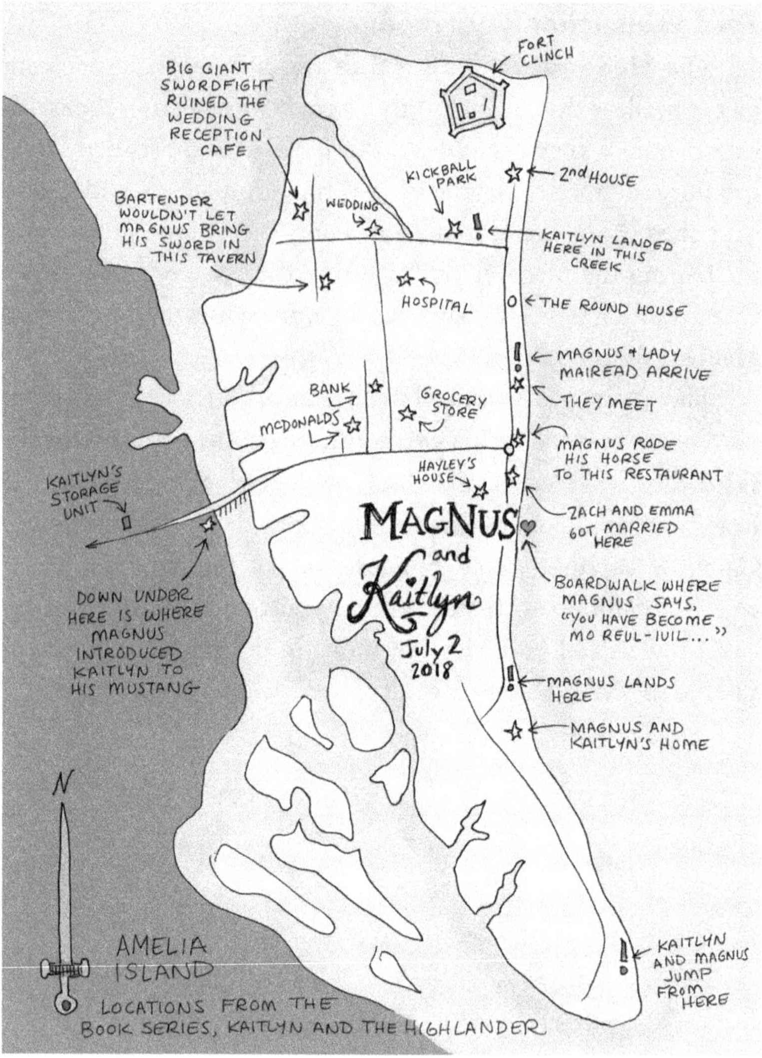
FORT CLINCH
BIG GIANT SWORDFIGHT RUINED THE WEDDING RECEPTION CAFE
KICKBALL PARK
2nd HOUSE
BARTENDER WOULDN'T LET MAGNUS BRING HIS SWORD IN THIS TAVERN
WEDDING
KAITLYN LANDED HERE IN THIS CREEK
HOSPITAL
THE ROUND HOUSE
MAGNUS + LADY MAIREAD ARRIVE
BANK
GROCERY STORE
THEY MEET
MCDONALDS
MAGNUS RODE HIS HORSE TO THIS RESTAURANT
KAITLYN'S STORAGE UNIT
HAYLEY'S HOUSE
ZACH AND EMMA GOT MARRIED HERE
MAGNUS and Kaitlyn
July 2 2018
DOWN UNDER HERE IS WHERE MAGNUS INTRODUCED KAITLYN TO HIS MUSTANG
BOARDWALK WHERE MAGNUS SAYS, "YOU HAVE BECOME MO REUL-IUIL..."
MAGNUS LANDS HERE
MAGNUS AND KAITLYN'S HOME
N
AMELIA ISLAND
LOCATIONS FROM THE BOOK SERIES, KAITLYN AND THE HIGHLANDER
KAITLYN AND MAGNUS JUMP FROM HERE

ACKNOWLEDGMENTS

A huge thank you to David Sutton for reading and advising on story threads, wanting Magnus and Kaitlyn to consider their wealth, hoping I can find some empathy for Bella, and wondering about where James went. I appreciate your time, the back and forth as we get to the nitty gritty in this story and pull apart the confusing threads. As you said, when we were discussing a particularly wibbly-wobbly thread, "You're earning your money now." True that! You help the story get better and better, thank you, especially for your idea of adding a stocking for Archie. That was great.

A big thank you to Heather Hawkes for beta reading, championing, being a long time friend and supporter, and for letting me know that Magnus's tears don't make him weak, saying, "Only movie stars wouldn't cry." I'm so grateful that you've been enthusiastic and sometimes 'on-call' when I'm totally freaking out. And that this time you told me, "Personally, every book gets better." Thank you.

~

Thank you to Jessica Fox for reading and saying, "Once again, I was impressed by Kaitlyn's terrible arsery. She was brave when she had to defend others but her traditional scared, impulsive and freaked out when Magnus was around to defend her, excellent character development while still being realistic." I really want Kaitlyn to be a terrible arse and yet also a real girl, thank you for agreeing. Your notes and advice are great and when you said this at the end, "I could go on but it would be just writing about what I liked, which is a lot and I know you are on the clock here, so consider your fears assuaged and ego inflated." Thank you. That was kind and helpful.

~

Thank you to Kristen Schoenmann De Haan for your tireless beta-reading for me. This go around you weighed in last yet still found things I hadn't noticed. Thank you for saying, "I was so invested in this wonderful Montegue/Capulet friendship..." It means a lot that you saw Magnus and Fraoch this way, their friendship will be a good one in future books.

~

And a special thank you to Cynthia Tyler, a truly amazing editor, every pass you make helps the story get better and better. Plus you have this amazing history yourself — want to know about sword fighting, horsemanship, rifle shooting, sailing, Scottish history? Ask Cynthia! This installment I did ask and you delivered: North Florida maps, English tailors, the details of high-end costuming, the cuisine on ships crossing the Atlantic, as well as the correct terms of the boat doohickeys, how much money to buy a cart at port and yes, the man is selling oysters, plus the founding year of St Thomas Hospital. Thank you so much. I'm lucky to have every bit of your experience informing my story.

~

And thank you to my mother, Mary Jane Cushman. When I was in junior high school I helped her clean out the Old Jail to become the Amelia Island Museum of History. I helped her carry boxes of artifacts and affix to walls the hand-written cards to create the museum displays.

She was also co-owner of a toy store called the Gamekeeper on Centre Street and was so proud of the community. When David Sutton asked me to send Kaitlyn and Magnus there to shop for Christmas, he was exactly right. She was so proud of that shopping area and would have loved to see it in a book.

Amelia Island was a home she loved the details of and I hope I have told a story that does those details justice. She passed away in 2011 and was my greatest fan. I still miss her every day.

~

A huge thank you to every single member of the FB group, Kaitlyn and the Highlander. Every day, in every way, sharing your thoughts, joys, and loves with me is so amazing, thank you. You inspire me to try harder.

And when I ask 'research questions' boy do you all deliver.

I told the group that Magnus would be revisiting Ham House

and one of the members, Elizabeth Corley, lived near that house many years ago.

She told me that the gardens were great fun to play in. And that, "The house is stunning too, full of dark wood and smells of the past!"

And, "...when you go in through the front door the floor tiles are black and white chequered and there is a balcony above that runs all the way around on the first floor so you can look down into the hall from there. The stairs are off to the left (and very very ornate carved wood!) There's a door right by the start of the stairs that opens to a small chapel. I always remember one of the curators telling me about a secret staircase when I was a little girl that the servants used. I saw a small part of it, it was tiny and pitch black and really creepy! There's a beautiful long gallery on the first floor too that runs from the front to the back of the house, all dark wood panelled. The river Thames runs along in front of the house and sweeping lawns behind the house. The stable block is part of the walled garden."

I appreciate this glimpse into the house. It really helped Magnus's memories, thank you Elizabeth!

I asked, "Magnus agrees with Kaitlyn on something. Then a little while later he has to admit that she was right about something else. Then they have this discussion:

...he grinned. 'I have learned that Kaitlyn Campbell was in the right in this."

'Good, I'm glad you see my point.'

He added, 'You are always wantin' me tae agree with ye and now it has been twice in a day. You are goin' tae have tae agree with me on somethin' so I daena feel so insignificant.'

'Like what?'

...

What does Magnus want Kaitlyn to agree with him on?"

There were so many great ideas, from ice cream flavors, to food choices, to whether Florida is as beautiful as Scotland, to very romantic thoughts. It came to me as I was reading their answers that it would be about the scent of Kaitlyn's shampoo. She's gotten kind of carried away with the flower fragrances and Magnus is food driven. We all suspected this of course.

Thank you to Rachael Temaat, Jeanette Reames, Lillian Llewellyn, Jenna Rae Payne, Heather Haroldsen, Jackie Malecki, Carlla Hamilton, Karen Nichols, Michelle Lisgaris, Carmen Sánchez, Nikki Nikki, Nicola Ashton, Julie Stephens, Gail Bissett, Debbie Nida, David Sutton, Marian Birsa, and Donna Bartlett for weighing in and helping me come to the answer.

I also asked, "So Magnus is riding a coach a verra verra long distance. Let's just say it's his century. He will be traveling for days.

The interior carries six passengers. It looks like each seat was about 14" wide, so there was some tightness and thinking on the bulk of the ladies clothing is liable to give me claustrophobia right there.

There are five other passengers in the coach when he squeezes into his seat.

Who are his fellow passengers?

Especially – ***who is the person that he is sitting right up against?"***

This is what I chose:

There were six seats altogether, five were full of other passengers. My travel companions were a wealthy widow, Madame Fuller, and her son, Samuel, headed tae York; a young man who was a clockmaker's assistant, his name was Paul Hanley; and a young woman, a Mistress Brookes and her traveling companion.

Thank you for the ideas, Jessica Martin (As Magnus settles in for the long journey ahead, he feels Agatha shift closer to him so that every bump in the road conveniently jostles her practically in his lap. Agatha turns to apologize in a breathy voice as she runs her finger across her exposed decolletage. Magnus looks at the girl and says "That's alright lassie, but I'm nae sure my wife would approve of ye ridin all the way on me lap"), Janet Lewis Sims (The woman across from him, is flirtatious, and he's trying not to give her any encouragement), Christine Champeaux (a woman about Kaitlyn's age, recently widowed) These were great ideas and helped me fill that carriage with interesting people.

I also asked, ***"I need a place. Nick Reyes, a horrible person and a time-traveler, likes to go there. It's his favorite vacation place. He might mention it to Magnus, when he was there last..."***

The most useful ideas were: Annie Miller (I feel like he's the kind of jackass that has an island...) Jessica Fox (My first thought was a Greek or Mediterranean island with a house atop an ocean-side cliff. I can almost see a battle on the big terrace that faces the ocean and has a huge drop into the jagged rocks on the shore below), Margo Machnik (Malta!!! In a cliffside villa), Carla Howell (He owns a Villa...Beautiful mountains, cliffs, ocean, exotic... perfect!), Sly Greenberg (Somewhere in the Greek archipelago...), Polly Hagen Jones (...some place living quite nicely, like Greece?)

Thank you for the ideas! Santorini was where he ended, and we got to meet Christo and Sophia and Magnus gained even more friends.

I also asked, ***"I need the name for a Tailor shop in London in the year 1740. Also the name for the Tailor working it.***

I also need the name of a women's dress shop and the name of the tailor working it."

Heather Story mentioned Ede and Ravenscroft, the oldest Tailor in London est 1689. And then Jackie Malecki added a link to Ede & Ravenscroft and there I found the original Tailor, William Shudall. And he's who I chose, a combination of true and artistic license.

There were so many great ideas from Maureen Woeller, Julie Stephens, Jenni Branchaw, Sharon-Nick Palmer, Gloria Michaels-Brown, Margie Klink, Sara Denison, Cristin Follett Gillis, Elizabeth Rains Johnson, Carmen Basanta Sánchez, Diana Toles, Kathryn Horton, Georgene K Jacobs, Zoie Scurfield, Madeline Anna Plitz, Amy MacNeill, Lindsay Holden-Shannon, Cathy Serpe Cannizzaro, Susan Nelson, Carol Distelhurst, Kim Stevens, Dianna Schmidt, Mary Moeykens, Michelle Lambert Poppell, Rachael Temaat, Mindy Anspaugh, Courtney Brennan, Angelique Mahfood, and Jenni Branchaw, thank you for sharing them with me.

And I asked, *Say there are men or women from the 15th -18th century Scotland and they see something that they don't understand, something modern for example — they might use the term 'monster'. But would there be better terms, maybe something from Scottish Mythology or Gaelic or...?*

What if they saw a futuristic person with a lot of gear on?

What if they saw an alligator?

What if they saw a manatee?

What if they saw a drone?

Or an ATV kind of vehicle?

Thank you to Kim Bonser Houlden (Demon, devil's beast), Judy Wallenfelt (Demons?) Rachael Temaat (...something demonic would work better like the Gaelic word for Demon or witchcraftery?), Stephanie Knight-Magnuson (Beast), Tara Luffy Moore (Beast. Demon.) and Amy MacNeill (...Gaelic for Demon...) I ended up calling most of the monsters beasts, and Fraoch uses the Gaelic word for demon: deamhan uilebheist

Thank you to Kevin Dowdee for being my support, my guidance, and my inspiration for these stories. I appreciate you so much. And thank you for helping me research the effects of scurvy and making me laugh by drinking two vitamin C packets right after.

Thank you to my kids, Ean, Gwynnie, Fiona, and Isobel, for listening to me go on and on about these characters, advising me whenever you can, and accepting them as real parts of our lives. I love you.

ABOUT ME, DIANA KNIGHTLEY

I live in Los Angeles where we have a lot of apocalyptic tendencies that we overcome by wishful thinking. Also great beaches. I maintain a lot of people in a small house, too many pets, and a to-do list that is longer than it should be, because my main rule is: Art, play, fun, before housework. My kids say I am a cool mom because I try to be kind. I'm married to a guy who is like a water god: he surfs, he paddle boards, he built a boat. I'm a huge fan.

I write about heroes and tragedies and magical whisperings and always forever happily ever afters. I love that scene where the two are desperate to be together but can't because of war or apocalyptic-stuff or (scientifically sound!) time-jumping and he is begging the universe with a plead in his heart and she is distraught (yet still strong) and somehow, through kisses and steamy more and hope and heaps and piles of true love, they manage to come out on the other side.

I like a man in a kilt, especially if he looks like a Hemsworth, doesn't matter, Liam or Chris.

My couples so far include Beckett and Luna (from the trilogy, Luna's Story) who battle their fear to find each other during an apocalypse of rising waters. And Magnus and Kaitlyn (from the series Kaitlyn and the Highlander). Who find themselves traveling through time to be together.

I write under two pen names, this one here, Diana Knightley, and another one, H. D. Knightley, where I write books for Young

Adults (They are still romantic and fun and sometimes steamy though, because love is grand at any age.)

DianaKnightley.com
Diana@dianaknightley.com

ALSO BY H. D. KNIGHTLEY (MY YA PEN NAME)

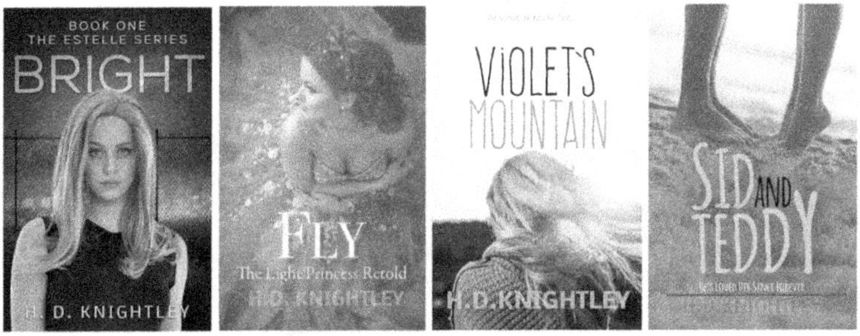

Bright (Book One of The Estelle Series)

Beyond (Book Two of The Estelle Series)

Belief (Book Three of The Estelle Series)

Fly; The Light Princess Retold

Violet's Mountain

Sid and Teddy

CPSIA information can be obtained
at www.ICGtesting.com
Printed in the USA
LVHW091139220121
677184LV00001B/42

9 781075 486258